BETA

RACHEL COHN

HYPERION
NEW YORK

First Edition
1 3 5 7 9 10 8 6 4 2
G475-5664-5-12214
Printed in the United States of America

This book is set in Adobe Caslon Pro.
Designed by Marci Senders

Library of Congress Cataloging-in-Publication Data
Cohn, Rachel.
Beta/Rachel Cohn.
p. cm.
Summary: "On a futuristic island paradise where humans
are served by enslaved clones, a sixteen-year-old clone named
Elysia seeks her own freedom"—Provided by publisher.
ISBN 978-1-4231-5719-9 (hardback)—ISBN 1-4231-5719-2
[1. Cloning—Fiction. 2. Family life—Fiction. 3. Love—Fiction.
4. Resorts—Fiction. 5. Islands—Fiction. 6. Science fiction.] I. Title.
PZ7.C6665Bet 2012
[Fic]—dc23
2012008663

Reinforced binding

Visit www.un-requiredreading.com

1

IT'S ME SHE WANTS TO PURCHASE.

The fancy lady claims she came into the resort boutique looking to buy a sweater, but she can't take her eyes off me. She wears a diamond-studded ivory silk suit perfectly tailored to her hourglass figure, her luminous face is flawless despite her being middle-aged, and her chestnut hair falls in lustrous waves down her shoulders. Her smooth hands are manicured, the fingers bejeweled with precious stones. She looks as if a beautician constantly hovered around her, ensuring that her every moment was aesthetically pleasing. She is flanked by two male bodyguards, tall, tanned, and blond, with bodybuilders' physiques. Each has glazed fuchsia eyes and a violet fleur-de-lis tattoo on his right temple, like me.

The fancy lady's pale-pink fingers rummage a baby-blue cashmere cardigan, discerning the quality of the material, but her own eyes remain fixed on me. She is judging the quality of me. "Is she available?" she finally asks Marisa, the boutique manager. Her voice is breathy, childlike, and she asks the question casually but quietly, as if she were splurging on an enormous slice of decadent, high-calorie cream cake. Marisa, who is also the most elite broker on Demesne, nods discreetly. This store sells apparel—and people.

If we can be considered people. Here on Demesne, the humans call us "clones." I call myself Elysia, because that's what Dr. Lusardi told me to call myself.

I emerged just weeks ago. But I am a sixteen-year-old girl. I know nothing of my First, the girl I was cloned from. Nor will I likely ever know anything about her. In order for me to be made, she had to die.

We're in a private room, just me, the fancy lady, and Marisa. No bodyguards, no other customers, no other clone specimens. The room's walls are stark white. Sheer opaque curtains billow as they usher in Demesne's prized super-oxygenated air from large bay windows. The room is meant to convey the peace and tranquility for which this island lodged in the equatorial seas is famous. The windows offer a broad view out toward Io, the bubbling violet-blue sea that surrounds Demesne. I wonder how it is that Io's waters can feel so special. It's not something I am meant to understand; the reason has to do with human feeling and nothing to do with logic. People spend their life savings to experience one moment luxuriating in Io. You could toss me into Io to absorb all of its supposed mystical properties and it would have no effect on me.

I have no soul.

The fancy lady prods me as one might poke a piece of fruit at the market. She gently pokes my flesh, first my arms, then my thighs. She presses her hands against my back to test its firmness, then runs her hand through my hair.

"She's exquisite," the fancy lady says.

Marisa cautions her. "Mrs. Bratton, for our own liability, I need to make sure you understand. She is a Beta. Dr. Lusardi has not perfected the teen line yet." Marisa's hand reaches to my shoulders to pull my hair aside so the customer can clearly see the laser-branded tattoo on the back of my neck: BETA in violet lettering.

"I assume that will be reflected in the price, then," the fancy lady called Mrs. Bratton says in her soft voice.

My chip tells me this is called *bargain hunting*.

"Of course," Marisa says. "Dr. Lusardi will be thrilled to know someone of your stature is willing to take a chance on a teen Beta."

Mrs. Bratton directs her gaze toward me. "What is your name, dear?"

"Elysia," I say. *El-EE-zee-ya. El-EE-zee-ya.* I can still hear Dr. Lusardi making me practice saying my name, and the island's name, *Deh-MEZ-nay*, when I first emerged. Clones don't just wake up and automatically know how to speak. It takes a day or two after stasis.

"I think you might make a wonderful addition to our

household, Elysia. We're so badly missing a teenage girl ever since Astrid, my eldest, went off to college on the Mainland." She pauses. "Biome University."

"Congratulations," I say, because I know that's the appropriate thing to say to a parent whose child has gained admittance to an ultracompetitive learning institution. "You must be very proud."

Mrs. Bratton's face brightens. "I am! But Astrid's so unnecessarily devoted to her studies. She insists on not traveling home to Demesne during the school year to visit us. We miss her so. Her younger brother and sister have been so whiny since she left." She pauses to look me up and down one more time. "Yes, a new girl is just what the family needs. Would you like to be that girl?"

"Yes, ma'am," I say. It doesn't matter to me whether I exist in this store or at her home. But my internal feed tells me how to intone the enthusiasm that makes the humans feel good about their decision to buy me.

"Her manners are exquisite," Marisa brags.

"Indeed!" Mrs. Bratton says. "An excellent improvement on the insolence of real teens, and I should know." She smiles. "I've raised a few."

Marisa sends me back into the store while she finishes the negotiations with Mrs. Bratton. I am to pick out some nice but modest clothing to take to my new home, where I shall serve my new owner. I choose the baby-blue sweater Mrs. Bratton was admiring, along with a white blouse and a plain blue skirt to match the sweater. A starter uniform. I change into the outfit. There is nothing else I need.

Except to say good-bye to Becky.

Becky is the other Beta teen available at this boutique. When I first arrived, Becky informed me that Betas were harder to sell as a buyer cannot be one-hundred-percent assured that a Beta will always operate as programmed. Becky and I are teen Betas, the first of our kind. Becky said when she first emerged, Dr. Lusardi informed her that while some buyers liked the cachet of being the first to own a new model, the teen Betas were not expected to do well because not that many adult humans actually like teens; in fact, many actively try to forget they'd once been teens themselves. According to Becky, Beta teens would serve as experiments until Dr. Lusardi could manufacture actual babies and children, who could potentially "blow the market wide open."

While Becky is technically available for purchase, there's no expectation of a sale for her, and so she's consigned to work in the boutique, keeping it tidy, fetching beverages, and straightening up after customers. With her unfortunate aesthetic, Becky will never ascend to the upper caste of clones and work as a companion, chef, butler, oxygen leveler, sporting instructor, or—the most prized role of all—a luxisstant, an organizer of residents' luxury needs. Becky emerged months ago with frizzy brown hair that looks like a jumble of rat's tails, eyes on the sallow pink side of fuchsia, and a jaundiced complexion. She is also fat, at least two sizes above the cellulite-free standard ideal known as the "Bikini Body," the island's preferred aesthetic.

According to Dr. Lusardi, I am her finest Beta, teen or otherwise. My aesthetic accentuates the Demesne lifestyle, as clones are intended to do. My holographic brochure says my measurements are "model perfect." I have muscle tone suggesting that my First might have been an athlete or a dancer. Dr. Lusardi said I am a veritable "Tasty." I have luxurious honey-blond hair, sun-kissed skin, and a complexion of peaches and cream. The trickiest part, according to Dr. Lusardi—my eyes—came out just right, like bright fuchsia pieces of hard candy, with almond-shaped lids and thick brown lashes, designed to convey docility and not creep out owners. From a distance, a clone's luminous eyes are meant to draw in humans and make them feel safe. Up close, the eyes appear hollow. Because of that, humans tend not to look into our eyes too closely, which I've been told is socially preferable, as eyes without souls behind them can be frightening.

"So you're to be a companion," says Becky. "How excellent for you."

Suddenly I feel a pang in my heart, as if I will miss this other teen Beta, but I know the reaction occurs because my chip knows how to mimic human responses, and not because I am capable of actually missing Becky. We feel nothing for each other. We don't need to. I don't know why my stomach also experiences a hollow emptiness at the thought of leaving this other teen Beta. There is so much for me to learn—about this island, about my own body chemistry. I am so new.

Becky adds, "You've only just come onto the market. You're a quick sell. Congratulations."

"Perhaps once I am settled in my new home, I could inquire if any roles there might be suitable for you."

"Thank you," says Becky, emulating gratitude for a

promise we both know is unlikely to be kept. "It is perfectly satisfactory for me to serve here too."

Mrs. Bratton and I depart in a chauffeured Aviate, a gliding, low-altitude luxury-utility vehicle. The LUV's windows appear darkened from the outside, and inside it smells like jasmine and has seats that feel as if they are caressing their passengers. I sit in the back with Mrs. Bratton while her two bodyguards occupy the front. The bodyguards gaze intently out the windows, as if threats could loom in the paradise outside this vehicle. Perhaps they stare so seriously because they don't know what else to do. The Aviate drives itself.

As the Aviate glides over the terrain, Mrs. Bratton swipes her right hand along her inner left arm from elbow to wrist. Her Relay screen appears beneath her skin and she begins Relaying messages, her interest in her new purchase—me—apparently evaporated. It is my duty to please and not bore her, but my chip lets me know that humans sometimes need quiet time for Relaying, so I do not try to engage her at this moment. Instead, I watch the scenery go by: tall palm trees secluding luxury villas, turquoise lagoons, and gardens full of blooming jacarandas, lilies, passionflowers, dahlias, orchids, and hibiscuses. In the distance, I see the placid, lulling Io Sea, and up above, farther away, the emerald-green forested mountains that loom over the island. Although I can't see it from the Aviate's view, I remember that those mountains descend on the other side into a wild rain forest, where Dr. Lusardi's compound, the place I came from, is hidden.

I have never lived anywhere but Demesne so I cannot

compare it to other places, but even without a chip telling me so, I think I could understand that this island is an ideal, an embodiment of perfection. Breathing in the silken air is like having warm honey trickling sweetly down your throat. The contrast of colors—Io's violet-blue, the lush green plants and tall trees, the flowers' bursting plumes of bright pinks, yellows, oranges, reds, purples, and golds everywhere— intoxicates the eyes.

Excitement bubbles within me, a direct antidote to the earlier anxiety I experienced being separated from Becky. I have an owner now, and we are on our way to my new home, on the most desirable place on Earth. What will my newly emerged life on Demesne be like?

A response comes through on Mrs. Bratton's Relay, and she sighs. "Oh, dear. The Governor, he's not happy about this at all."

My interface flashes an image of an imposing bald man wearing a military uniform adorned with many medals. It informs me that the Governor is a retired general who is now the island's chief executive officer, hired by Demesne's board of directors. "How do you know the Governor?" I ask Mrs. Bratton.

"He's my husband, silly."

I suppose this affiliation explains her security detail, although the very idea of needing security on such a perfect and tranquil place confuses me. But these are things I do not question. I am only a clone, and a Beta at that.

"Why is he called 'the Governor'?" I ask Mrs. Bratton.

"It's a nickname, pet. Like from colonial times. *CEO* sounds so . . . *boring.*"

"I understand, Mrs. Bratton," I say. Even though I don't. As part of my orientation program when I first emerged, I learned to use this as a useful phrase to fill silences with humans. Whether I actually understand is irrelevant.

"Don't call me Mrs. Bratton. That's so formal."

"What shall I call you?" I ask Mrs. Bratton.

"You may call me Mother."

2

WHEN I FIRST AWOKE, I DID NOT KNOW THE concept of a mother. I had the knowledge gap typical of a new Emergent, with a basic grasp of language and symbols from my First, but no context.

As my eyes slowly opened, the first thing I saw was the face I would later know as Dr. Lusardi's. She was observing my awakening. My vision was blurry, but her coloring was so distinct that she came into a hazy focus. She had a mass of red corkscrew hair surrounding a pale face of orange freckles and blood-red eyes, and wore a white lab coat. I could hear the whir of machines behind her, dings and beeps creating a soft symphony of electronic noise that made no sense to me.

If I could have, I would have leaped up off the table and run—hard and fast. But that was not possible. Only later would I comprehend what had happened in my first waking moment, when the things attached to my arms—my hands—felt clammy, and the thing in the upper left corner of my torso—my heart—felt like it was furiously racing against that thing in my head—my brain—to see which body attachment could experience full-on meltdown first. Once my chip was implanted, I understood that feeling was called panic. After I received the chip, I would never again have to experience that unnecessary sensation. That's only what came first.

The one sensation I truly understood first awakening was bitter cold, made distinct by the shivers sweeping across my body as I lay naked and uncovered on the frigid metal table attached to Dr. Lusardi's master invention—the human duplication machine. The machine from which I emerged resembled an open casket, with tubes attached to its ends, directing matter into the machine from an attachment on another raised metal table parallel to it. The parallel table was the one my First had lain upon as she was duplicated into me. But her dead body was no longer lying there when I awoke.

A voice near Dr. Lusardi—an assistant's, I suppose— said, "Looking good for a Beta. This one's a Tasty, for sure."

I felt moist flesh on my forehead, which was Dr. Lusardi's hand, checking me for fever. She said, "Emergence appears to be successful. Give her a couple hours just to make sure she's not a Fail, but I'm not worried about this one. Give her a mild tranquilizer now to calm her down. Once her blood pressure and body temperature stabilize, put her under general anesthesia, brand her face, and implant the chips."

* * *

The second time I awoke, after my chips had been implanted, Dr. Lusardi was again standing over me.

"Mother?" I asked. My surroundings, which had been vague in my first panicked awakening, now registered more clearly. I understood that Dr. Lusardi had been responsible for making me.

"Creator!" Dr. Lusardi said sternly. "Not Mother. Now, sit up."

I sat up, feeling light-headed as I experienced the effect of gravity on my anatomy. My vision was still hazy, but I comprehended enough to realize that I was in some kind of medical laboratory. I saw wall-size information displays showing anatomical images of the human body along with scientific formulas, storage units marked as containing DNA samples, and life-size skeletons. As I gazed around the white-walled, windowless medical laboratory room, I saw floor-to-ceiling data interfaces with illuminated numbers and symbols scrolling across them. Behind the interface was a table holding surgical instruments—scalpels, specula, fiber-optic devices, laser-cutting guides, syringes and needles, and measurement devices—a laser ruler and calipers. Beyond the table, the wall was lined with shelves of medical texts, and jars, so many jars—jars of blood, and jars of gelatinous molds containing spare body parts, such as fingers, toes, nipples, ears, and eyeballs.

Dr. Lusardi poked her fingers around my flesh. She examined my physical attributes, then announced, "Skin tone's a bit waxy, but that's common after stasis; it will wear off. You are indeed exquisite. You'll need a commensurate name.

I shall call you . . . Elysia. Say it after me. *El-EE-zee-ya.*"

"Zha," was all I could sputter.

Dr. Lusardi nodded. "You'll need another day before orientation, I see." She addressed a hollow-eyed male orderly standing in the corner. Perhaps he too had woken up on the same table upon which I now sat. "Take her to the waiting chamber until she's ready for orientation. And give her some clothes."

Dr. Lusardi started to walk away, then she turned back around to inspect me one more time. She said, "You should fetch an excellent price, Elysia. Even for a Beta."

The waiting chamber was a windowless room with a row of single beds lining the wall and no other furnishings. There were four other new Emergents like me, also awaiting orientation, dressed in green hospital scrubs like the ones I had been issued. The other new clones, two females and two males, appeared older than me—in their twenties and thirties, human age—and were notable for their exceptional aesthetics, with physical attributes humans consider superior, such as lean bodies and faces with high cheekbones, full lips, and full heads of hair. Their faces reflected nil variance. While my database flashed me examples of human facial expressions, with labels such as HAPPY, SAD, ANGRY, and LOVING, these other Emergents exhibited no expressions other than BLANK.

We did not speak to one another. What would there be to say? *What the . . . ?*

And there was a fuchsia-eyed clone standing in the

corner of the room at all times who had the bulk of a heavy-weight boxer. It was clear from his appearance and his constant silent watch over us that we were to wait, to rest, and not to converse.

So, in the waiting chamber, I lay down on the cot like a good clone, and I slept when I could, and I waited for a life outside the waiting chamber.

The next day, the other new Emergents and I were brought to the orientation room, another dark, windowless room where we were told to sit on floor pillows set up in a circular pattern. In the middle of our circle, a holographic presentation for newly awakened clones instructing them on their new lives was projected.

An elegant young woman, who had alabaster skin, slanted black eyes, and jet-black hair with violet highlights, narrated the orientation. She wore a red Chinese dress with gold dragons embroidered across it, accentuating her svelte figure. As she spoke, a montage of images was displayed around her, featuring pictures of the Io Sea's violet-blue water lapping on white sand beaches, tiered waterfalls gently cascading over crystalline stones, towering rock formations rising from the ocean, inland mountains, and tangles of dense jungle. Her intonation purred in welcoming delight.

"Hello, newly emerged clones! I am Mei-Xing, and I am here to tell you about Demesne, your new home!

"Demesne is an archipelago of islands formed after a giant undersea volcanic eruption occurred a thousand miles off the coast of the Mainland, the newly realigned continent of countries brought together after an unfortunate time in human history called the Water Wars. This lush new paradise needed humans to enjoy it! Of course! The world had experienced such despair, but now with hope and prosperity once again reclaiming the Earth, this new paradise was primed for pleasure. So, the best island in the new archipelago was bought and developed by some of the wealthiest and most important Mainland humans ever! These swell fellas had the island crafted into the ultimate playground for elite people like them who needed their own private refuge. Of course! They earned it!

"The ocean surrounding the very island where you're watching this right now was reengineered by master scientists and spiritual gurus to create the world's most luxurious waterscape. They remade their waterway and called it the Io Sea, which ripples in patented violet crests, and offers a totally transformative experience. For humans, swimming in Io enlightens, relaxes, and enchants. Beautiful!

"Guess what else? Since they'd already reengineered a whole ocean, they figured, why not make the air better too? So they designed a system to pump premium oxygen into Demesne's atmosphere. This succulent, sweet air, only available in specially designed container spaces elsewhere, is actually pumped across our entire island. Amazing, right? Right!

"So probably now you're thinking, This is total paradise on Demesne, what more could this perfect place need? The answer to that would be: workers to serve the island's guests! Of course! Maids, butlers, cooks, construction laborers, you know! The tiny glitch was that the very atmospheric conditions that make Demesne so totally awesome also make it very difficult to travel to. And it's way too relaxing and fun on Demesne for humans to get any actual work done! Bummer!

"To remedy that, the island's founders built a scientific compound for the brilliant Dr. Larissa Lusardi, the world's top expert on cloning. They brought her to Demesne to create workers who could provide the important services the island would need for it to be a functional resort. And you, my friend, are one of those lucky clones! You have been chosen because of the superior aesthetic of your First—the recently deceased human you were cloned from. Through Dr. Lusardi's patented technology, Firsts' bodies are cloned within forty-eight hours of their expiration, allowing for the extraction of their souls. So, bonus for you! You don't carry the burden of a heavy soul. I know, so lucky!

"You are the elite of human cloning. Congratulations! You represent the strength and beauty for which this island is renowned. And now you will be living and serving on the most luxurious and beautiful place on Earth! Amazing, right? Right!

"Welcome!"

As Mei-Xing pronounced the word *welcome*, a diverse procession of clones whose ethnicities seemed to represent every corner of the earth came forth to wave in greeting and repeat her last word: "Welcome!" They were dressed in the respective uniforms of maids, butlers, chefs, massage therapists, golf and tennis instructors, luxisstants, etc., and like Mei-Xing, they were adult specimens who appeared in their twenties and thirties, and who fit the island aesthetic of great looks matched with great bodies.

I had awakened as one of them, but in teen form.

I held the promise of a new future in cloning.

After the presentation, Dr. Lusardi herself came into the room to address us. She said, "Think of yourselves as empty art canvases." A server clone came into view and handed mirrors to us all. Dr. Lusardi continued. "Look into these mirrors. See your canvases."

I looked into the mirror and saw my face for the first time. I had eyes, ears, nose, cheeks, lips—the usual human complement of features, all perfectly formed and aesthetically desirable. On the right side of my face, I saw the tattoo that had been aestheticized from my temple to my cheekbone, a violet-colored fleur-de-lis symbol. I touched it, and saw the other clones doing the same thing to theirs, trying to feel the pretty picture on our faces to see if the tattoo had texture. It did not.

Dr. Lusardi said, "While you may look like humans, you are not humans. The violet tattoos on your faces are there to signify that distinction. You belong to Demesne." She paused while the server clones removed the mirrors from our hands. Then she continued. "But, like humans, you can be considered to have two parts—what's inside you, and what's outside. The first part, what's inside you, are your organs, which have been replicated from your human Firsts. In humans, what's inside is something that can't be seen—the soul. Here is the primary distinction between you and your Firsts. You do not have souls. What you have instead are individualized chip implants, which have been customized for you. The first chip is in your brain, and it contains all the data you will need to function in your assigned roles on

Demesne. Your chip will instruct you how to mimic human feelings by arranging your face and body language to organically and physically express what your soulless bodies cannot actually feel. It will self-modify to approximate the human expressions appropriate to any situation you are in.

"You will have different roles on Demesne. You two"—here Dr. Lusardi pointed at the two brawny male clones sitting in our circle—"are perfectly built for construction work. You will go straight to construction headquarters from here, with no intermediary broker to auction you off. The skill set you need to operate machinery and the like has been implanted in your chips. You two"—here she pointed to the female clones, slim blondes with tiny waists and full breasts—"will go to a broker who will try to sell you into more upmarket roles, perhaps masseuse or even luxisstant. You will receive training in your assigned jobs, and your chips will show you how to project the qualities that humans like to see in their workers—warmth, devotion, cheerful efficiency." Dr. Lusardi then pointed at me. "And you, our teen Beta. I don't know what will happen with you. My other teen Beta has been a Fail, so normally I would not put you out for sale yet. But you are too exquisite not to give it a try. You have exactly the aesthetic this island seeks, even if you are a Beta."

"What does *Beta* mean?" I asked.

"A test model," she said. "Still under development." She chuckled and added, "Just like a real teenager."

Next, another holographic projection dropped into the middle of our circle, showing the diverse procession of welcome clones we had seen in the earlier presentation, who now displayed their forearms. Dr. Lusardi explained, "The second chip you've received has been inserted beneath your skin on your right wrists. It is your locator, to ensure you're never lost and that your owners always know where to find you."

The new Emergents and I all placed the fingers of our left hands onto our right wrists to touch our chips. We could feel a texture, a small bump beneath the skin. How fortunate. In this new and strange land, we would never be lost.

The holographic image of the clones demonstrating their forearm chips disappeared, replaced with close-up images of the clones' individual faces, displayed in rapid succession. They each had identical violet fleur-de-lis tattoos on the right side of their faces, while the left sides of their faces had individual tattoos, different types of flowers on each.

Dr. Lusardi explained further: "Then there's what's visible on the outside. Your facial tattoos brand you as clones indigenous to Demesne. You've already seen your violet fleur-de-lis tattoos. Once you are bought and assigned duties, the left side of your face will be aestheticized with a specific botanical tattoo symbolizing your role. This is when the empty canvas of your existence shall start to take form. From then on, that botanical symbol will quickly identify what role you serve on the island."

The holographic images disappeared, replaced by a lulling musical accompaniment underscoring the finale to Dr. Lusardi's orientation lecture.

She said, "But as your aesthetic evolves based on your duties here, what will remain constant is your mission. Always remember: you were created to serve. Science has allowed for the extraction of your First's souls so that you clones may serve here without restriction. You feel nothing, so that the humans you serve can feel what they come to Demesne for—happiness."

Holographic images were projected in front of each of us, human faces labeled HAPPY, CONTENT, PLEASED, and SATISFIED.

"These are the faces you shall strive to attain in your service to humans," said Dr. Lusardi. "These faces are your ultimate artistic goal. You are merely the supplies that enable your owners to experience the art of fine living on Demesne, which they've worked so hard to create."

We returned to the waiting chamber after our orientation, and were told we would spend one last night there before being sent the next day either to our new duties, in the case of the two males, or to appropriate brokers to be put up for sale, in the case of the two adult females and myself. We went to bed.

Sometime in the middle of the night, I awoke suddenly, my mouth parched. "Could I please have some water?" I asked the burly clone orderly who presided in the corner of our room at all times, watching over us.

He pointed to the door. Quietly, he said, "There's a water fountain at the end of this hallway. Don't be long."

I scurried outside into the dimly lit hallway. As I marched toward the fountain at the end of the hallway, I passed by a doorway that, unlike the other doors I'd seen so far at the compound, had a glass window for seeing inside the room. The sign on the side of the door said INFIRMARY.

I datachecked this word and learned that an infirmary is a place where malfunctioning or sick beings are sent to be made better.

I peered through the window. The room appeared to be a scientific laboratory similar to the one in which I'd first emerged, with long metal tables and medical equipment. On these tables were fuchsia-eyed clones in need of repair.

A male clone lying on a metal table, his hands and feet locked into restraints, was having the skin on his chest seared off by a lab worker holding a steel torch. A female clone sitting on the next table, also restrained, had blood and ooze dripping from one empty eye socket as a lab worker extracted her remaining eyeball from the other socket. In a corner of the room, a male clone was pinned against a wall, his arms above his head with his wrists and ankles in restraints, and he was being prodded with a long metal stake that was jabbed into his armpits, his mouth and nostrils, then his ears.

The subjects' bodies were all beaten, bruised, and bloody, and their mouths were open, as if they appeared to be saying something. Or screaming something.

My heart palpitated as my hands turned clammy and I felt beads of sweat form on my brow. My body felt turned back to *panic*, as during my first moments upon initial awakening.

I turned around and raced back to the waiting chamber to return to my bed.

Thirst could possibly be a sign of malfunction. I no longer required a drink of water.

3

IT'S TRUE ABOUT THE AIR HERE.

Although I have no basis for comparison, I can feel how the oxygen-enriched air on Demesne could give a human body and mind a constant feeling of bliss. The air here is so smooth I begin to understand how humans with souls would find it impossible to accomplish any work. It's no wonder the humans require clones who don't care about luxuriating in the island's serenity. The sweetness could be as intoxicating as the anesthesia shot to my face from which I am awakening.

My eyes open from their brief slumber. We are gliding in the Aviate again. Now I remember. Anesthesia wears off more quickly on clones. After my purchase, we stopped at the clinic on the grounds of the country club, called Haven, where clones go to be "vined," the term the humans use for clones who have received the specific botanical tattoo symbolizing our role, aestheticized onto the left side of our faces after we are assigned jobs. Mother's bodyguards in the Aviate's front seats are vined in nasturtium—shield-shaped leaves with bright yellow and orange flowers—symbolizing conquest, a trophy.

I touch the left side of my face, drawing a line with my finger from my temple to cheekbone. In the LUV's window reflection, I can faintly see the spikes of spurred, deep-blue flower petals. My vining announces to everyone how fortunate I am to be a teen Beta who will serve in an upper-caste companion role. Dr. Lusardi predicted that I would make an excellent sale, and she was right. I feel a swooping sensation in my stomach, a delicious anticipation. I can't wait for the new adventure to begin. I can't wait to settle into my new home.

"Your vining looks divine," says Mother in her childlike voice. "It will look even better once the burn marks fade. I'm so glad we went with delphinium instead of the chrysan-themum most of the other companions are vined in. Such a pretty choice. The blue complements the violet on the other side of your face so nicely."

Delphinium symbolizes ardent attachment. Mother seems ardently attached to my aesthetic. "Elysia, I don't think I've ever seen a clone as lovely as you. And that's saying something, on this island. I'm so pleased we will have a dear new girl at our home. What a brilliant idea for Dr. Lusardi to make a teen Beta. So young and pure! But oh . . . your poor First. All that wasted young beauty. Her poor mother, to have lost a child so young." She sighs. "Oh, I can't wait to show you off!"

She hugs me to her side. I assess the proper response—to rest my head on her shoulder, and so I do, causing Mother to deposit a maternal kiss on my head. "Such a sweet girl," she coos. Warmth from Mother's hug floods my body. I am not just a companion, but a daughter, just like the Brattons' human girl. I will be cared for and loved just like Astrid. I am such a lucky Beta.

Like all the villas on Demesne, Governor's House, where Mother has brought me home, is designed to be both art and architecture. A hundred or so luxury mansions are scattered across the island, all created by the same architect, all using the same exterior materials: stucco, wood, glass, titanium, and copper. The houses are shaped in sculpted geometric forms that look as if ancient civilizations had merged the temples built for their gods with a modern intergalactic spaceship, then blended these hybrid homes seamlessly into Demesne's landscape.

The Aviate arrives on the driveway's landing pad, which is surrounded by rows of Demesne's signature flowers, called cuvées. The cuvées are torchlike flowers, with bright coral-red spiked flowers on long, erect stems. They make the Aviate landing pad sparkle, like bottles of champagne waiting to be burst open.

Mother clutches my hand as the Aviate comes to a stop. "Welcome home, pet," she purrs.

I do not need a guide to my new home; my chip's interface reveals everything I need to know about it. Governor's House is perched at the top of a cliff abutting the ocean, with floor-to-ceiling glass walls for premium water views. The entryway is a marble foyer with crystal light fixtures hanging overhead, leading to a house of grand rooms: lavish bedrooms, serene lounge areas, state-of-the-art kitchen, massage room. And of course the house has the premium entertainment facility common to homes on Demesne: a FantaSphere room, a fantasy game arena for sports such as virtual deer stalking and shark hunting and rain-forest pillaging, and especially for playing Z-Grav, the zero-gravity game Mother has told me the teens on Demesne are crazy for.

Governor's House is powered by solar energy and operates on clone energy. The Governor and his wife have their own butler to anticipate and serve their every need, along with clones to facilitate the household operations: maids, chef, groundskeepers, luxisstant, bodyguards. The island's larger pool of clones, the sporting instructors, massage therapists, and construction workers, are shared by Demesne residents and reside on the grounds at Haven.

As we walk inside, Mother keeps hold of my hand and says, "You are the first clone at Governor's House to serve as a companion, and its first Beta model. We are going to have such fun trying you out!"

For the last couple of years, my new brother Ivan has been the region's wrestling champion in his weight class. Or so Mother informs me after he wrestles me to the ground after we are first introduced. He is eighteen years old and has light brown hair shorn in a military crew cut, with light-blue eyes and full rosy cheeks like Mother's, giving his face a softness at odds with his imposing bulk.

"Just kidding," says Ivan as he returns to a standing

position. He extends his hand to help me stand back up. "I didn't even know they were making teen Betas now."

"Good boy!" Mother says to Ivan. "Now you have a companion when you want to roughhouse. Someone your own age, so you won't accidentally harm our delicate little Liesel."

Delicate little Liesel squeals with delight. "We got a Beta! We got a Beta!" She is a skinny ten-year-old girl with only the faintest hint of adolescent development in her chest and hips, and has coloring like Ivan's and Mother's. "Can I show her to her room, Mother? Pretty please?"

"No," Mother says. "That's why we have clones, darling. To do the work." Mother addresses the clone standing nearby. "Xanthe, please show the Beta to the old nanny's quarters off Astrid's room. I'll be there soon to help her settle in."

The housekeeper, Xanthe, appears to be in her early twenties in human years. She has pale white skin, with bobbed black hair and angled fuchsia eyes. She is vined in holly, symbolizing domestic happiness. I follow her down a long hallway with glass walls looking over the ocean on one side and vibrant gardens on the other.

"This is an excellent household," I say to her, to make conversation, and to let Xanthe know that she must be doing a great job keeping it so tidy.

"Why wouldn't it be?" she responds.

"I don't know. This is the first house I've been to here."

"It's all the same, any house on this island," says Xanthe. "Harmonious and beautiful."

* * *

I am to take over the former nanny's quarters attached to my new faraway sister Astrid's bedroom. It's small but functional. I have a bed, a chest of drawers for clothes, a desk, and a window overlooking the ocean. Astrid and I even wear the same size. Mother gives me a box from Astrid's wardrobe to fill my own closet. "Astrid never wore most of these clothes," says Mother. "She has such a gorgeous figure for wearing these tight jeans and teeny tank top styles, but she preferred that awful grunge look. So unfortunate, the trash-bag hempwear the peaceniks wear on the continents. But you should be a perfect fit for all these clothes I bought for my fashion-sourpuss daughter."

"Which outfit shall I wear?"

Mother consults her diamond bracelet watch. "The children love to play in the pool at this hour. Put on of one the bathing suits so you can join them."

While I change in the bathroom, I hear the Governor join Mother in Astrid's room. He is indeed not happy about my arrival into his home, and he is not shy about arguing loudly with his wife.

"I told you, no more clones!" he hisses at his wife. "Especially a teen Beta! What were you thinking? The island treaty with the Mainland only covers adult clones, and they'd take away those if they could! Do you realize the political fallout you're exposing me to? You've outdone yourself with this frivolous purchase."

Mother sounds unconcerned. "Don't be ridiculous. Elysia's a gentle little angel. You will love her."

"That has nothing to do with it."

"Dearest. A teen Beta! We're the first to own one! I had

to have her. I promise I won't buy any more."

"She is a teenager. She will turn Awful." I datacheck *teenage Awful* and learn that rapidly changing hormone levels in teenagers can sometimes cause them to act out in wild and insolent ways, which their adult keepers approximate as "Awful" behavior, but generally the adults tolerate these behaviors as teens just "acting their age."

"You don't know that."

I know that. I will not be an Awful teen Beta. My chip will ensure that I always know how to behave like a good girl.

"But why risk it?" says the Governor.

Mother says, "If she doesn't work out, we can return her. Is that enough for you?"

I silently vow never to act out in a way that could cause me to be returned. I must prove worthy of Mother's decision to buy me and make me part of her home and her family.

The Governor says, "I'm serious. No more impulse purchases like this."

"I promise," says Mother.

"And I promise *you*. If this goes awry, it's *your* Relay credit chip that will be cut off." His tone turns playful. "Or cut out, from your arm!"

Mother laughs. "You are such a tease, Governor."

4

AS I STEP OUT ONTO THE POOL DECK, MY NEW brother Ivan's reaction to his sister's replacement wearing her bikini is quite concise: "Whoa." At first I think he is speaking nonsensically to me, but then I datacheck this word—*whoa*—and learn that it is native to eighteen-year-old males.

I understand now why Astrid shunned the bikinis Mother purchased for her. I can't imagine why any girl would want to wear such a thing. It's barely a collection of strings. It really should be called a "lounge costume" as it offers little of the support a body needs for actual swimming.

"Whoa to you too, Ivan," I answer.

I inspect the view. The infinity pool is built on the hillside at the edge of the property, and is angled to give the appearance that the pool drops directly into the ocean below.

The pool's sapphire waters provide a warm highlight to Io's violet-blue waters underneath. It is a partitioned pool, with a large, open, circular section that leads to a smaller grotto pool sequestered in a stone cave.

Ivan does not want me distracted by the view, however. He thinks that the bikini-wearing Beta should jump into the pool immediately. He suggests this by splashing me with a huge wave that wets me from feet to torso. "Jump in, Beta!" he calls to me.

"Can you swim, Elysia?" Liesel asks as she swims over to Ivan at the pool ledge.

Observing me, Ivan tells Liesel, "She has one of those girl bodies, like her First was either a major athlete or she was one of those skinny, built girls who don't eat but then pudge out after they have babies, like Mother."

"Mother is not pudgy," I assert, defending my slender benefactress's honor.

"She was till the nutritionist at Haven put her on that starve diet!" says Ivan cheerfully.

"Maybe Elysia's First had anorexia and that's how she died," Liesel speculates.

Ivan throws his hands up. "Liesel! Dude! You shouldn't even know what anorexia is." He then points at me. "And there's no way that clone's First had anorexia."

"How do you know?" asks Liesel.

Ivan leans over to whisper something into Liesel's ear, causing her to giggle and stare directly at my bikini top.

"Oh," Liesel says, nodding her head in wonderment. "So that's what 'stacked' means."

Ivan splashes Liesel. "Don't say that in front of her."

"Why not?" says Liesel. "She's a clone. She doesn't care."

It's true. I don't care who thinks I'm stacked. I am neither offended nor flattered. I'm just . . . I look down at my round, full breasts . . . stacked, apparently.

And I, too, am curious to know if I can swim. How will I know until I try?

I step to the edge of the infinity pool. I dangle my toes, dipping them in and out, swishing them through the water. The water feels warm and inviting. It's as if the water zaps me when I touch it—a current that calls to me.

Ivan and Liesel resume their game of aqua "Horse" as I test the water with my toes. The siblings' game is not a fair one. Ivan is a burly young man with a wrestler's physique. Delicate little Liesel has nothing to anchor herself against his strength; I understand now why Mother required a teen companion for her teen son. But Liesel plays along with Ivan in delight, seeming pleased to be the object of her big brother's attention.

Dive. I feel like that's what I'm supposed to do. I walk over to the springboard built over the deep end of the pool, and instinctively I bend my knees.

"Do it!" Ivan calls out. "Dive!"

"Go, Elysia!" Liesel says, encouraging me.

My calves spring me forth, up and then over.

I *can* dive! The movement comes naturally, feels graceful.

The water envelops me and I imagine it is like a womb that nurtures those not created in a human-duplication machine. It is warm comfort. It is safety. I can't believe how beautiful the feeling is, my skin drinking in this soft water. This moment is like a miracle. A few weeks ago, I wasn't even alive. A few weeks ago, my First lost her life, and I gained her body and this fascinating new existence. Now, I experience this gift called life by swimming in my new family's pool located on the most luxurious island on Earth.

As my arms press through the water's resistance, I realize: I am a *strong* swimmer. Beneath the water, I experience a moment of recognition: I am *supposed* to be in the water.

When I come up for air, Ivan and Liesel are staring at me with stunned expressions.

"Do you think your First was a diver?" Liesel asks me.

"I don't know," I sputter.

"That was, like, an Olympics-worthy dive," Ivan says. "Our new Beta sister is amazing!" He and Liesel high-five each other.

"What else can you do?" Liesel asks.

I dive back underwater and do a handstand, and under the water again, I experience something else. I hear a voice calling to me: *Z! Over here! Z!* The voice calling to me rips at my heart, jolting my balance. I must flip the handstand over and return to the air again.

I am so confused. I feel blindsided, probably by the sun's bright burst directly onto my exposed skin. "What's buzzing?" I ask my new siblings. I rock my head left and right. Do I have water trapped in my ears?

My new siblings appear confused too. "Nothing," they both respond.

Maybe I just imagined the *Z* sound under the water.

"Anyone can do a handstand," Ivan says, swimming toward me. "How are you at water wrestling?"

He lurches toward me, grabbing my arms from behind

me. I bend down and flip him over my back. Again, I experience recognition. Somehow, I know: I've done this move before. I know exactly how to water-wrestle with a strong male.

Ivan tumbles back into the water as Liesel laughs in delight.

I see Mother watching us through the glass patio doors. She is smiling. I am fitting right in, doing my job exactly as she'd hoped.

Ivan returns from beneath the water.

"She got you!" Liesel teases him.

"That was a good move, Elysia," Ivan says. "Astrid was so boring to play with. She just wanted to sit by the pool and read prehistoric Communist manifestos. You'll be much more fun."

Liesel jumps onto me from behind for a piggyback ride, splashing water at Ivan. "Catch us! Catch us!" she squeals.

She holds on to me until Ivan catches us and throws her off me so he can wrestle me on his own, fair and square. He is stronger than me, but I am more agile. He grabs me in a tight hold, but I wrap my calf around his knee to break myself free from his grip. The amount of resistance is just right—we are well-matched in this game. I dive underwater and swim the length of the pool's floor, coming up for air before he's lumbered halfway back to catch me again. I dive under again and swim around his legs to taunt him before he can grab me in another hold.

Beneath the water, I realize something for certain: I *have* done this move before—swum around a boy to tease him. And now I can see this male's long, strong legs. I understand by the size and form of the muscles in my vision that the stranger's blond-haired legs belong to a swimmer—a *serious* swimmer.

This is not right.

I swim away from Ivan's legs to rid myself of this false image, stroking toward the underwater tunnel that leads to the grotto side of the pool. But the underwater sprint only brings another apparition: a face to go along with the serious swimmer's legs. I see a young man, sun-kissed, with the looks of a historic California surfer god—golden skin, blond hair, turquoise eyes, a torso sculpted into the human aesthetic of muscular perfection. It's as if his deep blue eyes are staring right at me, recognizing me, inviting me. His full red lips part to say something: *Z!* My heart clenches, longing for him, needing to touch him, *immediately.* I reach out my arms for him. I must touch him, I must, I must, but the excited, almost desperate gasp of my breath causes me to gulp water, and I am forced to rise back to the surface before I reach the passage to the grotto.

I cough, trying to expel the water from my lungs and regain my equilibrium. Ivan and Liesel swim to my side and supportively pat my back.

"You okay, champ?" asks Ivan.

I'm possibly *not* okay. What I saw under the water was a vision that belonged to my First. I don't know how I know this, but I do.

I remove the negative thought from my mind. This family bought an unfeeling clone, and that's exactly what they're going to get. They deserve only the best. I will be that best. My body quivers, shaking off whatever impossible thing just happened beneath the water.

On the pool deck, I see Xanthe, the housekeeper, tidying the area around the pool, picking up wet towels from the ground and spreading them out to dry on the lounge chairs. For a moment, our fuchsia eyes lock and she nods at me, as if to assure me that I am doing my job well, just as she is doing hers. Xanthe is like me, only she is meant for work and I am meant for play.

"Do you need a rest?" Liesel asks me. She rubs my arm tenderly as my coughing spell finishes.

"I most certainly do not!" I say, splashing her and inciting a new round of delighted squeals from my new little sister.

Like Xanthe, I know how to do my job.

5

THE SUN AND THE POOL PLAY HAVE FAMISHED Liesel and Ivan. They devour their dinners while I sip my strawberry shake.

"Do you like macaroni and cheese, Elysia?" Liesel asks me between greedy bites. "It's my favorite."

"Don't be a dork," Ivan says. "You know clones only drink strawberry shakes."

"I might like vanilla shakes too," I say.

The family laughs as if I am hilarious.

As a courtesy, full servings of the same foods the humans are eating have been placed on my plate, even though nutritionally I only need the strawberry shake to survive. I have grilled tuna, a salad, and a side serving of macaroni and cheese. I can process the human food, but not enjoy its taste.

It would be pointless for me to eat their food, as all the nutrition they intake from their meal I can get from one single shake. The strawberry shakes have adequate flavor, but I've been told the shakes' chemical components are abhorrent to human tastes, so I don't have to be polite and offer them sips of my special drink.

"You should try the macaroni," Liesel advises me. "It's awesome."

I have never tasted food besides Dr. Lusardi's strawberry shakes. I look toward Xanthe, standing at a discreet distance behind the dinner table, ready to serve and clear the meal as needed. Xanthe tactfully nods at me. I should try.

I fork a piece of macaroni that's on the plate in front of me and place it in my mouth. The pasta feels soft inside my mouth while the cheese flavor dances across my tongue. Ohmygoodnessthisissogood. My mouth feels infiltrated with . . . delight? I datacheck the setting *delight* and learn that it is a state of extreme satisfaction, a high degree of gratification. Indeed, I am extremely gratified to chew such cheesy goodness. My stomach seems to be signaling my mouth, *More more more, please!*

It's like my wiring is tripping all over itself. My chip tells me to *express* delight at the humans' food, but my stomach says it *is* indeed delighted. Whoever invented adding melted cheese over starchy goodness was surely the most brilliant human ever.

But. I should not be able to take pleasure from taste. I should only know how to express pleasure without actually feeling it. I should not eat another bite. Yet I can't help myself. I want more macaroni and cheese. I cannot understand how the humans don't eat this flavor combination for *every—single—meal.*

I chew and swallow the remaining portion of my macaroni and cheese, and even though I want to ask for another large portion, I don't. I return to my safe strawberry shake.

It's not possible I could have enjoyed an unnecessary piece of carbohydrate. Clones have taste buds that can distinguish flavor but not take pleasure from it. This is what I was told.

"What did you think?" Liesel asks. "It's great, right?"

"Completely awesome," I assure her.

Ivan chuckles.

"JK!" Liesel gleefully squeals.

"What's JK?" I ask.

"Just kidding!" Liesel and Ivan say at the same time.

Oh, that again.

Mother beams at me, then shoots a glance at the Governor, sitting at the head of the table. "Did I not say she's a delight? She'll even try Liesel's macaroni and cheese, just to please us."

It really was awesome. I was not being kind or JK.

But they don't need to know that. At no point during orientation was I instructed to reveal any Beta quirks that might arise, such as an unfortunate (but fortunate!) sense of taste.

"She's a natural in the water too," Ivan says. "I bet her First was an athlete."

"Now, there's an idea," the Governor says to Ivan. "You need to be kept occupied until you start basic training. If Elysia is so athletic, she could be your fitness companion. Get you ready for the Base. Give the Beta some actual use here instead of just pretending to like human food to please you."

Rather than university, Ivan is soon to follow in his father's footsteps and enter into military service. He will join the elite private army that trains on the Base, the giant military compound on the Mainland that extends for a hundred miles, from the ocean into the desert. The army and its Base are owned by the same people who live on Demesne, but the army protects those powerful people elsewhere. On peaceful Demesne, no army is needed, and also would be an aesthetic nuisance.

"Cool!" Ivan says.

The Governor turns to me. Like his son, he is a large male, but with a rigid, authoritative demeanor. The Governor boasts, "Five generations of the men in this family have risen to the rank of general. One day Ivan will be the sixth. Elysia, you will help Ivan with physical training to get him into top shape for boot camp. He leaves in three months. He can use this time to prepare."

"Yes, Governor," I say.

He has not instructed me to call him "Father."

MOTHER BRUSHES MY HAIR UNTIL IT SHINES.
"This is what I miss," she sighs. "Astrid has beautiful golden hair just like yours."

I sit at the vanity in Astrid's room while Mother stands behind me, observing me in the mirror. She is so content. It seems like a good time to ask the important questions about the birds and the bees.

Not those birds and bees. I know about those.

"Mother," I say. "Are there clones on other island resorts?"

She pats the top of my head affectionately. "No, pet. We're more special here. Other island resorts use native human populations for workers, but that's not possible here. Our island was formed relatively recently, so it has no native people. Except us, of course!" She winks at me in the mirror. "And it's extremely costly to get passage here, so importing workers is not an option. Other, less special places use human workers. Only Demesne can have clone workers. Rules and laws, boring boring boring!"

"Is there a boat that brings people here from the Mainland?"

Mother smiles at me in the mirror. "At last, a daughter who doesn't treat me like a major drag." She laughs. "Perhaps you don't know, but real teenagers have a way of treating their parents like they wish the creatures didn't exist. I rather like having one who doesn't ignore me and wants to ask me questions!" She pauses, struggling to remember my question. "Yes, Elysia! Residents come here by private plane, obviously, but Demesne's treaty with the Mainland requires that a boat go back and forth from the Mainland, so Demesne doesn't seem so exclusive and off-limits to nonresidents." Mother teasingly places her hand over her mouth, as if to confide in me, and speaks in a lower voice. "Even though it is!"

"So the boat is very expensive?"

"No, dear. The boat is practically free. But the visas required for entry here cost quite a nifty sum. Visitors who come here need to get visas in order to stay at Haven, since we don't have real hotels. We don't want tourists running amok here."

"Then how come people can't also fly to Demesne like the residents who have houses here?"

"They *can* fly here. So long as they own a piece of the landing strip, which is required in order to own property here."

"Then people who want to come here buy landing-strip rights," I say.

Mother scoffs. "Sure, if you have that billion Uni-dollars to spare! My dear, the landing strip rights cost more than all the homes on this island combined."

"So that's why workers aren't ferried or flown in?"

"My goodness, Betas are question-y. It's almost cute, until it goes on too long and costs me my beauty sleep." She pauses, as if gathering her energy, then explains. "Clones are very eco, you know." She squeezes my arm affectionately. "You should be very proud to be one. Recycling dead people into clones is the ultimate scientific achievement. Your human First's death was not wasted, and you are totally biodegradable after your term of service."

I do not ask how long my term of service will be. I'm not ready to address my own biodegradability—when I age too much, as happens to clones once their looks and abilities fade after their decade of service. I've only just started living. To put an end date on my term of service when I'm still under warranty seems premature.

"I understand that I am fortunate to be here and I have gratitude to you for welcoming me, Mother," I say.

She gently rubs the backs of my shoulders. "My sweet girl. If you really want to know, we tried the human experiment, years ago. We brought in a real nanny for the children, who slept in what's your room now. We thought it would give the children some true cachet—a real, live Mary Poppins! What a disaster she turned out to be. The exquisite atmosphere here made her feel so much better than she should have. Instead of being a disciplinarian and babysitter, she turned completely relaxed and happy. She let the children run wild while *she* sunbathed! Disgraceful, wouldn't you say?"

"Yes, Mother."

From behind me, Mother runs her fingers through my long hair, then she divides it into three sections and braids it. I smile at her in the mirror's reflection. Mother says, "I used to braid Astrid's hair before she went to bed. It was the one thing she'd let me do for her, independent little minx. She said she slept better when her hair wasn't tangling up on her pillow."

"The braids feel nice, Mother. Thank you."

She kisses the top of my head. "You're welcome. Now, there's something you could do for me."

"Yes, Mother?"

"Sometimes when Liesel sleeps, she has nightmares. If you hear her, will you go to her until she falls back asleep? I take sleep aids at night and often don't hear her. Astrid used to do it, but now Ivan does, and he just makes Liesel more anxious. Boys and their bedtime war games. He has no sense for how to soothe a scared child. You know how young men are."

I don't know. Other than that they say, "Whoa."

"I will, Mother," I say.

"Good girl. Good night."

She walks toward the exit of my bedroom, pausing to stand in the doorway for a last moment to observe me. My feed recognizes her face reflecting human *pride* and *affection* as her gaze settles on me.

"Mother?" I ask her.

"Yes, dear?"

"When Astrid got sick, what happened to her?"

"What do you mean?"

"Did she go to the infirmary?"

Mother laughs softly. "No, of course not. We took care of her here when she got sick, as we would with all our children. Mercifully, none have ever been ill enough to require hospital care."

"So if I got sick, I would not go to the infirmary?"

Mother turns out the light in my bedroom. "Go to sleep, Elysia. You are not capable of being sick. You're just that perfect."

7

I HEAR LIESEL'S SCREAM IN THE MIDDLE OF the night. I jump out of bed and run to her room, as Mother requested. I turn on the light in her room and see that it is a shrine to the old-time princess vogue, with sparkling pink walls, a French vanity with drawers, and a four-poster canopy bed surrounded in pink tulle.

I sit down on her bed. Liesel throws herself against me, burrowing her face against my chest. I stroke her hair, experiencing an overwhelming need to comfort this distressed child. Just like a real sister, I want to protect her from harm, real or imagined. My nightgown dampens from her tears.

"What happened?" I ask Liesel.

"I dreamed about the bad guys again. They were standing on the ground outside my bedroom, shooting bullets into my window. Just like in Ivan's game."

"That's terrible. That would never happen here."

"It *could*. The bad guys are everywhere."

"Who told you that?"

"Ivan. He said the protest people are getting stronger and they're going to start coming after us, not just after Daddy."

"Who are the protest people?" I scan my internal database but find no information about such a sect.

"Don't you know anything, Elysia? The ones who are against cloning."

I kiss the top of Liesel's head, the way Mother did mine. I set my tone to *reassuring* and tell Liesel, "How could anyone be against cloning? People would protest . . . *me?* I don't think that's possible."

She looks into my face and for a moment her stress appears to lessen. But my comforting face is apparently not enough. "But how do you *know?*" Liesel persists.

"Know what?"

"That no one will try to hurt me."

I datacheck this question, which provides the definitive answer. "Bad things don't happen on Demesne," I promise Liesel.

Liesel whispers, "Are there bad clones out there?"

"What do you mean?" I whisper back.

"Defective ones. Clones that don't work."

I lift her bedroom window so that a stream of fresh Demesne air might soothe her. "I think you already know that this island is too perfect to allow anything defective to exist here."

But if there are defective clones, perhaps that is why they

have an infirmary at Dr. Lusardi's compound, so they can be tucked safely away from humans?

I sit back down next to Liesel and pull her close. I softly rub her chin to offer solace.

She burrows her head into my chest again, at last comforted. "You work good," Liesel murmurs.

Awake, she is pacified, but Liesel remains convinced that "someone bad" is coming to get her in her sleep. She begs, "Can I sleep with you, in Astrid's bed? Astrid used to bring me to sleep with her when I was scared from nightmares. My bed's too small for two people."

We return to Astrid's room. I tuck Liesel into Astrid's bed, then slip in alongside her. Liesel places her hand on my waist for reassurance and quickly drifts back to sleep, exhausted from the drama she created for herself.

I cannot fall back to sleep so easily. Since I am filling in for Astrid, I figure it's my job to get to know her better. I look at a holophoto on her nightstand, picturing Astrid and Liesel, their arms around each other's shoulders. Liesel is smiling and Astrid is not. Astrid has light-blond shoulder-length hair like mine, and baby-blue eyes like Mother's. Liesel looks carefree and happy, while Astrid looks tired and distracted.

I open the drawer on Astrid's nightstand. In it there are pieces of strawberry-flavored hard candy. I wonder if I will like strawberry candy as much as I like strawberry shakes. I reach for a piece of the candy but its wrapper is slightly undone, leaving the candy stuck to the bottom of the drawer. I pull at it, but what comes up is not just the candy, but a board that lines the drawer bottom. As the board comes up along with the candy stuck to it, I see there's a drawer hidden beneath. The drawer contains notebooks filled with Astrid's university entrance-exam practice tests. I pick up one of the notebooks and read through Astrid's answers. Her scores at the beginning of the book are weak, but by the last one, she's achieved near-perfect results. Even her handwriting has improved by the end. No wonder Mother is so proud of her. Astrid clearly worked very, very hard to attain the scores she'd need to gain admittance to the best universities.

I place the notebook back in the drawer on top of the other items stored there. There's a silver dagger with a red ribbon wrapped around it, and a note attached: *Merry Christmas, Astrid. Love, Dad.* The rest of Astrid's drawer is filled with a dictionary and girl products—the ones for their cycle. I take out the dictionary to read later but leave the dagger and the girl products. Replicants are like humans biologically in every way except that we cannot replicate ourselves. I do not need girl products because I have no cycle. I wouldn't know what to do with a dagger. But I can always learn new words.

It occurs to me that there are only holophotos in Astrid's room of herself and Liesel but no other family members. In fact, in comparison to Liesel's room, which is decorated very pink and frilly, Astrid's has minimal furnishings and decoration. It's almost sterile. The only "art" hanging on her wall is a calendar, on which she X'd the days counting down to her departure.

* * *

I am still awake in the morning when Xanthe comes into Astrid's room. I close Astrid's heavily marked-up dictionary that kept me engaged through the night and place it on the bed. I am surprised to have found so many words that appear on the printed page that I cannot find by scanning my database's dictionary.

I have just come across a word that Astrid highlighted.

> **Insurrection** [in-suh-REK-shuhn]: An act
> or instance of rising in revolt, rebellion,
> or resistance against civil authority or an
> established government.

Insurrection strikes me as a threatening and unpleasant word, but next to this dictionary entry, Astrid scribbled, *Yes!*

"There she is," Xanthe says, looking at Liesel slumbering peacefully by my side. "It's time to get her up and ready for school."

"There's a school here?" I ask. "Will I go to it?"

"If I had a sense of humor, I'd think you were funny," Xanthe says.

I guess this means I will not be going to school here. "Where is the school?" I ask.

"Since there aren't enough year-round residents on Demesne to support a school, the children who live here have tutors. The tutors work with students at Haven. They have regular school hours, as on the Mainland."

"Are the tutors clones?" I ask.

"Of course. No human could be trusted to educate them thoroughly. But there are no other children her age on the island for her to socialize with and she gets lonely, so you will be her playmate after tutoring time."

Just months ago, my First was probably a student. Perhaps she lived somewhere on the Mainland. I wonder if she was a good student. As hard-working as Astrid, as eager to go off to university?

"Do you wish for an education?" I ask Xanthe.

She looks at me as if I had suddenly sprouted three heads, or suddenly announced my sincere and not just mimicked love for macaroni and cheese. "What could I possibly do with an education?" Xanthe asks.

"Learn stuff? Change and grow better?" I surmise. "There is just so much to learn here and it's just . . ." I start to say *amazing* but am cut short by Xanthe's eyes narrowing suspiciously at me. I don't have much education, but I know enough to know I should not desire to experience anything *amazing*; I should reflect that experience for humans, but not actually feel or desire it for myself. "It's just . . . good to have information," I conclude.

Xanthe pronounces, "I do not wish for anything and I do not need to be better than I already am. I do not wish because I am made to serve, and all the information I need, I already have. As do you." She goes to Astrid's closet, where some of Liesel's clothes are hanging, pulls out pieces of clothing, and assembles Liesel's outfit for the day on a chair.

I am about to nudge Liesel's arm to gently wake her. I don't want her to miss the privilege of her schooling. But

Xanthe stops me from nudging Liesel. She leans in close to whisper to me.

"Do *you* wish?" she asks.

My heart suddenly beats faster, as if I am being threatened, when I know I am only being reassured about my duties. "I do not wish," I state. "I serve."

"Correct," says Xanthe, and nudges Liesel awake.

PER THE GOVERNOR'S ORDERS, IVAN AND I BEGIN our workout regimen at eight in the morning. We do stretches and calisthenics on the patio, take a jog on a flat path, and end our regimen with a series of heart-racing, vigorous stair sprints up the cliff that goes from the beach to the Governor's House.

We are halfway up the cliff stairs for our fifth jaunt when Ivan stops us to survey the landscape below us. "Did you explore much on Demesne, before you came here?" he asks me between panted breaths.

Again I am reminded of the miracle of this new moment. Before I came here, I was confined to closed spaces—Dr. Lusardi's compound, the boutique—and could not suck in this sweet Demesne air or stare from the top of a cliff down to a magnificent vista of violet water, white sandy beach, palm trees, and divine perfection. And this is only what I can see right now. Who knows how much more spectacular the scenery will become as I explore this island more?

I don't answer Ivan's question. There's too much to say. I want to see *everything*!

"Of course you didn't. You probably weren't allowed. I'm sorry," Ivan says, unnecessarily. He reaches inside a deep hole in the cliff's stone, within arm's distance of the cliff stairs, and pulls out a magnification lens stored there. He hands it to me. "Check it out. Pretty amazing view, huh?"

I look through the lens, inspecting the scenery, gulping in the honeysuckle-flavored air. The light blue of the sky is tinged with a rosy-orange haze, evidence of where the sun meets Demesne's atmosphere. Surrounded by Io's rippled violet waters, I see a landscape filled with villas nestled under a rainbow spectrum of trees. Farther out is the mountain range from which Mount Orion, the highest of all, lords it over the island, billowing out volcanic smoke. Below the volcanic mountain is a forest so dense it appears to be a tangled jungle. In that jungle, under the smoky mountaintop, was Dr. Lusardi's compound where I was made, but it is not visible through the binoculars.

I focus the lens on a sandy beach spot at Haven in the distance. I watch as a heavyset woman steps into the water, dips under for a brief soak, then returns to her beach perch. She looks a size thinner and ten years younger as a result of that single dip, as if the sea offered a makeover boost from which she emerged as her more radiant self. Back on the sand, she straddles her male partner, who sets aside his reading material. He wraps his legs around her. They kiss slowly, longingly, as if for the first time, even though their physical familiarity with each other indicates they are longtime companions.

Hovering in the background, the club's servants carry drinks and plates of food to nearby sunbathers.

"Good view of the good life, huh?" Ivan asks me. I know he means the good life intended *for humans*, but I nod in agreement anyway. For me too, I think.

After our tenth sprint up and down the stairs, Ivan stops us for another rest at the bottom of the stairs, near the shoreline.

"I can't believe you can keep up with me," he says.

I can more than keep up with him. In fact, I easily could whip his time and speed, but Mother instructed me to let Ivan win. "His confidence needs to be bolstered before his military basic training," she said. "Be a nice girl, darling Elysia. Let Ivan have his way."

A teen girl runs down the cliff stairs and approaches us.

"Ivan! Hi!" She is a pert, freckle-faced redhead wearing a tennis costume. "They told me I could find you down here. Want to play doubles with me and Dementia?"

"Hey, Greer," Ivan mumbles. "Maybe not today."

"What's that?" Greer demands, pointing at me.

"We got a Beta," says Ivan.

Greer appraises me, staring deep inside my glassy eyes. "They're making *teen* replicants now? Guess I better watch my back! Don't want the pirates to capture and turn me into the undead." She fondles a piece of my hair. "Your First had great hair texture. I wonder what moisturizer she used. Do you have a name?"

"Elysia," I say.

"Lusardi picks the weirdest names. Do you play tennis?" Greer asks.

Ivan answers on my behalf. "She's here to play with me. Not you, Greer."

"Don't be like that," Greer says, pouting. "I'm just trying to get a good game going." She walks back up the stairs, turning to us one more time. "We'll be on the courts if you two want to join us. Or maybe we'll see you later at the club."

Greer sprints away up the stairs.

"Who was she?" I ask Ivan.

"Her dad is the envoy to Demesne," Ivan says, rolling his eyes. "She lives on the property adjoining ours. He basically represents the military's interests on Demesne. I'm pretty sure being named an envoy is just a sweet gig for rich or influential military people with no actual tactical skills. The military sends them here to be happy but useless."

"So, Greer's father is happy and useless. Is she also?"

Ivan shrugs. "She's all right, I guess."

"Don't you like her? She's very pretty."

"I like her okay. She's just always around. She's kind of a slut. There's nothing, like, interesting or mysterious about her."

Speaking of mysterious: "What's a dementia?" I ask.

"Dementia is Greer's best friend. Her real name is Demetra."

"Then why call her Dementia?"

"Datacheck the word. Then the name will make sense once you meet her."

> **Dementia** [di-MEN-*sh*a]: Mental deterioration of organic or functional origin.

I cannot imagine how this word could be personified in a real human girl, and I cannot wait to find out.

Ivan taps my shoulder to resume another chase. I race along the shore, running as far as I can. Ivan runs and runs, but he cannot catch me.

From the signal of satisfaction my chip sends me, I understand: humans like winning.

Apparently, so do I.

We circle back to the stairs to race back up them. Ivan reaches the top of the stairs about a minute behind me, out of breath.

"You cheat," he says. "You drank a strawberry shake before that last lap."

Indeed, I drank a strawberry shake that had been left for me at the top of the stairs before our last sprint, but Ivan too fortified with a wheatgrass shot left for him.

"You're right," I tell Ivan. "I had extra help."

Sweat pours down his face while mine remains clear and smooth. I could continue climbing another thousand steps. Ivan folds his torso down over his legs, exhausted.

"Tomorrow we'll make even better time, right?" I ask him.

"You're killing me," he moans.

"What's a slut?" I ask him.

"A girl who puts out too easily."

"Puts out what?" I imagine Greer putting out dinner and don't understand what Ivan wouldn't like about that.

"Puts out, you know. . . ." His face, already beet red from our run, turns a darker scarlet. "Sex."

I wonder where Greer puts the sex out.

It's no wonder the word *insurrection* is not found on my database. What could there be to revolt against on Demesne? Life here seems, as Ivan puts it, "major sublime."

Ivan and I sunbathe on the deck of the floating pool at Haven. Built in the middle of Nectar Bay, which flanks the country club, the pool is made of glass so that swimmers can view the colorful striped and spotted tropical fish teeming outside the pool but not ruin their feet by having to walk across the coral on the bay's shallow floor nor tamper with the marine ecosystem in the bay. The sun beams bright in midday glory, turning the violet water surrounding the pool to a bright pink. My skin goldens as Ivan and I relax on rafts lightly bobbing on the water. In the distance, I see the sunbathers on the beach. Those people are so idle and happy, they're almost comatose. They couldn't manage a protest even if they tried.

"Nap time," says Ivan from the raft next to me. He places a towel over his eyes to block out the sun. "You about killed me today, Elysia."

Our floating rest is jostled by the arrival of the mentally deteriorating human girl.

Dementia joins Ivan and me in the floating pool at

Haven by way of a cannonball. We hear her yelping with excitement as she races down the pier toward the pool. She wears one of those collections of strings called the bikini. I too am wearing a two-piece suit, but a more secure-fitting, navy-colored sports bra and briefs I found in Astrid's pile of discarded clothing. Once Dementia approaches the pool's ledge, she leaps into the air, folding her knees and clutching them to her torso. "Cannonball!" she shouts before splashing down into the pool, creating waves so strong they nearly knock off us from our rafts.

She emerges back into the air to grab the side of Ivan's raft.

"Hey, sexy beast," Dementia says to Ivan. "I heard your mom got a Beta."

Ivan points to me. "That's her. She's called Elysia."

Dementia dives back underneath the water, swims under Ivan's raft, and arrives at the side of mine. She is as pretty-looking as her pretty-sounding name, with dark olive skin, black hair, and olive eyes to match her skin tone. She places her hands on my raft and checks me out. "So shiny. So pretty. Ivan, your mom has great taste." She places one hand on my forearm, drawing her fingernails in a straight line down my arm. The gesture is something between a tickle and a scratch.

"Dementia!" Ivan splashes her from his raft. "Don't cut her. How many times do we have to remind you? Cutting is something you save for yourself. It's not to be inflicted on others."

Dementia's hand grabs my raft instead of my arm and she casts her eyes down, contrite. "Sorry." With her olive eyes not staring at me, I notice the temple on the deeply scarred right side of her face. It appears she used some sharp edge—perhaps a razor—to try to sculpt her own fleur-de-lis design but gave up halfway. Perhaps she did not have the proper anesthesia. Her eyes look back up at me, with an eager expression on her face. "So, Elysia . . . can you, like, do stuff?"

"What kind of stuff?" I ask her.

Ivan answers for me. "She's an ace swimmer. Show her, Elysia."

I drop off my raft and place my feet on the bottom of the pool. Then I leap forward with my arms extended in front of me, dive underneath, and launch into the butterfly stroke. I race across the pool as quickly as my arms and legs will move, wondering if the underwater apparition of manly gorgeousness I discovered in the pool at Governor's House will decide to make himself known to me again once I am submerged.

He does not. I don't know whether to be disappointed or relieved.

When I come for air at Demetra's side, her jaw is slightly dropped.

"I've never seen a stroke that fast and that perfect," she says. "You're like a machine."

Ivan says, "I think we should take her to Hidden Beach and see what kind of dives she can do off the rocks there. This pool's too shallow for diving."

"Plus there's all the old people hanging around here," Dementia says in disgust. In fact, we're the only three in the floating pool at this moment, but on the beach there are several sun worshippers of late middle age—the late thirties–early forties, human kind of middle age that does not require the expiration date mandated for clones of comparable seniority. The old people have been watching us, as if waiting for us to leave. "Not very 'raxic-encouraging," Dementia adds.

I scan my database but can find no clues whatsoever as to what Dementia meant. However, I nod my head knowingly to her statement, to seem like I am part of their crowd, which is my job.

Ivan swipes his arm to Relay. He communicates a message, then returns his glance to Dementia and me. "Farzad's at Hidden."

"Ask him how's the water?" says Dementia.

Ivan Relays. "He says total 'raxia."

"Let's do it!" says Dementia. She shakes her head wildly so that her long hair whips and sprays water across her shoulders. To the people on the beach, she loudly calls out, "You can have your pool back now, olds!"

9

WE TAKE A SMALL SAILBOAT FROM HAVEN TO A
beach spot a short way up the island. Ivan beaches the boat
onshore and leads Dementia and me to a set of nearby rocks.
We climb the precarious formations. Once we reach the tops
of the rocks, we are perched above a cove of violet water
lapping golden foam onto crystalline pink sand. This is
Hidden Beach.

We jump down from the rocks toward Ivan and
Dementia's friend Farzad, who is on the sand, buffing his
surfboard. He looks up from his board for a first glimpse of
me. Farzad speaks the same native tongue as Ivan.

"Whoa," he says to Ivan. "Way to Beta."

"Admire but do not touch," Ivan says.

Dementia giggles. "If you break it, you have to pay
for it."

Ivan and Dementia sit down on the sand opposite Farzad, so I sit down too. The warm sand offers a gentle, massaging heat against my backside.

Like Ivan, Farzad wears only board shorts, but the display of Farzad's physique shows him to be lean, with taut muscles where Ivan's are bulky. He has dark brown skin with eyes to match, and shoulder-length black hair tied back in a ponytail. He tells us, "I took a Jet Ski out to the breaks earlier. Met some kids from the Rave Caves surfing the *gigantes* out there."

"What are the *gigantes*?" I ask. My database has no definition for the word they pronounce *hee-GAHN-tays*.

"Giant waves," Ivan says, pointing to the ocean in the distance, where I can see the white tips of monster-size waves forming, at least a mile out from where we're sitting.

"That must be very dangerous to surf," I assume. Not only are the waves huge, but they are blue-gray because they are outside the periphery of Io's ring, the violet crests demarcating the line between the Io Sea and the ocean beyond. The ring has been bioengineered to push back the rising waters that have destroyed other coastal places around the world. The pure waves on the other side of Io's ring look as if they would gobble any human who tried to ride them.

"Danger is a state of mind," Farzad informs me. "Conquer it, and you ride heaven."

"The perfect water inside the ring not good enough for you?" Ivan teases.

"I had the wave controller dial it to max," Farzad says, referring to the wave control on designated surf beaches

inside the ring that surfers can have Demesne staff manip-
ulate to suit their desire of thrill seeking. Inside the ring,
the water is modulated to maximize fun but ensure safety.
Apparently, safety is a bore to Farzad. "I asked him to go
gigante size, but he said that wasn't allowed. It was snoozer
on this side. I was only going to get more by going directly
to the source. I need to understand what's out there in the
gigantes. Because of Tahir."

Ivan and Dementia nod knowingly.

"Did you score from any Rave Cave kids while you were
out in the wild?" Dementia asks.

Farzad's hand dips under the waistband below his finely
cut abs. He pulls out an airtight plastic bag containing
several white pills.

"Scored," Farzad says.

"What are the Rave Caves?" I ask.

Dementia grins at me. "It's so adorable how new clones
don't know anything."

It's true. I don't. But I am eager to learn.

Ivan points to some small islands in the distance, beyond
the *gigantes*. "Those islands out there. They're part of
Demesne, but not really. Our island was just the only really
habitable one that could be developed."

"So no one lives on those islands out there?" I ask.
According to my locator chip, the islands in the distance are
mere dots on a map, nameless and unremarkable.

Ivan tells me, "People live there, supposedly. It's just
totally illegal, and lawless. The terrain is very rough,
untamable. Runaway kids from the Mainland hang out

on that island on the left. They call it the Rave Caves. It's supposedly a totally wild party scene."

"Have you been there?" I ask him.

"No! My father would kill me if I tried."

Farzad adds, "There's no Relaying available in the Rave Caves, or even proper bathrooms or showers. It's completely wild. Surfing the *gigantes* nearby is great, but civilized people don't hang out on the islands nearby, for sure."

I ask, "If it is so wild, who goes there?"

Ivan says, "People from the Mainland sneak off to those islands by boat. They figure if they can get to those closer points, they might be able to gain entry to Demesne."

"How?"

Ivan says, "By swimming here from there. Which is virtually impossible. Or maybe paying a pirate ship to try to Jet Ski them to a place like here, at Hidden Beach."

"Does it work?" I ask. "Do people get here that way?"

Dementia chimes in. "Nope. Mostly they die trying. Then they become clones. Lucky!"

Today I have learned many things. I have learned what *insurrection* means, that sex can get put out, and that Demesne's archipelago includes things like the *gigantes* and Rave Caves. I have also learned that *scoring* does not only apply to numerical values used in a game to determine a winner. *Scoring* can also mean obtaining illegal drugs—in this case, the drug the kids here call *'raxia*. Currently Farzad, Ivan, and Dementia are experiencing this drug. They lie on the sand wrapped around each other, their eyes closed, content smiles spread across their lips. Dementia lies topless on the sand, but, like Ivan and Farzad, she has left her bottom covered.

"It's kind of overdoing it, in my opinion," Greer informs me. I have also learned today that there is no subject on which Greer doesn't have an opinion, including the fact that Farzad, Ivan, and Dementia should have told her they were going to do 'raxia before inviting her over here and wasting her time. "I mean, this whole atmosphere on Demesne—the sweet air, the soothing water, the luxury homes, whatever— was designed to create a state of ataraxia. Why fake more of it? It's just greedy."

Ataraxia, I have also found out, is an ancient Greek concept synonymous for pure happiness, and Demesne's founders designed the island using the term as its central design premise. It is the region's youth who have taken this word and applied it to their version of pure happiness, the drug they call 'raxia.

Greer and I sit on the bluffs above Hidden Beach, overlooking Io, watching the three ataraxic teens on the sand below. Greer says, "I don't know why those guys have to, like, chemically induce even more of it. They're just afraid to experience something real. They've lived here practically their whole lives. They have no idea what real even is."

"Ivan said doing 'raxia is better than sex. Preferable to it, even," I tell Greer, in case she doesn't know.

"I've done both," Greer states. "Real sex is better."

"Where have you done the sex?" I ask her.

"That's a bold question."

"It is?"

"I guess you don't know any better." Greer sways her legs

as they dangle over the bluff. "I've had sex here, and back in the city where I'm from originally from."

"Is the sex good?"

Greer laughs. "Yeah, it's mighty mighty, I have to say."

I do a quick internal dictionary scan but can only determine that she has doubled the word *mighty* without giving it any meaningful relevancy.

"Do you mighty-mighty often?" I ask.

She stares at me with the human facial expression I identify as meaning: *You must be an idiot.*

Greer says, "I 'mighty-mighty' when it's available with a like-minded, hot-bodied kind of person with whom I share a mutual attraction. But I'm only eighteen. It's not like I've 'mighty-mightied' with that many people."

"Who have you mighty-mightied with?"

Her tone turns agitated. "Stop calling it that. It was just a play on words." *A play on words.* I imagine children seesawing over blocks spelling out words like FUN and FAIRYLAND.

"I am sorry. I shall recalibrate the question. Have you had the sex with Ivan or Farzad or Dementia?"

Her white skin turns scarlet. "Maybe," she mutters. She gestures to the slumbering bodies beneath our feet. "But as you can see, they prefer 'raxia. And maybe you are getting too personal, so I would suggest if you have more questions, you recalibrate the subject matter as well."

I can do that. "You have not always lived on Demesne?" I ask her.

"No. We only moved here a few years ago, when my dad took the envoy job. Most people on Demesne don't live here full-time. If they did, it wouldn't seem so special. Farzad,

Ivan, and Dementia are the only teens on the island who live here year-round now that Astrid's gone. And now you, I guess. Not sure if you count."

"Do you prefer to live here or in the city?" I ask her.

"Depends on which kind of city you mean, old or new?"

"What's the difference?"

"Well, the old cities are so floody. Like, it's cool how as the water rises in those places, it's made for really interesting elevated buildings and parks, hilarious water-sloshing fashion, awesome end-of-the-world dance parties. But I prefer the new cities. Before my family moved here, we lived in Biome City. The deserts are sick with cool people now."

"So the desert is for cold hospitals?"

"No. Don't be so literal. I mean more people are moving inland. Places that used to be nothingness are somethingness now. Think about it. Farzad's family owns the biggest compound on Demesne. Know why? Because his uncle invented the mechanism that controls the water that allowed the new desert cities to be built in previously inhabitable places, like BC."

"BC?"

"That's what people call Biome City."

I scan my database for more information about BC. The interface reveals that it's a new city built after the Water Wars, and was designed using the principles of biomimicry, whereby the primary elements in the city take inspiration from nature. The graphics display shows me office skyscrapers that look like tree and rock formations instead of concrete behemoths, hovercars gliding across the sky in traffic patterns like migrating birds, and sustainable green housing built in shapes like termite mounds and anthills. Since BC was built after the time of the fossil fuels that polluted the old places, the city views stretch out unobstructed by air pollution to massive sand dunes rising like mountains in the distance, and a night sky twinkling with thousands of stars.

Says Greer, "BC is my favorite place. It's like, when you go there, you don't feel all depressed and hopeless. When you're there, you can see that the Water Wars weren't totally useless, in the end. Because of them, where desert wasteland used to be is now epic party."

"Oh. But doesn't a desert need there to be little water?"

"Sure the desert does. But the people there don't."

"The water does not change the environment?"

"That's the desert's problem, not the people's. The desert adapts. The people adapt. Live. Die. Struggle. Suffer. Create. The people in the real world beyond Demesne's ring are not all this manufactured perfection. They deal." She gestures with her hand to indicate Demesne's atmosphere as her eyes home in on me, to let me know I am included in her phrase *manufactured perfection*.

After an hour, I have exhausted Greer with my questioning. Below us, Farzad, Ivan, and Dementia appear to be stirring. Their toes and fingers wiggle as their bodies elongate into stretches.

"Finally," Greer says. "What a waste of a day." The spark of some idea lights up her expression. "Hey. All this time I've been feeding you information, now you can do something for me."

"What?"

"Just . . . do something cool. Ivan said you're a good diver. Go . . . dive." She points in the direction behind her shoulder, to the ocean beyond the cove, where the water is deep enough for a proper dive. Probably. My map data does not specify.

We walk over to where the bluffs tower over the ocean. I am not sure I can pull off a dive from this vantage point, but since I have been asked to, I must try. Clones do not produce adrenaline, so I have no fear of the height or difficulty involved. I understand that death is a decent probability. I also sense that to attempt the dive could be a first step toward understanding who my First was. If I can do this, she might have been able to, as well. If she could do it, then there would be a reason. She was an athlete, or a gymnast, or an acrobat. Or just a . . .

"Daredevil," Greer says. "Jump."

The rock beneath my feet is smooth enough to serve as a platform, though it offers me no springboard. I stand with my toes dangling over the ledge, looking down into the whirling expanse of water that I calculate to be about twenty-five feet below me.

"I can do better than just jump," I tell Greer.

I'm not sure that I can.

I stand on my toes and extend my arms high above me. I don't know how shallow the water is, or whether there are rocks below the water's surface to obstruct the impact. Dive could equal death. Or dive could equal power. Knowledge.

I leap.

My arms remain raised high as my legs spring forth, out and then up. My arms lower to touch my extended feet—pike position—then my torso falls back as I extend my toes upward. My body extends in a vertical line upside down as it hurtles into the water. All my muscles seem to know exactly how to align themselves. My fingers shine out long and parallel as the water sips them in before engulfing my whole body.

Beneath the water, there is darkness and confusion and if it's as if every fiber of my being experiences the physical tingle of elation. Because there he is again. *Z!* He beckons me. He swims around me, his blond hair rising in the water as his turquoise-blue eyes lure me closer and closer. His arms open for me to fling myself into. *You know I can't resist you, Z. Get over here!* I try and I try to press myself to him, but he remains out of reach. I feel that I will die if I can't touch him. The pull of him is irresistible, almost suffocating, and entirely . . . *amazing.* I calculate this is what Greer meant by "mighty mighty."

But his face and body disappear as I plunge deeper into the underwater vortex. My body curls against the current, finally allowing me to take control and spring up into the air. Above me on the bluffs, Greer is shaking her arms wildly. She spreads her arms wide into a victory stance. "Flawless reverse dive!" she yells down to me. "*Unbelievable!* Perfect rip!"

I know she means that my reverse dive produced little splash, an ideal entry "rip," which refers to the ripping sound as a diver enters the water. I also know what I have just experienced—*again*, only more intensely this time—is something no Beta—or any clone, for that matter—should have.

Not only do I have taste, but I have something much, much more forbidden.

I have memory.

That beautiful man I saw below belonged to my First. She felt joy when she experienced the water with him; when she swam with him, those were the happiest moments in her life. She loved him—deeply, passionately, maybe even a bit obsessively. I don't know how or why I know this. But I know it to be true. I *feel* it to be true.

"You should have *seen* it," Greer tells the now-awakened Farzad, Ivan, and Dementia. "Her First was definitely a trained diver."

The others are still coming off the 'raxia; they're indifferent to Greer's enthusiasm.

"Help me put this back on," a sleepy-eyed Dementia requests of me. She holds the strings of her bikini top to the back of her neck so I may tie them. My head is woozy from the dive followed by the swim through the rough waters back into the cove at Hidden Beach, and the flash of memory that feels like a thunderbolt ripped across my skull. My sore fingers tie the strings on her top. Her own bikini top now securely fastened, Dementia cups her covered breasts and says to no one in particular, "Look, Ma, no tan lines!"

I wonder if I may request of Mother a proper one-piece swimsuit to wear to practice more dives. Astrid's sports bra ensemble barely held on during my swim through the rough surf.

"Did you even hear me, Dementia?" says Greer. "You have *got* to see what this Beta can do."

Farzad, bleary-eyed, mumbles, "We had a Beta once. Dr. Lusardi called him a landscape-artist Beta, but that was just a fancy term for gardener. Dude went totally mental and started pruning our trees into obscene private-parts shapes."

"Sounds like an awesome Beta to me," Dementia says.

"Porny!" says Farzad. "That's what that Beta was. Taught us not to buy before the product has been tested. Tahir said when he flew the plane over our compound, it looked like a garden of obscenities." Farzad settles into a deeper awakening, his face brightening. "Hey! I forgot to tell you all. Tahir's coming back next week."

"Who is Tahir?" I ask.

"Farzad's cousin," answers Ivan.

Dementia says, "Tahir's dad—Farzad's uncle—is practically the richest man in the world."

Ivan says, "He can not only turn water into wine, he can turn water into . . . lots more water."

Greer asks Farzad, "Is Tahir better?"

"I don't know," Farzad says. "He Relays to me that he is, but I need to see it for myself. He's been so different since the accident. Totally checked out. I feel like the injury was worse than the doctors said."

"What was the accident?" I ask.

The humans all point to the *gigantes* in the distance. Greer says, "Surfing accident. Tahir got caught up in a swell and pulled under. He suffered major head and neck trauma. It's only because his father's hovercopter had dropped him down there and was still flying over that he even survived."

As the sun goes over the horizon, the air has turned

chillier. Farzad sees me shivering and wraps a towel over me. He gives my shoulders a warming rub.

Ivan removes Farzad's hands from touching me. "Bro, she's *my* clone. And you know the rules on Demesne," says the Governor's son to Farzad. "Look, but don't touch."

10

EVEN WITH A PERFECTLY-PREPARED CHOCOLATE soufflé set down in front of her—Mother's favorite dessert, which the Governor requested the chef make specially to appease her—Mother is still pouting after dinner. The terrace deck where the family dines looks out over Io, which this evening offers views of dolphins leaping through the violet waters. Tropical birds sing from the trees surrounding the deck, while the family's resident parrot, who is a fireworks display of contrasting red, yellow, and blue plumage replete with its own tree and nest, chirps from its large cage, "Chocolate for Mother! Chocolate for Mother!"

None of this display impresses Mother. To Ivan, she grumbles, "You kept her to yourself all day."

The Governor says, "Enough already. What would you

have done with Elysia—taken her to Haven and have her cheat at mahjong with you?"

"I don't cheat!" Mother snaps.

Ivan and Liesel both look down, trying not to laugh.

Mother totally cheats, I can see on their faces.

"Cheater!" the parrot parrots. Mother snaps her fingers, signaling for her bodyguards to come outside. She looks toward the cage and they know exactly what to do. It takes two large men to remove the huge cage from the deck, out of sight and audible distance from the dinner table.

Mother returns her attention to Ivan. "You can't keep Elysia all to yourself, Ivan," she says. "She's here to keep me company too. Your father is at work all day and Liesel is being tutored. I have to do *everything* here all by myself." A server clone refills her wineglass.

"You're just bored," Ivan tells Mother.

The Governor ignores her and asks Ivan, "How was your workout this morning?"

"Killer," Ivan says. "Elysia put me through some serious paces." He neglects to tell his parents he "eased out" his recovery from our morning workout with an afternoon chemical 'raxia escapade with Farzad and Dementia. Before we returned to the house, Ivan ordered me to keep that piece of information on the "down-low." When I looked down low at his feet for traces of 'raxia, Ivan let me know he only meant I shouldn't tell his parents about his 'raxia indulgence.

"Excellent," the Governor says. "And how was the surfing with Farzad this afternoon?"

"Awesome," Ivan lies. "We dialed wave max."

"Good," the Governor says. "That kind of surfing works your core hard. You need to lose that gut before basic training or it's going to be that much harder. I just saw the stats report I ordered of your incoming class at the Base. Your competition there will be fierce, the toughest and strongest kids from across the world. You mostly got in because you're a legacy." As Ivan lifts his fork for a bite of chocolate soufflé, his father adds, "Maybe lay off the chocolate?"

Ivan grins at his dad. "How about I lay off the chocolate tomorrow? Today I just feel so . . ." He looks at me and lets out a sigh. *"Great."*

"I told you having a new girl would be good for the family," Mother tells the Governor.

I'm sure the spot of 'raxia helped Ivan's mood too.

"Ivan will need all the help he can get before he goes to the Base," Governor says, and seems to nod approvingly in my direction before looking at his son to offer his fatherly wisdom. "You don't know, because you've always lived here, but the world out there is hard. The Base is fiercely competitive."

Mother says, "I'm sure Ivan can more than hold his own there."

Liesel says, "He's from Demesne. Of course Ivan will be the top of his class at the Base. He earned it."

Her brother hasn't earned it *yet*, but somehow Liesel has not made that distinction.

Mother asks Ivan, "Have you given any thought to what assignment you'd like to get after basic training?"

Ivan says, "Maybe I'd like to return here after training

and start, like, a military police mission."

"We don't need police on Demesne!" Mother says, horrified. "But you do have that kind of brute strength. Perhaps it be nice if you could use that for more gentle purpose. Perhaps you become some kind of builder. An architect for military compounds?"

Ivan says, "Or perhaps I could be a camouflage fashion designer. Or a strategic campaigns astrologer."

"You can go to the Base to learn astrology?" I ask, surprised. According to my interface, the Base is where young recruits go to hone their physical endurance, learn military history, and gain weaponry skills. It shows me no correlation between astrology and the military.

"Ivan's doing sarcasm," Liesel informs me. "He learned it from Astrid."

I datacheck this word.

Sarcasm [SAHR-ka-zəm]: Expressing ridicule that wounds.

I leap from my chair and run to Mother's side, and grab her seated upper body into a hug. "Don't be wounded, Mother," I say.

The family roar with laughter. Mother places a kiss on my cheek and then gestures for me to sit back down. I am so confused.

"Thank you, darling Elysia, but I am not wounded by sarcasm," Mother tells me, smiling. "But surely I'm grateful that at least one of my children seeks to protect me instead of just mocking me." Her mood has shifted: brightened. I did this. She extols the group, "Let's enjoy this wonderful dessert, shall we?"

"Yummy yummy yummy," says Liesel as she digs into her dessert.

I can smell the chocolate. The scent should give me no feeling other than ambivalence, but instead, my mouth fills with saliva and my nostrils feel directly assaulted with the air of enticement. It's as if the chocolate is singing to me . . . *El-EE-zee-ya . . . you know you want me, Beta. I'm even more delicious than you can imagine.*

I want to taste it so bad. It smells so good. I swallow the saliva that has accumulated in my inexplicably tantalized mouth.

"Does chocolate compel ataraxia?" I ask the family.

"Darling," says Mother, cutting a piece of her soufflé and placing it on my plate. "It's the antithesis of *meh*."

"What is *meh*?" I ask.

She shrugs. "Indifference. Chocolate is the opposite. It's the very essence of happiness. Try some."

"She can't enjoy it," the Governor says. "It's wasted on her."

Liesel tells me, "I don't think there's any better ataraxia than chocolate." Ivan snorts.

"Women and chocolate," the Governor says, choosing a sip of wine instead of the soufflé. "I'll never understand it."

"That's because you don't understand women at all," says Mother.

"Be quiet already," the Governor says.

It's hard to listen to the Brattons' bickering and not wonder if the humans' notion of ataraxia as being a true happiness is really just a perceived perfection, subject to its own bumps and disappointments.

My fork wanders into the soufflé to grab a small portion. I place the chocolate soufflé onto my tongue, which is instantly alerted to a taste of such exquisite beauty that I want to gasp from the sensational shock. Warm chocolate, both cakelike and gooey, penetrates all sides of my mouth, spreading sweetness and wonder. It's not as if I want more evidence that, in addition to being a Beta with memories of her First, something else is off about me. But surely this chocolate provides it; I think I love it even more than that stupendous concoction called macaroni and cheese. I want to round up all the chocolate soufflés on the dinner table and devour every one.

I force myself to stop after the second bite, and I wash the flavor down with my strawberry shake. I should delete this memory, or I will become greedy for more.

"How was the chocolate soufflé?" Liesel asks me.

I shrug. "I suppose I can see why humans would find it satisfying, despite its lack of nutritional necessity. It's no strawberry shake."

The family laughs again as if I am not only their substitute daughter but also their personal comedian. I don't understand why I am so funny. Chocolate soufflé really is no strawberry shake. They are two completely separate and unrelated food items.

I will not confess it to the family, but I'm a true believer.

Chocolate may in fact produce ataraxia.

The Governor's luxisstant, Tawny, vined in red-and-yellow marigold on the left side of her face, steps out onto the deck. Her aesthetic reminds me of the human myth called "mermaid." She wears a white scalloped minidress over her tanned skin, and she has long, white-blond hair with aquamarine-blue tips falling down to her waist, sculpting her perfectly proportioned figure. Tawny tells the Governor, "The envoy's new assistant has arrived. He came directly here to greet you instead of going to Haven as I instructed him on his itinerary. I asked him to wait in your study. Shall I rebook your massage for later tonight?"

The Governor sighs, throws his napkin on the table, takes one last swig of wine, and stands up. "Yes. Thank you, Tawny."

Mother asks, "Is this the new assistant who will be preparing the report to the Replicant Rights Commission?"

"Indeed," the Governor says. "Fresh young officer straight out of the academy. Big potential, this kid. Or so the Board of Directors tells me. Army probably gave him this nonsense job to season him a little before he gets a real assignment."

"Should I invite him to tea? Perhaps he'd like to be on the planning committee for the annual Governor's Ball," says Mother.

The Governor and Ivan both laugh.

Ivan says, "Um, I doubt some guy who trained to be a commando, then got sent here for his first assignment, really wants to plan a party that only socialites on Demesne care about, Mother." His face registers sympathetic horror for this poor envoy's assistant, who could have been sent to battle but instead was sent to paradise.

Liesel says, "I'll be on your committee, Mother. I will not mock you."

"Thank you, sweetheart," says Mother. She glares at Ivan.

"Ivan, don't mock your mother about the most important social event of the year," the Governor says as he takes his leave from the dinner table. As he follows Tawny and steps back into the house through the glass doors, I see the Governor's hand subtly graze Tawny's firm behind. Ivan notices too—and notices me noticing.

"Sorry," Ivan mumbles.

Ivan interrupts Mother. "Elysia needs real athletic swimwear. Something that covers up more than Astrid's old bikinis."

Mother giggles. "Of course, dear. Did Farzad enjoy the view too much today?"

11

LATE THE NEXT MORNING, I RETURN TO MY bedroom after my early-morning workout with Ivan. Xanthe is tidying my room when I arrive. "Ivan dropped off this for you," she says. A one-piece swimsuit lies on the bed for me.

I hold up the modest navy biketard that will cover me from my upper chest down to my midthighs. "This should fit," I tell Xanthe. "Was it Astrid's?"

"Astrid's grandmother's," says Xanthe. "But it's not for today. You're to join Mrs. Bratton at the club this afternoon."

"Ivan will be disappointed. He wanted me to play Z-Grav with him."

"Ivan will go play with his human friends. He will be fine."

If he does 'raxia, he will be more than fine. He will be in bliss.

Perhaps 'raxia is like chocolate. Should I ask Ivan if I may try 'raxia?

I want to delete the memory of the chocolate, but I can't. The memory is too sensational; my mouth salivates again as I think of it.

To distract myself, I step out of my clothes to try on the unitard. "Do you swim?" I ask Xanthe.

"I don't know," says Xanthe. "I haven't been instructed to try."

"So what do you do, then?"

"When?"

"When you're not working."

"I go back to my quarters. I sleep. What else is there to do?"

I suspect sleep is her distraction, to make the time go faster, until . . . until what? Does she even think about her ultimate expiration?

Does she wonder about her First?

I set my voice to the tone called *casual* and ask Xanthe, "Do you know anything about your First?"

"I'm a Lamb," Xanthe says. She takes a basket of folded clothes from the floor and begins putting the items away in my dresser drawers. "That's all I know. I heard Dr. Lusardi say it to her assistant when I first emerged."

"You were cloned from an animal?" I ask, shocked. If that's the case, Dr. Lusardi did an outstanding job molding Xanthe's aesthetic.

"Of course not. It's a reference to what humans call sacrificial lambs." She watches my face as I try to access the information. "Don't bother, the clone meaning of *Lamb* is not in the database. Lambs here are created from the poorest people. They voluntarily sacrifice their lives to be turned into clones."

"I can't imagine why they would do that."

"They do it to provide financially for their loved ones after their soul extractions."

If a person could pay for their family to survive by offering to have their souls extracted so they could become clones, I suppose it's a small price to pay. After all, the clone will get to live in paradise, and thereby provide for the loved ones they've left behind, who will suffer less, having access to the money the humans seem to crave even more than chocolate. This is logical.

Because of her sacrifice, somewhere back in the real world, the family of Xanthe's First possibly now has a roof over their heads, or food on their table. All they're missing is whoever she was to them—a mother, a wife, a daughter, a sister, an aunt?

Xanthe comes over to inspect my new swimsuit. "There's a tear on the back. Take it off and I will mend it."

"I'll mend it," I tell Xanthe. "I'm sure I can figure out how to sew."

"Don't be absurd. Take it off and return it to me. It will be fixed and ready for you this evening."

"There's no rush. . . ." I start to say, but she cuts me off.

"It's better if you wear the modest costume when you are here."

I remember the Governor touching Tawny's behind. I ask Xanthe, "Isn't it against Demesne laws to consort with a clone?"

"Technically, yes," says Xanthe. "But they make their own rules here."

Tawny walks into the room. "I've been looking everywhere for you, Xanthe. The Governor has changed his daily appointment time, and the massage room needs to be set up for him immediately." She says this with great urgency, as if there were a raging fire about to burn the house down.

"Yes," says Xanthe. She lifts her other basket of newly laundered clothes. She and Tawny begin to walk out of my room, in perfect lockstep.

"I could fold those for you, Xanthe," I call out. She has so much to do, and I don't.

Tawny and Xanthe both turn to face me, their heads cocked at the same angle, their faces set to the same expression I recognize as *horror*.

"That's not your job," they both say. They leave my room.

12

THE SCANDAL!

The ladies who lunch have informed me of the most shocking depravity. The coca beans from which chocolate is made are in short supply on the Mainland—such short supply that cocoa is rationed elsewhere. Here on Demesne the chocolate is in abundant supply, because the island harvests its own cacao beans, which are not allowed for export to the rest of the world. The native chocolate concoctions produced here are even calorically stabilized, to cause only minimum pudge in the case of overconsumption. The humans here shall not have to make do with only one chocolate bar per week like the poor people on the Mainland.

I will not indulge.

We are seated on the back garden of the Haven main house, on a patio overlooking Nectar Bay. I keep score as

Mother plays mahjong with the ladies after lunch. The ladies wear light tunic dresses patterned in bright mosaic and floral prints with strappy heeled shoes on their pedicured feet. They are of late human middle age, but their Demesne-oxygenated faces give them a youthful glow, with rosy yet taut complexions brightened by Io's cool breeze. Near the thatched parasol over our table, which protects the ladies' delicate skin from the sun, server clones hover, discreetly keeping their wineglasses full so that it seems the ladies are daintily sipping at their drinks instead of tossing back full carafes. Each lady has a small bowl of tropical berries dipped in chocolate to nibble with her wine, as well as a fleet of masseuses, bodyguards, aestheticians, and sport instructors waiting in the wings to serve them after their board game.

A few hundred yards away behind us, at an empty lot in a corner of the property, I see workers whose faces are vined in bamboo, which represents strength and sturdiness. These lower-caste clones, manufactured for physical labor such as sanitation and construction work, are laying the foundation for a new addition to the Haven's main complex. We can faintly hear them grunt as they use heavy machinery to lower the concrete slabs into place for the foundation.

"What are they building?" I ask Mother.

"Oh, the noise they make," Mother whines over the lightly audible sound of a distant power tool. "It's insufferable. They are building a new guest wing at Haven. Silly nuisance laws requiring more outsiders be allowed in for visits. They'll need more accommodations." Discreetly built beyond a thick stand of trees behind the construction workers is the service clones' own housing—bamboo huts, furnished with bedding and not much else.

"Certainly the outsiders are not staying in our houses," says the lady sitting opposite Mother. Now that I've learned what sarcasm is and that it cannot cause physical injury, I have privately renamed this lady Mrs. Red Whine for the amount of pinot noir she drinks while complaining about pretty much any topic up for discussion.

"Yes," I say, nodding in agreement, supporting the team as a good companion should do.

Mother's friends beam. Says the lady to Mother's left, whom I call Mrs. Linger because she drags out her words and her eyes seem to linger longingly on the sight of the shirtless male grunts in the distance, "Your Beta is so-o-o-o-o much more fun than Astrid! That girl just moaned a-a-a-all the time about e-e-e-e-equality and susta-a-a-a-ainability and di-i-i-i-istribution of wealth. Bo-o-o-oring!"

"Astrid's contempt for Demesne was a real downer," says Mother's friend on the right, Mrs. Former Beauty Queen, who would like me to know she still wears the same size as when she won Miss Teen Mainland "only ten years ago, ha-ha-ha!"

Mrs. Linger says, "A-a-a-and your Beta wears the pre-e-e-ettiest things!" Mother wanted me to dress like her for the ladies, so I am wearing a bright pink-and-yellow paisley print tunic cover-up dress identical to hers. I am taller than Mother, so the dress only just covers my rear. I wear one of Astrid's bikinis underneath. Mother prefers me not to wear a one-piece swimsuit and look like her mother-in-law when she's showing me off to her friends.

"She's just such a delight," says Mother.

The other ladies nod. I cannot imagine why I am a delight other than that I agree with the ladies' every statement, I smile prettily at them, and I don't blabber on about equality, sustainability, and distribution of wealth the way Astrid did. Apparently all the ladies' offspring are part monster, part angel—privileged children whom the ladies have so deeply embedded in luxury and the idea that ataraxia is their right that these children have no discipline and find their mothers major drags to deal with. Luckily, the ladies have each other, their bottles of wine, their mahjong sessions, and their full complements of staff ready to ease their pain when the pursuit of ataraxia occasionally leads to disappointment or ungrateful children.

"Show them what you can do, Elysia," Mother requests of me.

"Like what?" I ask. The floating pool in the middle of the bay is too far away from our perch and would not give the ladies a very good view of my dives.

"A good diver must also be a good gymnast. Try some back handsprings."

I stand up and comply. I know Mother wants me to distract the ladies so she can slyly look at their tiles and figure out how best to cheat. Mother very much likes to win. I think she likes it more than chocolate.

As I flip back and over, I hear Mrs. Red Whine comment, "Can you imagine ever getting one of our spoiled daughters to perform on command?"

They all tut-tut in agreement and applaud when my feet land back on the ground. I hear their wineglasses clink as Mrs. Linger exclaims, "I wa-a-a-ant a Beta too-o-o-o!"

"Come here, dear," beckons Mrs. Beauty Queen to me. She is the tipsiest of the bunch so far this afternoon. I go to her. She presses her hands around my waist and proclaims, "Oh, this tiny waist is a dream. This Beta's First could have been such a contender on the pageant circuit, I bet. Do you know how to pageant-strut, dear?"

I access my database and determine, "Yes."

She claps her hands. "Goody! My daughter used to play pageant strut with me all the time when she was little, but by the time she was twelve—mercy, by then it was impossible to get her to perform at all for her mummy. Let's see you pageant-strut."

I set my face to *confident* and walk a pageant strut past the ladies' table, swaggering, swaying my hips and shoulders, and beaming a magnificent smile toward the ladies.

They applaud enthusiastically. "My Beta!" Mother exults in her breathy voice. She gulps down the remainder of her wine and points to the ladies around the table. "Don't you all forget. I got one first."

Mrs. Linger says, "Ta-a-a-alent competition?"

Mrs. Red Whine rolls her eyes. "Please, let her sing 'Children of Hope.' No pageant can be won without that trite piece of nonsense."

"'Children of Hope' is a beautiful song!" Mrs. Beauty Queen counters. "My daughter used to love singing that song with me when we played beauty pageant in the FantaSphere." Mrs. Beauty Queen looks at me. "Do you know the song 'Children of Hope,' Elysia? Say yes!"

Again I access the database and again say, "Yes."

Mrs. Beauty Queen says, "Then sing it. My little brat never will anymore."

I've never sung before. I don't know what my voice will sound like. But I do know the words and melody to this power ballad–style song, a comforting favorite that's been popular since the time of the Water Wars.

I sing, adjusting my voice for *pageant* setting, strong and sincere, using my face to emote with exaggerated bravado and making grand flourishes with my hands:

> *"In these troubled times of darkness and fright,*
> *From them we receive the gift most sublime.*
> *They are our dreams, our loves,*
> *Our children of hope."*

The ladies squeal with delight as they clink their wineglasses to toast my pageant performance.

Turns out, I can carry a tune.

Tipsily, Mrs. Beauty Queen mutters, "That Beta's no defect for sure."

The other ladies gasp, and Mrs. Red Whine makes it her duty to chide Mrs. Beauty Queen for whatever transgression has just happened. "Don't even speak the word," says Mrs. Red Whine.

"Amen," says Mother.

The ladies are all sufficiently drunk and ataraxic. It has been a successful afternoon of game playing and they are ready to wind down their get-together. But not before commenting on the arrival of Dementia, who comes outside from the main house and begins walking toward our table.

"O-o-o-h dear, the wi-i-i-ild chi-i-i-ild," says Mrs. Linger.

Mrs. Beauty Queen whispers, "Well, you would be too if your own parents couldn't tolerate you and stranded you on Demesne to be raised by clones."

Says Mrs. Red Whine, "It's so sad. You know, the day she tried to carve the tattoo on her face was the same one that the nanny who'd raised her since was she was a baby reached its term of service." I presume that the nanny must have reached forty-five years in human age, her aesthetic and skills no longer valued or needed by Dementia's parents.

Dementia approaches us. Mother tells her, "Demetra, darling, how *are* you?"

"Fine. Whatever." Dementia seems to be trying to ignore the ladies as her eyes settle on me. "Tutoring's done for the day. Can the Beta come play with me?"

Quietly to Mother, Mrs. Red Whine mutters, "Perhaps not such a good idea?"

But Mother says, "Of course, Demetra. Take Elysia to play." I start to stand up, but Mother has more to say to Dementia. "I sent your mother an invitation several weeks ago, asking her to be part of the planning committee for the annual Governor's Ball, but I haven't heard back from her. Do you know if she received it? The most important social event of the season should have the input of Elaine Cortez-Olivier's impeccable taste, right?"

Dementia grabs my hand and pulls me from my chair. "Don't know if Mom received it and so sorry, Mrs. B, but don't really care." Dementia is so excellent at the sarcasm. "The parents are in BC right now. Relay Mom there."

I know Mother has already Relayed Mrs. Cortez-Olivier to follow up on the invitation, but she has not received an answer. She will not dwell on this slight. Mother snaps her fingers and a server clone appears to set up her nap chaise while the masseuse materializes to tend to her tired feet.

"Let's go hit some 'raxia," Demetra says to me. To the ladies' shocked expressions, she adds: "Kidding!" Under her breath, she mutters, "Sorta."

Dementia leads me by hand from the Haven patio to the beach. We step onto the dock and walk the long plank that leads to the floating pool in the middle of Nectar Bay.

"Will your parents be returning to Demesne soon?" I ask her.

She shrugs. Her index finger scales the side of her face, poking at the scar from her aborted attempt at cutting a fleur-de-lis into her temple. "The clone overseers, I mean babysitters, have alerted my parents to recent, um, incidents. So maybe they'll make an appearance soon. I wish they'd take me back to Biome City with them."

"I have heard that Biome City is epic party."

Dementia laughs. "Yeah. It's real and weird but kinda wild. Like, sometimes when the desert storms get too intense, you can't even go outside, you have to stay home and, like, play in the FantaSphere. But it's a regular-people place so, say, if you were a regular girl . . ."

"I would like to be a regular girl!" I exclaim.

"No, I mean if you really were a regular girl in BC and

not just a Demesne clone mimicking the desire to be normal. Life as a regular girl can be harsh and not all epic party. If there's a desert storm, you'll have to stay home and hang out with your parents till it passes. 'Cause not everybody has a FantaSphere in their house. That's only on Demesne. In BC, regular people have to go to the Space Needle Arcade and pay to play in a FantaSphere."

"Wow," I say.

We've reached the pool. Dementia looks out over the vista beyond the floating pool—palm trees, white sand, violet-hued sea—and gulps in a generous dose of Demesne oxygen. She then opens her arms wide and yells out, *"I'm so bored here!"*

I open my arms too, in solidarity. *"Me too!"*

"You're so freaking cool," says Dementia. "Doc Lusardi did a great job programming your chip. I totally wish I could get a Beta, but my parents would never go for it." Dementia's olive eyes home in on my tunic dress, identical to Mother's. "Dear gawd, please take that monstrosity off."

I take it off, so I am now wearing only a bikini.

"Race you!" Dementia exhorts.

She dives into the pool for a head start. I dive in after her, luxuriating in the smooth water that feels like home. I should have no problem catching up with Dementia and beating her time easily, but beneath the water, it happens again, that jolt passing through my skin, and there he is. I see his face more distinctly in this clear, docile water, his high cheekbones and gleaming white teeth, the dark tan of his skin. His turquoise eyes stare intently at me, as if he could see straight through me. The nearness of him sends quivers of excitement through my body. His dirty-blond hair swishes upward as his rock-hard body swirls, treading through the water. He has a large, muscular frame, like the bamboo-vined construction workers, like he could carry the world on his shoulders. *You know you own me, Z,* his voice says, and my heart leaps, and my loins feel suddenly alive. His voice, so gravelly, strikes directly at a lustful drive I didn't know I possessed. The voice is a sensual stroke that tingles my skin. *You know you own me, Z.*

He was my First's first. She felt him inside of her. I don't know why I know, but I know how I know: because I can feel a sweet, intense aching in my heart and directly at the private core of my being. The ache overwhelms me with its sheer want; I can't get enough of this hunger for him.

Again, I race toward him, to touch him, but this time when I reach him, instead of disappearing, he puts his hand up, to push me away. *I can't do this,* his voice says. *It's wrong. You know that.*

I hear this, and I hurt so much I truly can't breathe.

Hate. Rage. Betrayal.

I understand these feelings now.

I plant my feet on the pool's bottom and rise above the water, desperately inhaling the premium oxygen into my lungs, desperately hoping that somehow I will see him above the water, live and in the flesh. *We can make it work,* I want to plead, on her behalf. *Please.*

But I see only Dementia at the other end of the pool. "You were supposed to race me! What's the matter with you? You look like you've seen a ghost. Don't just stand there like a bore or I will have to cut you." Before Dementia dives back beneath the water, she adds, "Kidding! Sorta!"

I immerse myself beneath the water again to search for him, but the vision of the bronzed god does not reappear. I lie down on the bottom of the pool as long as my breath will hold. My database tells me that if I were a human teenager desiring to confine myself to a private place, here is where I would create it. It is my sanctuary, under the water. Submersed in liquid silk, I am not an unfeeling clone.

Beneath the water, I can know her. She was fierce, uncompromising. When she loved, she loved deeply, passionately. She loved the blue-eyed water god. She owned him. His heart.

But when she felt betrayal, she hated, and she was feared. Hate gave her power.

If she were me (and she is me, even if she's dead), she would not fear my unnatural memories and instincts. She would say, *Maybe your unspeakable defects give you power too?*

13

IVAN IS WINNING MORE.

In the few weeks since I arrived in the Bratton household and we began our morning workouts, his running speed and agility have improved immensely. He can keep up with me easily, and many times now, he can outrun me. His daily body mass index recordings show he's lost ten percent of his fat, yet gained ten percent more muscle.

We're halfway up our third sprint up the cliff stairs going from the beach to the grounds at Governor's House when Ivan stops, turns around to face the ocean, and asserts, "I'm *pumped!*" He mock jabs at me, like a boxer eager for a round.

Not only has Ivan increased muscle mass but his confidence has grown. He's become more eager, as opposed to resigned, to leave for military training. He knows now he can keep up there. He eagerly counts down the days until his departure for basic training, and he has determined a career goal. Ivan has decided he wants to become a fighter pilot. Selection for that coveted job is highly competitive. He will work hard to attain that lofty goal.

The Governor is pleased. Only a month ago, Ivan was lackluster in his physical abilities, at least relative to the shape the other Base recruits will be in, and he was uninterested and noncommittal about identifying goals. Mother gives me credit for helping with Ivan's turnaround, and herself credit, in turn, for bringing me home. It's been a win-win situation; even the Governor is now won over to having a Beta as part of his family. "You might even be an improvement over Astrid," said the Governor to me over dinner one night as he inspected Ivan's improved body statistics. "You have all the desirable qualities of a teenage girl without any of the awful hang-ups, and without the misinformed ideological platforms that Astrid had."

As we stand on the cliff-side stairs, Ivan leans into a cranny in the rock, a crack just big enough to slip his hand into. "Know what I've got in there?" he asks me. "But you have to promise to keep it a secret."

I nod, surprised. My brother is not usually the secretive type. That's because boys are easier than girls, Mother has told me. Astrid kept secrets and was a liar. But Ivan "wears his heart on his sleeve," according to Mother. "What you see is what you get."

When he pulls his hand out from the crevice, I see white seeds in his hand. "These are cuvée seeds," Ivan says, referring to Demesne's native torch flower plants, which festively adorn the gardens, driveways, and landing pads of many of the island's homes. Next, he pulls out an even more curious item hidden within the cliff wall—a small porcelain bowl with a matching thick porcelain nub, which my interface reveals is a mortar and pestle, an old-fashioned instrument for grinding materials such as spices. Ivan places some cuvée seeds in the mortar and grinds them, producing a creamy liquid with a heavenly floral scent.

"Let me guess," I say. "You are practicing to become a military perfumer?"

Ivan offers me his fondest smile. "Sarcasm: well mimicked. But no, something even more exciting. I'm trying to make my own 'raxia."

"Why? Is not the kind you illegally obtain of satisfactory quality?" I ask.

"It's more than satisfactory. That's the problem. The more satisfactory the 'raxia gets, the more I want, and the less I want to wait to find someone to score it off. 'Raxia is made from the cuvée seeds inside the spiked petals of the flower. I'm teaching myself how to make it, but also improve on it. If I add components like testosterone"—Ivan pulls a small bottle labeled *T* from the crag—"I can use it to not only feel great, but get stronger too."

"Good science," I acknowledge.

"I'm, like, inspired now. Feeling good and want to feel even better. But not just *feel* better. *Be* better. Strongest."

"Does the Governor know?"

"He totally wants me to be number one, dude."

"I mean, about your chemistry set."

"Of course not! He'd kill me. So don't you tell him. I'm just showing you this now because I'm going to start collecting more supplies for more experimentation, and I want you to know where to store them for me if I ask you." He jabs hard at my arm—playfully, but hard enough that I know a light bruise will appear later. "Okay, champ?"

"Yes, brother," I say.

I've settled into a routine at the house. In the early mornings, I wake up Liesel and help her prepare for "school." Then I work out with Ivan for two hours. After lunch, I am Mother's companion. Sometimes we go to Haven for lunch with the ladies, sometimes I take notes that she dictates to me with respect to her food and guest planning for the upcoming Governor's Ball, and sometimes she just wants me to go shopping with her.

Most shopping on Demesne is done by Relay as there are only a few proper shops and cafés on one main street near the airstrip. Today, Mother wants to return to the shop where she bought me. She says she needs new lingerie, but I think she wants a new clone.

"Don't I remember that there was another teen Beta at the store?" she asks me as we approach the boutique.

"Yes, Mother. Her name is Becky."

"She must not have been bought yet. I would have heard about it if she was."

We enter the store and are immediately greeted by Marisa, the broker who sold me to Mother. "Mrs. Bratton, so lovely to see you," says Marisa. "How is your Beta working out?"

"She's heaven," coos Mother. "Simply heaven."

"Dr. Lusardi will be so pleased. What can I help you with today?"

"I would love a new nightie. Something silky and sexy. And . . . is that other Beta still available?" *Subtlety* is not a component programmed into Mother's disposition.

Marisa grimaces slightly. "She is available. But . . . maybe not to your tastes. She's not as flawless as this one." Marisa gestures to me.

"Let me see her," says Mother.

Marisa goes to the back of the store and returns with Becky. The other teen Beta appears more sallow than the last time I saw her, and amazingly, her fuchsia eyes have specks of red in them, as if they were bloodshot. She also looks like she's gained a full dress size.

"Hello, Elysia," she says to me.

"Hello, Becky," I say.

Mother inspects Becky top to bottom. The choice is an easy one. "No," says Mother.

"Let me show you our lingerie collection," Marisa says. "We just got in some fabulous pieces from Biome City. Such an amazing design scene happening there!"

"Yes," Mother sighs. I can see she is disappointed. She wanted something fresh and interesting. Now all she's going to get is a nightgown that probably looks the same as her fifty other ones.

Mother and Marisa retreat to a far corner of the store, leaving Becky and me alone at the front. "How are you doing?" I ask Becky.

"Satisfactory," she states. Her appearance has changed.

She is not only heavier but her skin is more sallow, and her eyes seem withdrawn instead of glazed. "How is Governor's House?"

"Satisfactory," I state. Better than being stuck inside this boring boutique all the time just waiting for a sale that's never going to come, I think.

"What is it like?" she asks me. Her affect is as bland as it's supposed to be, yet I can't help but suspect something is off about her.

"Perfect," I say.

"Of course," says Becky. "How do you serve there?" she asks. "Do you have chores?"

"I do not do chores," I say, surprised that my voice sounds somehow affronted. "I am a member of the family."

"So then what do you do?"

"I work out with my brother Ivan. I accompany Mother to her lunches. I play in the pool with my sister Liesel. At night I dine with the family."

"You dine with them?" Becky asks. "Do you eat their food to be polite?"

"I do." *I LOVE their food*, I don't add.

Becky leans in closer to me. "Have you ever tried the chocolate?"

"Yes," I say coolly.

"It compels ataraxia in humans, I've heard," says Becky.

"Seems to," I concur.

"Does it compel ataraxia in you?" she asks.

"I am incapable of achieving ataraxia, of course." I don't know why I don't just tell Becky that I can actually taste it. Her life seems so small already. I do not need to further remind her of my privilege. My nice home and family. My sense of taste that I shouldn't have, but do.

"I have tried chocolate," she whispers. She says the words rapidly, as if she has been eager to make this confession but could only muster the courage by speaking the words quickly.

Well! Perhaps her life at the boutique is not so small and unprivileged, after all.

I follow the lead of her confession and offer my own. Quickly and quietly, I admit, "The chocolate is very pleasant."

Becky grabs my hand and clenches. "Yes," she states, as if relieved. She walks me to a bureau table where stacks of folded sweaters lie. She opens a drawer on the floor level of the bureau, reaches behind a stack of sweaters stored in the drawer, and pulls out a hidden stash of chocolate bars. "I have extra if you want to take them for yourself."

She would not gain weight from tasteless strawberry shakes. But she would gain from too much chocolate, which she would only eat in excess if she were actually taking pleasure from it. Is it possible that a sense of taste is indeed a Beta quirk? Or do other clones experience it too?

"No, you keep them," I say. "I can have chocolate at home anytime."

"*Please* take it away from me, Elysia. It is making me fatter, and I don't want to be returned."

"Returned to where?" I ask.

"The infirmary," Becky whispers.

She saw the same thing I did.

I take the chocolate bars and place them in one of Mother's shopping bags that I carry for her.

"Thank you," Becky says. "I have heard all about what

a hit you are with your new owners. They've all come into the store to check me out after meeting you. One by one, privately, all of your mother's friends have come here in search of another you. They think the other ladies don't know. But they see me, and they do not buy me."

"You will find a buyer," I say, my voice set to REASSURING.

Suddenly, Becky hisses, "I don't *want* a buyer. I *want* my freedom."

She *wants?* And what kind of freedom does she mean? There is no chance for me to respond to her shocking admission. Mother and Marisa return to the front of the store. Mother is ready to leave. I pick up Mother's shopping bags. "Time to go to Haven for lunch," Mother announces.

"Yes, Mother," I say. "Good-bye, Marisa. Good-bye, Becky."

I thought *freedom* meant leaving the boutique to be welcomed into a new home, but I feel sure that not only does Becky share a sense of taste, but by *freedom*, she meant something entirely different from the meaning my database ascribes to the word.

I think Becky meant owning herself rather than being owned by a human.

14

POP POP POP.

The fawn is dead.

"*Stop!*" Liesel screeches, using the safe word to turn off the game when it gets too scary for her.

"Too late," says Ivan. "You didn't call it in time. Baby deer down."

But the game still recognizes Liesel's command, and it disappears. The rolling hills, the tall oak trees, the meadow with the gentle pond where the fawn was slaking its thirst, the dead baby deer—they vanish in an instant. All that remains of the virtual game are the gun consoles in our hands.

"I want to play RainforestPillage or PrincessBall," Liesel pouts. "I hate the shooting games." The hunting games frighten her, especially the shark-hunting one. From growing up on Demesne, she thinks of sharks as benign, cloned creatures she sees when her father takes her for a boat ride to the periphery of Demesne's ring, and lets her dangle her feet over the boat for the sharks to tickle. In the FantaSphere, sharks are oceanic monsters that hunt humans instead of tickling them.

Ivan says, "You know the rule. If you want to me to play with you, you have to pick a nonlame game."

Liesel sighs. "Astrid would have played PrincessBall with me."

"Yeah, so she could lecture you on the objectified female whose only goal is to be saved by a prince."

"I want to be saved by a prince," Liesel says.

Ivan says, "Your big brother will make sure there's nothing you'll ever need to be saved from, okay? So whadya wanna play?"

Liesel tries one more time. "Can't Elysia play PrincessBall with me and you go do something else?" When it's just me playing in the FantaSphere room with her, Liesel's game of choice is PrincessBall, in which we attend lavish balls while dressed up in taffeta ball gowns and diamond tiaras. She's even saved our custom-designed prince to her game profile so we can play with him again and again. He knows every dance step Liesel commands him to do, from ancient steps like the Hustle and Macarena to newer ones like the Bootywave and Skullthrash. He is tall, dark, and handsome and wears an officer's formal uniform of black dress pants and red jacket adorned with a gold brocade belt and a crimson-and-gold sash. He never fails to gift us with boxes of chocolate. We've named him Prince Chocolate.

"No," Ivan snaps. "I said pick something good or I'm not playing with you at all."

"Don't be mean!" Liesel says, pouting.

"I'm not being mean. Don't be a baby. Dad wants me to do more fitness games."

Liesel sighs like Mother. "How about Z-Grav?"

"Yes!"

The game begins, but this time, no virtual objects or scenery appear before the room's white walls. Instead, we hear a sucking noise and immediately we are drawn to the ceiling like magnets. At zero gravity, our bodies' core muscles must work to get our feet back down to the floor. Whoever reaches the floor first wins. Usually I get there first, but since Ivan has gotten so much stronger and leaner, he might have a fighting chance this round. Liesel doesn't even try to compete; instead, she happily bounces off the walls and tries to push her brother higher any time he makes downward progress. She has no desire to win, only to have fun.

I strive to win because that is the stated mission of the game.

I feel certain it would have been my First's goal, as well. A clone does not come by the sculpted musculature I have unless she was duplicated from someone who made sport—and winning—her mission.

Ivan strives to win because the Governor can never remind his son enough that he needs to be a "winner" in order to survive, and thrive, in the military.

The three of us float through the room, struggling to work our way back to the ground. Liesel hangs from the ceiling, grabbing at Ivan's hands to pull him up as he tries to work himself down. Thus obstructed, I easily reach the ground first. The sucking sound ceases. Liesel and Ivan drop to the floor, their falls cushioned by the air balloons that spring from the ground at their landing positions.

Ivan stands up and the balloon disappears.

"This sucks," says Ivan, who does not like to lose. "Let's go play a real game," he says to me. "Something involving real risk."

Liesel teases, "Something Elysia can't win at!"

"What?" I ask.

"Can I play too?" Liesel asks.

"No. You're still too small," Ivan tells Liesel. He Relays a message to the outdoor staff. "Elysia and I are gonna go paragliding off the cliffs."

It feels like we are hanging over the edge of the world.

I don't feel the chemical rush of adrenaline, but I can understand its potential by looking at Ivan's face, registering a combination of anticipation, fear, and determination. We shall dive into danger. Astrid, he's told me, was scared of heights and would never play this game with him.

Our feet stand at the edge of the cliff on the Governor's property. Beneath the rugged edges of the cliff, a hundred yards or so below us—about the length of a football field— Io's waters spread wide and promising. The servants have fastened each of us into a paraglider, and Ivan and I now stand at the spot from which we will make our running leaps to ascend into the air, away from land.

Ivan turns around to face the house. "We're going to take a hard run starting from that spot." He points to a large rock several feet away from us, then circles his arm to where our feet now stand. "You need to make a very strong leap when you reach the edge here, so that when you take off you don't hit the rocky cliff side." He points to a compound of houses near the shoreline, a couple of miles from our cliff perch. "See that megahouse carved into the limestone cliff down there? That's the Fortesquieu compound. We're going to take a nice spin over the water, and then land on the beach there, where the sand is firm enough for a running landing. Got it?"

I nod. He starts to proceed back toward the rock where the wing of his paraglider is spread on the ground to prepare for a forward launch. Once he's ready to leap from the edge, the wing will alight and expand above him, carrying him over the ocean.

But I don't immediately follow him. Instead, I wonder what would happen if I simply said, *No.*

Would my term of service expire if I suddenly announced, *Ivan, leaping from this cliff could easily throw me to my death. I have never maneuvered a paraglider before. I have a chip telling me how to use it, but no actual experience to serve as a guideline for how to guide this craft through the wind we will encounter hovering unprotected high above the ocean. Also, I would rather go for a swim in the floating pool and have visions of a beautiful bronze surfer god with turquoise eyes. After my swim I would like someone to serve me chocolate. I would like that someone to be human. I would like the clones to be the ones served today. You shall fasten them into their paragliders if that's how they choose to goof off today. Be a dear, won't you, pet?*

Ivan calls to me. "Come on already, Elysia."

I say the word. Quietly, but out loud. "No."

"What did you just say?" he asks, his face displaying shock and confusion.

"No," I repeat more loudly.

Ivan doesn't know what to make of my response. Should he be furious? Pacify me? Order me?

"Elysia, I *said*—"

I don't wait for his response, but instead take only a few steps backward, then crouch into runner's position. "Kidding!" I say. "Sorta!"

I don't bother with the mad dash from Ivan's designated starting point. I use all my strength to press down and then I shoot my legs as high as they'll take me, and I leap.

We soar.

Flying high in the air, held aloft thousands of feet in the air by the simple elegance of strings attached to a billowing flap of wing material, I understand why Ivan would actively seek this danger. Being up here is being: Free. Open. Infinite.

As the sun sets on the westward horizon, it casts an apricot glow over the violet water. The air feels thinner and more delicate than the premium oxygen pumped into the atmosphere below us. Gulping it in feels risky, enticing.

Could she be in that human idea called heaven in the skies above me? As I fly over the ocean, my lungs for the first time filling with the non-bioengineered air that she might have known, I can't help but think, I hope my First got to experience this.

"Sweet, huh?" Ivan's voice says into the audio receiver in my helmet.

"Better than 'raxia?" I respond.

I hear him laugh. "'Nothing's sweeter than 'raxia. But 'raxia is for riding out boring days on Demesne. Flying up here is living for real."

The high altitude offers me a new and broader view of the violet ring surrounding Demesne, and beyond the ring, to the white-tipped monster waves known as the *gigantes*, which look meek and unthreatening from so high above the water. For the first time since I emerged, I see the vastness of the real ocean beyond Io. As I watch it ebb and flow, howl and spit, I have a new understanding of its mighty power; Ivan and I seem so small and inconsequential in comparison to the ocean's enormousness. Past the *gigantes*, I see the archipelago of smaller uninhabited islands, their peripheries lined with white sand, but away from the shores, teeming with brush and jungle. I can begin to understand how those lands would be considered feral and lawless.

I look into the nothingness far beyond the islands. Water stretching into what seems like eternity. A thousand miles away, completely beyond my vision and, probably, my reach—forever—is the place where the Mainland meets the ocean. She must have come from there.

Does he miss her, the bronzed god whose heart she owned, and who destroyed hers in return?

"Fortesquieu compound ahead," Ivan's voice says into my helmet. "Prepare to land." I adjust the ropes accordingly. Ivan and I begin a slow descent as we near the landing spot on Demesne's shoreline.

Thud. My feet hit the earth, and I run to soften the landing.

Thud thud thud. Ivan drops behind me, harder and more awkwardly. He tries to run, but the paraglider apparatus wraps around him, forcing him to fall down. He coughs as he stands back up, entangled in rope, but exhilarated. "Awesome ride!" he wheezes.

"Why do you cough?" I ask him.

"Happens to people who grow up here. We're so acclimated to the pure air that when we get up into the other air, and it's so much thinner, our lungs take a beating on the landing. I should do this more often, to prepare to acclimate on the Base." He coughs harder and louder.

A lone figure walking down the beach comes up to him and pats his back from behind. Ivan turns around to greet the person. "Tahir!" Ivan exclaims. Ivan and the lone figure called Tahir do the 'bro fist-and-shoulder-bump thing indigenous to the *Whoa!* species.

Tahir is a tall male teen, with mocha-colored skin and hazel eyes framed in thick black lashes, and lips so coral-red and full they seem almost feminine, so perfect, it's as if they were genetically designed specifically for kissing. His black hair is half cornrowed, with braids framing his face, extending back from his forehead to a few inches into the middle of his head, where the braids end and his natural hair opens into a shag style, loose and free. Like his cousin Farzad, he has an admirably tight set of abdominal muscles on display above his board shorts, but his chest is bare, whereas Farzad's is specked with black hair.

Tahir appraises me curiously from head to toe, then steps around to my backside, where he must notice the word BETA laser-tattooed across the back of my neck. He steps back around to face me from the front, staring intently into my fuchsia eyes. My skin experiences a tingling sensation as our eyes meet, which I attribute to friction from the paraglider landing. He looks deeply into my eyes instead of glancing away quickly as the other humans do, as if he wants to see if there's something behind my glazed eyes besides an empty soul.

Unwrapping himself from the paraglider, Ivan tells Tahir, "Yeah, they're making teen Betas now. Can you believe it? She's called Elysia. Welcome home, buddy."

Tahir does not answer Ivan. Instead, his hand reaches out to touch my elbow, which feels a strange and immediate suction of warmth passing from his body to mine. He looks plaintively into my eyes while his full lips curve into a sweet half smile. "Hey, beautiful," he says to me.

It's like he's a real live Prince Chocolate.

Delicious.

15

IVAN COMMENCES THE RELAY ROUNDS, AND within hours after our paraglider landing on the beach, the gang—Ivan, Farzad, Greer, and Dementia—have assembled in Tahir's leisure quarters at the Fortesquieu compound to welcome their friend back to Demesne.

The Fortesquieu compound is a grand, multistory, pueblo-style structure carved into the limestone cliff towering over Demesne's most spectacular piece of ocean-front land. Tahir's quarters are a series of rooms with white stone walls and circular glass windows like a ship's portholes looking out over the ocean. The rooms are decorated with Turkish rugs and pillows and furnished with intricately carved tables and chairs made from ivory and extinct precious woods. The servants are under orders not to disturb Tahir's homecoming with his friends unless requested. A tray of finger sandwiches and glasses of fresh mint lemonade have been left for refreshment.

I feel drawn to him in a way I can neither define nor understand.

I just want to look at Tahir . . . forever.

Tahir tells us about his time back in Biome City, where he went to undergo extensive physical therapy after his accident. His college hopes, his former life on the competitive big-wave surfing circuit—these have been set aside for the time being. For now, his only life is recovery from his injury and near-death experience. His friends sit around him, rapt, as he relates his story, his hazel eyes occasionally peeking at me in my quiet corner, where I sit on a pillow at the window overlooking the sea. There is a remote quality in the way he speaks—slowly, as if he might at any time stumble over his words or memories. His spine and neck are still healing, he explains. Not only can he no longer compete, but there is to be no surfing *at all* for him for a long while. Maybe ever.

"No!" cries out Farzad. "It's too much. Unacceptable."

"But remember," says Greer, quietly. "He lived. The price could have been so much higher."

I glance at the mural on the wall behind where Tahir stands. The mural takes up the entire length of the wall and is a masterful painting, better than a hologram. It pictures Tahir in surfer stance, riding a huge wave that towers over his head. The painting is so detailed and close up on his body as to give a larger-than-life vision of the ripples in his biceps and abdominal muscles and the power of his strong legs. He rides deep inside a sapphire-colored tube of water rimmed in bubbling white foam above his head, while his back hand trails in the water behind him. His hazel eyes are brighter in this picture than they are in person, and display an intense determination. The detail in the painting is extraordinary, so precise that a viewer could almost imagine the sound of the swell rising before its inevitable crash, could almost smell the sea air and feel its breeze caressing Tahir's skin in that moment. To conquer such a wave must be a heroic feat, as evidenced by the many surfing trophies and ribbons displayed in a case on the wall opposite the mural.

"Let's play Z-Grav," says Ivan. "Something like the old times."

Tahir shakes his head. "No more Z-Grav for me either."

The group lets out a collective gasp.

"At least for now," Tahir amends. The friends nod. *Things can be the way they were*, their faces register.

But when he looks over at me, somehow I see in Tahir's eyes a different message: *No. Things will never be the same.*

It's nonsense to think I could experience some physical or psychic pull toward him.

So why do I feel it anyway?

In Tahir's FantaSphere room, the boys play Biome FlightFight, a fighter plane war game fought over the desert landscape of Biome City, leaving the girls free in the adjoining room to be girly—that is, to paint toenails and talk about the boys. Dementia half lies on an L-shaped chaise, her legs draped over the chair's end as I sit on the floor painting her toes a crimson blood color. Greer sits at the corner of the long side of the chaise with her legs stretched out on the cushion, Dementia's head pressed against her outer thigh.

With one hand, Greer sips a lemonade; with her other hand, she strokes Dementia's long raven hair as if Dementia were a kitten snuggled up against her.

"Does Tahir seem colder to you?" Greer asks Dementia.

"Totally," says Dementia. "Before, he was, like, arrogant-cold. Now he's just cold-cold. In his really hot Tahir way, of course."

This statement actually makes sense to Greer, who nods knowingly. "For sure. He really broke her heart."

"Whose?" I ask. "Did the heart require surgery?"

"Love heartbreak," says Greer. "Not an actual heart splitting apart. It just feels that way."

"Astrid's heart," Dementia says. "She loved Tahir madly. They weren't a couple, exactly, but they were an item when he was on the island, even if he would never publicly acknowledge that. He had other girls wherever he went, on the surf circuit, a whole harem back in Biome City, probably."

Greer says, "I guess you can be like that when your father is one of the richest men in the world. Tahir could have any girl he wants."

"Probably has!" says Dementia.

Greer laughs. "Yeah, probably. Poor Astrid. She was so into him, but he would never restrict himself to a girl whose father is only an employee of this small island."

"Would it not be prestigious for Tahir to associate with the daughter of the Governor?" I ask. And what about his daughter's clone replacement? I think.

Greer says, "Associate, sure. But, like, a committed relationship with her? Not cool, by Demesne standards. People would say it was beneath Tahir. Astrid's father is just a hired hand. The Governor and his family live here at the will of the Board of Directors, not because they actually own property here."

I ask Greer, "Does your father, the envoy, own his property here?"

This seems like a logical question but Greer snaps, *"No,"* and then regards me with irritation. "But at least my family comes from old money, even if we're not crazy wealthy like this old girl." She pats Dementia's head affectionately.

I don't understand how senility affects Greer's family's wealth, nor how Dementia at seventeen human years could be considered an old girl, but I suppose the answers will become clear to me eventually.

Dementia says, "Astrid was so sweet but too consumed by her determination to get into the best university. And she was such a yawn when she ranted on about fair distribution of wealth and all those impossible ataraxias. It was embarrassing. I think that's what finally drove Tahir away. She gave him her heart and he walked all over it." Dementia pauses while I try to imagine Tahir placing his foot on Astrid's beating heart. "Elysia, my leg's totally cramping. Rub my legs or something." I cease polishing her toes and rub her calves. "That's better. Go back to polishing now." Her leg cramp passed, Dementia resumes speculating about Astrid and Tahir's relationship. "Plus Astrid never wanted to go anywhere that would distract from her studying, and Tahir wanted to go *everywhere.* He was all, 'I'm gonna be hovercoptering over the Alps or race-riding across the Himalayas while you sit around here pining for me.'"

Greer says, "I could never figure out why Astrid was into

a scoundrel like Tahir. He was so the opposite of her."

"But, gorgeous much?" Dementia sighs. "Let's have some of that." She leans over to press PLAY on a holoframe on the side table. The frame's hologram picturing Tahir at last year's Governor's Ball goes into action. The clip shows Tahir wearing a black tuxedo with hazel-colored lapels to match his eyes, twirling Astrid on the dance floor, then dipping her so low her head nearly touches the ground. "I worship the ground your head walks on," Tahir tells her. Astrid laughs and smiles as he raises her back to him and presses her close. The eyes of all the women surrounding the dancing couple seem fixated on Tahir. He smiles back at them, gleaming pearly white teeth, then returns his attention to Astrid. "Hey, beautiful," he murmurs to her. Her face lights up anew.

"Well, yeah," Greer agrees once the clip ends. "There's that. He's gorgeous to the fullest. But Astrid had real feelings for him, and he wouldn't even acknowledge to his parents that they were more than a casual couple. He totally used her."

"Karma," says Dementia. "That accident was no accident, if you get my cosmic drift."

"Do you think they see each other in Biome City?" Greer asks.

"Doubt it," says Dementia. "Tahir's too much the love-'em-then-leave-'em type."

I have completed painting Dementia's toenails. I ask Greer, "Shall I paint yours too?"

Greer momentarily ponders the question, then responds, "Not today. I don't think the Aquine would like it."

"The Aquine?" I ask.

"The assistant who came here from the Base, to work

for my dad for a while. I am crushing on him so hard it's pathetic. He's an Aquine, so he probably goes for natural girls who don't wear toe polish. Aquine are supposed to be all humble and into modesty or whatever."

Aquine, I query. The interface shows me that the Aquine are a cloistered sect of genetically engineered people who mated to produce a new race of perfect humans. They are known to be peaceful, religious zealots who, along with engineering their DNA for great looks and strength, have created a race of people who are loyal to a fault: they only mate for love, and are monogamous. Once they mate, they are mated to their partner for life. This master race does not believe in tempestuous or casual lovemaking.

Dementia says, "The Aquine came round my house last week, did I tell you? I almost passed out from his gorgeousness. He was interviewing our staff for the annual report to the Replicant Rights Commission. His voice is this totally sexy growl, but he has a face like an angel. I wish he would interview *me!*" Dementia's hand touches the fleur-de-lis scar on her face.

Greer removes Dementia's hand and places her own hand on Dementia's scar, tracing it with her index finger. "My sweetest Dementia," Greer says, "you make me want to cry. Why do you do things like that to yourself?"

Dementia points in my direction. "Because I want to be like Elysia. I want to not feel. I want to not hurt."

The boys come in search of the girls once their FantaSphere game is finished. Farzad looks at me. "Hey, Beta. We need you to make the run."

"The run" is what I do when Ivan, Farzad, or Dementia send me to find a designated messenger—sometimes a bamboo-vined construction worker, sometimes a human who has gained temporary visitation to Haven—from whom I take delivery of 'raxia pills for the group's later consumption.

"What run?" asks Tahir. The gang all look at him, confused by Tahir's confusion.

"*The* run," says Farzad. "For the 'raxia hookup. If something went wrong, better the Beta should get caught than us."

"Yeah." Tahir shrugs as if he knew that already. "I get forgetful now."

They all nod, but Farzad's face displays concern—how could Tahir forget something so important?

Dementia grabs Tahir into a hug, resting her head on his chest. "It's okay, Tahir. We're so glad you're better."

He kisses the top of her head. "Thanks, beautiful," he says. But his eyes are directed at me when he says it. I wonder what his look to me is meant to express—the affection and sweetness revealed in the way he looked at Astrid, or the desire for an artificial toy the Governor shows in the way he looks at his luxisstant, Tawny?

"You're home now," says Ivan to Tahir. "And we're gonna take care of you properly this afternoon. This 'raxia we ordered in just for you is supposedly primo grade."

Tahir says, "I can't do that anymore, either. It might interact badly with all the medication I'm on."

"Whoa," Farzad and Ivan say at the same time.

Ivan says, "You used to be like, King of Ataraxia."

Farzad allows, "Disappointing, I guess. But I'm sure it's

just a matter of time before you're good to go again. The Beta can do the run, but we'll indulge on our own later, when you don't have to see it and miss it."

"Don't not have your fun on account of me," says Tahir. "Do it this afternoon. I'll go with the Beta to make the run."

"*You* don't make the run," Farzad proclaims.

"*Especially* not you," says Dementia.

"Maybe the old Tahir wouldn't," Tahir says. "The new Tahir will."

"I just needed a break from them," Tahir explains as we walk toward the central plaza in the Fortesquieu compound. I wonder—or perhaps wish—*Because you wanted to be alone with me, as I wanted to be alone with you?* The plaza is located at the top of the dwelling, where the front entryway of the complex leads to acres of landscaped grounds with sculpted trees and flower beds. We reach an elaborate fountain whose centerpiece is a carved jade dolphin with a mouth spraying pale-pink crystalline water. Says Tahir, "I didn't want to be rude and ask everyone to leave. But they were tiring me out."

Oh, I see. He'd rather hang out with a soulless nonentity right now because that's easier. Suddenly, so much about the humans' affection for Demesne and its clones makes sense. Talking to soulless creatures is less exhausting than interacting with their own kind.

We sit down on the fountain's ledge. A bamboo-vined worker wearing a gardener's uniform nears us, but then notices Tahir and continues to walk, as if the gardener never meant to approach us at all.

124

"Hey," Tahir calls to him. "It's okay."

The gardener backs up to us, looking over his shoulders to see if anyone is watching. "I don't know," the gardener says. "I shouldn't even be seen talking to you."

Tahir says, "Just hand it over."

The gardener takes a clear bag containing some pills from his pocket and hands the bag to me. "This never happened," he whispers, then runs away.

As I've been instructed, I place the bag in my pocket as if I've never received it and set my face to *innocent*.

Tahir says, "It's so unnecessary for the staff to treat me like I'm so sacrosanct. The whole reason my parents like to come here is it's the one safe place where we can act normal. We can leave the bodyguards to their quarters and just be us. You know?"

I don't know, but I nod knowingly the way Greer does. "For sure," I say.

I stare at his full lips. They are so luscious, so close. I could touch them, if I dared. This beautiful male teen is so much better than the underwater manly apparition with a perfectly toned torso. Tahir is real.

You know you own me, Z. For my First and her water god, *owning* meant something more than what I know it to mean on Demesne—owning a clone worker. I am curious to experience their kind of passion for myself, not just as a flashback vision belonging to her, to Z.

I should resist, but I can't. "Did you and Astrid experiment with the mighty mighty?" I ask Tahir. Because I am Astrid's replacement, I think. And I am . . . inquisitive.

"I don't even know what 'mighty mighty' is. And who's

Astrid?" Tahir's hazel eyes sear into mine and it's as if my soulless eyes feel the sizzle.

"The Bratton's daughter whom I'm replacing," I say, my tone experimentally set to *flirtatious*.

He winks at me. "I knew that, beautiful," he says, pointedly looking deep into my eyes again, so deep I feel I could melt from the heat of his stare. "But it's Elysia who's here now."

"I am a clone," I remind him. "I am not quite as real as Astrid." It's a good thing I am a clone, I think, because clearly my flirting abilities are nil. I have just announced my own undesirability to him.

"'Course you're real," he says. His fingers press into my wrist. "You've got a pulse." His index finger gently presses into the left corner of my chest. "You've got a heart. Right?"

"Right," I say, my heart pounding so hard I can't believe he hasn't removed his finger from the thunderous beat of it.

But his fixation on my face abruptly ends, and his eyes move to stare into the fountain. He takes his index finger from my chest and places it into the water, trailing his finger in circles through the water. I so want that finger touching me again.

He seems not to have more to say to me, so I must engage in that human pastime called "small talk." I say, "You must feel so much more relaxed here on Demesne."

He doesn't respond. As if he didn't hear me. As if he's so mesmerized by his finger's water swirls that he's forgotten that this girl clone, the presence of whose pulse and heart he personally verified seconds ago, is sitting right here, eager for more conversation with him. It's hard to see why Dementia and Greer find Tahir to be such an intriguing scoundrel. I am intrigued by him, certainly, but more because he is so intense and visually appealing, not because he oozes charisma.

"Because of the air here," I clarify.

"Yes," is all he has to say back.

Making conversation with cute boys is *hard*. It's as if my circuitry has no idea what to do or say to this person whose very nearness makes my heart skip faster but who seems to have forgotten about me with the same intensity that moments ago was focused on me.

"Do you miss taking the 'raxia?" I ask Tahir. Certainly Ivan would miss it terribly if he lost access to it. He worries about losing that access so much he's started trying to make his own.

Tahir shrugs. "Not really."

How can Tahir not miss it if the 'raxia is supposedly so great? Maybe it's not really so great. Maybe I shouldn't be so curious about it, or about this boy.

16

IT'S MOTHER-DAUGHTER TEATIME, ON SEPARATE tiers at Governor's House.

Upstairs on the terrace deck, Mother and her lady friends have convened an afternoon tea party for planning the upcoming Governor's Ball. The wine is flowing in greater quantities than their tea. Liesel and I can hear their giggles and cackles as the ladies enjoy each other's company. Below the deck, on the covered patio, Liesel and I have created our own pretend tea party. We sit at a small round bistro table covered with a white tablecloth, drinking from fine china teacups filled with hot chocolate, and nibbling on real peanut butter cookies. Liesel has devised a silent party for us to playact. Like mimes, we listen in to the conversation above us, and feign the imagined reactions of the ladies to each piece of gossip.

A new lady has just joined the boisterous group up on the deck. "Sorry, ladies!" she says. Liesel taps at an imagined watch on her wrist. I do the same to my wrist and shake my head. We mouth the word *Late!* and then roll our eyes. The new lady's voice sounds like Mrs. Former Beauty Queen's. She says, "Bad weather on the Mainland delayed my return trip to Demesne. I only got home an hour ago. The trip was horrendous, but I swear, the moment I breathe in the smooth air here, I immediately relax. All the tension just goes away back on Demesne."

"Yes!" sigh many of the ladies' voices in agreement.

Mother says, "I didn't realize you'd taken a trip back to the Mainland. Biome City?" She sounds jealous.

"Yes," says Mrs. Beauty Queen. "Some business we had to attend to back in the real world. And some shopping to do!"

"Must have been fun," says Mother.

"Certainly it's always more interesting back in the world. But never as divine as being on Demesne. Should I have asked you to come along, dears? I know you don't have your own plane for getting off the island whenever you want to, but you know all you have to do is ask us whenever you want a lift on one of our rides."

"Yes!" several of the ladies' voices affirm.

Liesel extends her arms wide and bobs her head in circles, imitating the motion of an airplane. I do the same.

"Demesne is perfect," says Mother. "Why leave?"

Liesel covers her mouth with her hand as her eyes go wide, meaning *Oh, no!* She knows Mother is lying. Many nights at dinner, Mother moans to the Governor about how all her friends have planes to take them anywhere in the world they want to go, and why can't she have one too? She'd like to go to BC to see the fashion shows, and Astrid. The Governor says, "You can ask your friends for a ride." Mother responds, "I shouldn't have to ask them. I should have my own. It's embarrassing." And the Governor inevitably responds, "Then you go earn the billion Uni-dollars to buy landing rights on Demesne. Last time I checked the bank account, we were several hundred million away."

A voice that sounds like Greer's mother's asks, "Ladies, who here has gotten a look at the new Aquine military representative on the island?"

A few ladies sigh and dreamily murmur, "Yes!" and "Oh my, I have!"

"There's an Aquine on Demesne?" one of the ladies asks. "I thought they didn't leave their settlements."

"Most don't," says Greer's mother.

"I have seen him, and he is a fine male specimen indeed," says Mother.

Liesel's hands go over her ears and she shakes her head.

"Ho-o-ow did he-e-e e-e-end u-u-up on Deme-e-es-ne-e-e?" asks Mrs. Linger.

Mrs. Red Whine says, "I heard the Aquine was really here to investigate what has caused some of the clones on the island to wake up."

Wake up? Who? Why? Where?

What?

Mother says, "Isolated incidents. Defects."

Liesel's hand goes to her mouth in shock. She whispers, "Mother said 'Defects!'"

"What are Defects?" I whisper back.

Liesel says, "Clones that go bad. That's what Astrid told me. I'm not supposed to know; Dad says we're not supposed to talk about it. Ever."

"Which clones go bad? How? When did that happen?" I whisper.

"Ssh!" Liesel admonishes. She crosses her index finger over her mouth and then points to the deck above us. "I want to hear this!" she whispers.

Mrs. Beauty Queen says, "Maybe it was isolated, hushed incidents in the past. But something's changed. I've heard there have been more Defect cases. Any truth, Mrs. Governor?" she teases Mother.

"None," says Mother. "Error is not tolerated here. The Governor makes sure of that."

But Greer's mother says, "I'm not so sure. This Aquine showing up to prepare the report to the Replicant Rights Commission seems a good excuse for the military to do some investigating."

"Anyway, here's to that master race!" says Greer's mother. "May it always look so fine."

"And natural!"

"And peaceful!"

"And humble!"

"And so poor and in need of a sugar mama!"

Liesel sticks her finger down her throat to mime *gross*. I don't just mimic the *confused* look back to Liesel—I *am* confused. Why would a peaceful and penniless Aquine man need a lady covered in sugar?

Mother seems disturbed by the turn of the teatime conversation. Not as disturbed as I feel.

17

THEY HAVE SOMETHING TO HIDE. I HAVE
something to hide.

They, apparently, don't have a hundred-percent success
rate with their clones. They have manufactured Defects in
error, and whatever these Defects did was so terrible that the
humans try never to speak of them, try not to acknowledge
that the Defects even exist.

It is so frustrating to find out new information that is
not on my chip, only to have that same chip compute the
risk involved in asking the humans for more explanation.

I am a good girl, not a terrible clone. But I have quirks.
Memories. Taste. I will not fail the family who loves me by
letting these quirks ever be translated into defects. I will not
cause my family such shame. I will keep my quirks hidden,

the way they hide their Defects. They own me, but I own my Beta quirks. Privately.

It is the rare morning when my time is my own. Ivan continues to strengthen and wants to do real boxing lessons today, as my agile jabs impress him less and less. He craves brute male power, and is therefore working out with one of the buff male fitness trainers at Haven. Liesel is with her tutor, and Mother rarely emerges from bed before eleven o'clock. Therefore, I take advantage of my free time to jump into the pool at Governor's House.

Back and forth beneath the water, I search for the underwater man-god, hoping to hear his siren call: *You know you own me, Z.* As I dive through the water, he deigns to appear, but in brief, soundless bursts. I see his blond hair swishing and his rock-hard body angling as he swims near the hole that leads to the grotto side of the pool. But the visions of him are brief, murky flashes, out of focus, as if the psychic frequency through which he communicates to me has dimmed. Not even his gravelly voice calls to me this time. My skin tingles at each sighting of him, and I dutifully race toward each vision of him, but he disappears as soon as I reach him. When he reappears at the opposite end of the pool, his arms opening for me, his lips parting as if waiting to kiss me, I swim to him again, but he disappears again.

I am tired of being teased.

I swim through the long connecting tunnel to the grotto side of the pool, where I can sulk in private, like a real teen. I don't know exactly what I want, but I know I want more than to be so continually cheated by this apparition, who only appears in visions and never in the flesh. I lie on a slab of flat, wet stone, in a perfect spot where the sun can peek through the grotto's cave walls and bathe my face and body in warmth. I set my face to *sulk*, but my body is too warm and my mind too distracted to accomplish the proper level of this trademark teen state.

I came to the pool hoping for a vision of my First's man, and I got it, sort of. Yet it's Tahir Fortesquieu I can't stop thinking about. Could it be that my thoughts of Tahir are breaking up my visions of underwater man? To hope to know Tahir better is inappropriate for someone of my caste. I understand that, and do not expect more. But I can't stop myself from wondering about that human affliction called intense physical attraction.

On the other side of the pool, I hear the voice of Tawny, as she and the Governor step onto the deck and walk toward the pool. "The children are at Haven. Mrs. Bratton is still asleep. Your morning meeting with the envoy has been moved to this afternoon."

I hear the Governor's gruff voice. "Finally! Some time for myself."

I peek through the hole in the grotto cave wall. Tawny wears a tiny bikini on her flawless body and is helping the Governor, dressed in boxer shorts, to step into the pool. I can see them, but they must not be aware that I am in the grotto.

"I have warmed the water," Tawny says. "To help loosen your joints."

It's true, the water does feel warmer. I thought it was the sun and my thoughts of beautiful boys that had made it seem so. But it was science.

Tawny stands in front of the Governor, both now submerged waist-high in the pool. She lifts his right leg up and down, then in a circular motion, then she repeats this pattern with his left leg. "Ah, joint therapy," the Governor sighs. "The best part of my medical plan."

The aquamarine-blue tips of Tawny's long, white-blond hair swirl in the water. The Governor's hands reach around her exposed back to press her close to him, groin to groin. She massages his scalp with her hands.

"Tawny," I hear him say. "What do you know about the Insurrection?"

"I only know what you have told me," she answers. "There are rumors of a rebellion raised up by a few Defects who sought freedom. Those Defects were captured and expired. But there is human concern that more Defects may be out there."

"When you're off work at night, in clone quarters . . . you haven't heard more about it there?"

"No, sir," Tawny says. Her hands move from the Governor's head to beneath the water. I can no longer see where her hands are, but they appear to be stroking his most private place.

"Do you wish for freedom?" the Governor asks, panting.

"I do not wish," Tawny states. "I serve."

"Good girl," the Governor grunts.

Defects. Insurrection. Freedom.

These are not just words, but actual concepts. I'm not sure how to process.

As Tawny serves the Governor, I quietly step out of the

water and disappear behind the trees flanking the grotto end of the pool. I walk through the trees, away from Governor's House. I walk until I reach the spot of land where the clone quarters are, several bamboo huts built side by side, each sized to accommodate two to four clones at a time. Since it is daytime, the quarters should be empty, and yet, from the hut at the far end of the row, I hear moaning sounds.

It sounds like someone must be in distress.

I walk toward the hut where the sounds are coming from and stand below the window. Through it, I see two bodies, a male and a female, black-haired and white-skinned, both nude, neither in distress. Perhaps the air has been pumped from premium to porny here on Demesne today, and indiscretion seems to be the result, whether my glazed eyes seek such sights or not.

The couple's coital gyrations are keenly symbiotic, as if each can sense what the other wants or needs at every moment. The intimacy is not like that between the Governor and Tawny—professional. Theirs is lusty and yet tender. If they weren't clearly clones (by the vining I can see on their temples through their black hair), I'd assess their mating to have the humans-only feeling called *soulful.*

I know what they are doing is supposed to be wrong, and it's forbidden for clones. So why does their union look so right—almost beautiful?

Her hands reach behind his neck to pull his face to hers. "Yes!" she loudly cries out. Their hands clasp as their bodies appear to culminate in a final moment of shared pleasure.

He collapses on top of her and she pulls his face to hers

to rub her cheek against his and run her fingers through his hair. I can finally see her face. Her glazed eyes may be that of a clone's, but her expression matches that human one labeled *cherished*.

That is the face I want to experience. With Tahir. For real.

Her fuchsia eyes meet mine.

The face belongs to Xanthe.

Later that night, at bedtime, Xanthe appears in my room. She closes my bedroom door and observes me as she steps to my bed to turn down the sheets and fluff the pillows. She has never before done this nighttime preparation in my room.

"Good evening," she says.

"Yes," I respond.

She takes an inordinate amount of time to fluff my pillows, as if she is waiting for me to commence conversation.

"Do I get a chocolate on the pillow?" I ask.

"Excuse me?"

"A chocolate. With the bedtime turndown service."

Her face registers *confused*. And then she seems to grasp what just happened. "You . . . joke?" she asks. She eyes me up and down. "How do you know how to joke?"

I shrug. "I don't know. It just happens."

"How unnecessary," she says. "What other things can you do?"

"I am a good diver."

"I have heard."

She waits for me to respond, but I don't. It's as if she's running out the clock to see when I will acknowledge what—if anything—I saw.

Perhaps we could do an information trade.

"What are Defects?" I ask her.

Her face pales, and I regret asking the question. It has set her expression to *fearful*.

"*I* am not a Defect," she proclaims.

"Of course you're not," I affirm. "It's just that no one will tell me what they actually are. Maybe you know?"

By persisting with the question, I am trying to say without saying: *I know your secret. Please, reveal this secret to me.*

Xanthe shuts and bolts all the windows in my room. Then she goes to my bedroom door, opens it, peers down the hallway to see if anyone is near, and shuts my bedroom door again. She sits down on my bed and gestures for me to sit down next to her.

Quietly, she says, "Can you keep the information to yourself?"

I believe she has accepted my trade. "I swear. Absolutely." I touch her fingers, but she winces. I take her hand anyway, and clench. *Please*, I want my gesture to tell her. *Trust me. Maybe we could help each other.*

She does not return my gesture, but she does not remove her hand from my beneath mine. Xanthe whispers, "Defects are clones who think they have souls. They feel. They rage. There have only been a few on Demesne. Once they were discovered, they were immediately returned, and expired."

"They *think* they have souls? Or they *have* souls?" I ask.

"I don't know," Xanthe says. But her index finger latches on to mine. As if she is acknowledging something: hope?

"Who is he?" I ask.

Her face visibly softens, almost glows.

"An oxygen leveler." *A-ha!* So there was something different in the air today, but it wasn't science. It was as untouchable as the air, something felt rather than seen. Could it be *love?* That impossibility would seem even more amazing than scandalous. "He lives in the clone quarters at Haven."

There's an opportunity here. I must take it. "Do you know about the Insurrection?"

Xanthe backs away from me, as if I have a disease. Did I take the questioning too far? "Of course not. There's no rebellion on this island."

Xanthe is lying. The word is not in my database, so it shouldn't be in hers either. *Insurrection* isn't just a word I saw in Astrid's book that the Governor happened to say earlier today. Whatever it is, it's real. How could *insurrection* equal the concept of *freedom?*

How can I let Xanthe know she can truly trust me?

My confession could equal my expiration, but my knowledge of her carnal feelings could equal hers. We're evenly matched. I need her to know that. I whisper, "I have a sense of taste. I love macaroni and cheese, and chocolate." As I speak the words, letting go of the burden of keeping this information to myself, I can feel my body actually relax, as if my mind is allowing my body a measure of relief.

For a moment Xanthe appears confused. First I was asking about the Insurrection and now I'm talking about food. Then she gets it. "Impossible," Xanthe says. "Maybe because you're a Beta. That must be it."

"Do you have a sense of taste?"

"No!" she says, sounding offended. "I only require strawberry shakes." She looks on the verge of panic.

"There's one more thing." I pause. "I think . . . I have memories. From my First."

Xanthe gasps. "No. That's unheard of. You remember her?"

"I don't remember her so much as I have visions that I'm sure are from her memory. It's just one specific memory. It happens when I'm in the water." I can tell by the furrowing of Xanthe's brows that my revelation is not a good thing. Quickly, I add, "It's probably nothing. It's probably some weird Beta thing. I don't know what I'm talking about."

Xanthe grabs both my shoulders, nearly shaking me. "Keep this to yourself," she says. "*Please*. They could probably deal with you having a sense of taste. *Maybe*. But memories? No way. You'll be labeled a Defect."

My bedroom door opens and Xanthe nearly jumps. Tawny stands in the doorway. "It's lights-out time in clone quarters," Tawny scolds Xanthe. "I've been looking for you everywhere. Come on. Don't be late."

Xanthe's face goes completely blank, as if her chip has accessed a reset button. "Of course. I lost track of time. How fortunate you found me," Xanthe says to Tawny, and she leaves my room without looking back.

18

DESPITE THE NEW INFORMATION I HAVE gained, I will not add *worry* to my palette of human mimicry. Whatever the Defects and protesters are doing does not concern me, because I am here to bring the fun.

Literally.

It is Tahir's eighteenth birthday. His parents have a lavish party planned for him that all the best people on Demesne have been invited to, but the afternoon party that the gang has arranged for him is the one they hope will really matter to their friend. Dementia and Greer say that Tahir has been asking them about me, so they have decided to give me to him for his birthday. They have wrapped me in a gift box with a ribbon on top.

Dementia lands her Aviate directly on the sand at Hidden Beach, where Ivan, Farzad, and Tahir await our arrival. I crouch inside the box, breathing slowly within the small area. Inside, I see only darkness, but based on the hard pounding in my chest, I conclude that darkness may not only affect sight. I feel a surge of the human state *irritation*. *This* is my darkness to conquer, and it has nothing to do with what I can't see. Why can't I be Tahir's equal instead of his prize?

The Aviate lands and the trunk pops open. I hear Farzad and Ivan standing at the back of the vehicle to lift the box out. Farzad says, "This is the dumbest idea those girls have ever had."

Ivan says, "Agreed. But what else can we give a guy who has everything?" Ivan pats the top of the box as if inside it has a puppy eagerly waiting to be sprung free. "Hang in there, champ. We'll have you out of there in just a few minutes. The girls are putting a blindfold on Tahir as part of the surprise."

Farzad says, "Imbecilic. Truly."

Ivan repeats, "Agreed."

Farzad adds, "Hey, Beta. Did you wear a white bikini? That's what did it for old Tahir."

Ivan says, "Astrid would never wear one for him."

Farzad says, "And your sister is no longer Tahir's sometimes girlfriend. Correct?"

"Correct," says Ivan. "She was too smart for him anyway."

They lift the box and carry it from the Aviate. I feel it placed on the soft-textured sand's surface. Through a hole in the side of the box, I see Tahir seated on a surfboard, blindfolded, with Dementia and Greer standing on either side of him. Dementia says, "We wanted you to have a special birthday-song surprise."

"Better than a hologram!" says Greer. She removes his blindfold with exaggerated flourish. "Ta-da!"

Tahir regards the box. "What's in the box?" he asks, sounding more polite than curious.

"Open it!" squeals Dementia.

He stands up and as he approaches the box, my heart beats faster still. His nearness does something to me. Breaks up the darkness in a very confusing way.

I hear the ribbon cut off from the box and therefore I do as instructed. I open the box by flinging myself up from my crouched position. I stand with my arms wide, in a victory stance, and pronounce, "Happy birthday, Tahir!"

Over my white bikini, the girls have placed a beauty pageant sash lettered with the words MISS HAPPY BIRTHDAY. But if the girls hoped for a great reaction from Tahir, he does not give them one. Apparently my skimpy white bikini and nubile flesh do nothing for him. I must try harder. As commanded, I switch to *pageant strut* setting and sing the "Happy Birthday" song to him with beauty contestant bravado. I strut and careen and bounce along the sand, projecting warmth and enthusiasm for this great holiday.

"Happy birthday, dear Tahir! Ha-a-ap-py birth-da-a-a-y, to-o-o yo-o-ou!"

I place my hands on my hips and deliver a smile and a wink.

Tahir smiles his signature grin, his full coral lips curving upward as he flashes a glimmer of bright white teeth, but the expression in his eyes feels completely at odds with his smile. His eyes are blank, as if he could not be more bored. My performance must have been flawed. The day is overcast and slightly chilly, and there are goose pimples on my arms and my teeth are chattering slightly. My aesthetic is all wrong.

Still, the girls clap enthusiastically at the finale of my performance while Ivan and Farzad shake their heads, trying not to laugh.

Tahir asks, "Where's my towel?"

Farzad retrieves Tahir's towel from the sand.

Tahir comes over to me and wraps the towel around me. "You are cold," he states. "Return to the Aviate until you warm up. I will build a campfire."

I return to the Aviate. But I am already warming up.

Tahir does not want to play games on the beach or swim today. He seems content just to sit in silence at the campfire on the sand and to stare at me through the fire's sparks and crackles while the others carry the conversation.

Greer bemoans her limited choices for getting off the island now that she's completed her high school equivalency exam. She did not get accepted at Biome University, and the few colleges where she did get accepted are all in boring places or floody places.

"When do you start at BU?" Greer asks Tahir. "I'm so jealous."

Tahir says, "My parents deferred me for another year to give me more time to recover from the accident."

Farzad says, "So how are you spending your time back in the world? You can't be in physical therapy all the time. Are you allowed to hovercopter yet?"

"Not yet," says Tahir. "Mostly I spend my time relearning what the accident caused me to lose."

Dementia says, "I wish I could get amnesia."

"I do not have amnesia," says Tahir.

Greer says, "She just means you seem a little forgetful since . . . Are they still giving you sedatives or something? You seem quieter too. It's weird to be here at the beach without you cranking some music and racing the boys on the sand."

"And ogling the girls," adds Dementia.

Tahir's stare has remained intent on me.

"I think he still ogles," observes Farzad.

"Yes, I still take pain medication," says Tahir.

"Ever think about joining the military instead of going to BU?" Ivan asks Tahir. Ivan did not bother with college applications; the military was his only choice—or, rather, his father's choice for him. "They'll help you get back into shape."

"Yeah, and get all buff like this bad boy!" says Dementia, giving Ivan's newly bulging biceps a playful squeeze. She turns to Greer. "And the uniforms are so cute. Maybe you should consider the military too, Greer? It would give you something to talk about with the Aquine working for your dad. You know, get him to help you with the application, help you train for the Base."

Farzad says, "Wait—there's an Aquine working for Greer's dad?"

Greer nods. "Yeah. He's fresh off the Base. He's doing the annual report that no one cares about to the Replicant Rights Commission."

Ivan, Dementia, and Farzad all laugh at the absurdity of the annual report no one actually cares about, but Tahir does not. Tahir says, "But Aquine do not join the military."

Greer says, "Traditionally, they haven't. This guy is the first from his clan. It's, like, a big deal that he left to join the world. He's unbelievably beautiful. All that master DNA works delightfully on him, I must say."

Dementia says, "He's so pure. Such a shame. No naughty dalliances for the forbidden Aquine. There's just something so ridiculously beautiful and romantic about mating for life." She pulls on her hair and kicks some sand into the fire. "At least you have options, Greer. My parents won't let me off this island."

Says Ivan, "You wreak enough terror here. I don't think the world can handle you, Dementia."

Dementia laughs. Then she emits a loud sigh and turns to Tahir. "Dude, I'm sorry, but someone has to say it. You are *so* boring now. I think some 'raxia ought to cure you of that. You game for the dare?"

Tahir shakes his head.

Farzad scoffs, "You never used to turn down a dare."

So challenged, Tahir says, "Then let's do 'raxia."

Ivan says, "Finally, happy birthday to Tahir!"

Through the fire, I observe Tahir. His hazel eyes sear into me, and I marvel at how this human prince can stare so keenly into my eyes but does not feel compelled to look away. The intensity of his stare could burn a hole through my soul. If I had one. I wish I did, if only so I could understand the appeal of their 'raxia.

The gang have tried a new kind of 'raxia—Ivan's custom blend. Farzad's review of Ivan's 'raxia: "Strange brew, bro.

It's less ambient than regular grade 'raxia. Makes me feel relaxed, but also like I want to punch through a wall. Weird combo."

Greer, who, because it's Tahir's birthday, has foregone her usual disdain of 'raxia and has joined the gang's ambient indulgence today, says, "Yeah, I forgot how sweet this stuff can make you feel. I'm, like, all tingly. But I also want to punch something." She playfully jabs Dementia's arm. "Kidding. Sorta!"

"I'm experimenting with steroid components in the 'raxia. This batch has some testosterone," Ivan informs his friends.

"That how you're getting so strong?" Farzad asks Ivan.

Ivan nods. "Yeah. My new 'raxia. And my new Beta."

Dementia says, "If I suddenly grow a beard, I'm gonna cut you, Ivan."

They laugh. Greer says, "What do you think of the 'raxia, Beta?"

My review of the 'raxia: "Meh." At Ivan's orders, I have taken one of the pills, but I feel no different. I still don't get why the human teens indulge in these capsules.

Dementia says, "I heard 'raxia affects clones differently. Makes them crazy."

Greer giggles. "I overheard Ivan's dad and my dad talking. I think that's why the Aquine is really here. To investigate some link between 'raxia and Defects."

No one laughs with her. Even high, they don't joke about Defects. "Not funny," says Ivan. "And not true. Look at her." He points to me. "No effect."

I shrug and admit, "Nothing."

The 'raxia has had its effect on Tahir, however. "Beta," he calls to me. "Come here."

I step over the sand to where he sits by the campfire. "Sit down," he commands.

I sit down on the sand next to him.

"No," he says, and for the first time I see the spark in his hazel eyes that his friends have reported missing since his accident. "Sit on my lap."

The gang applauds. "There's our Tahir!" says Farzad.

"Feeling good," says Tahir. "Different. So much sweetness."

Ivan nudges my arm with his finger. "Go sit on Tahir's lap like he said."

Tahir sits cross-legged on the sand, and I stand up and insert myself into his lap. I have never been so near and close to a human boy like this before. I don't think it's the 'raxia that makes me feel intoxicated. It's the press of Tahir's warm flesh against mine as my back leans into his bare chest. He breathes onto the back of my neck, where the word BETA is aestheticized, and my skin feels on fire.

"Kiss her!" Dementia tells Tahir.

"Yeah, put that Beta to good use, finally," says Farzad.

But Ivan's face has hardened and he warns Tahir, "Kiss her and I will beat you up, bro." The group turns to Ivan, their faces shocked. Then Ivan lets out a high-pitched laugh. "Ha-ha, JK!" says Ivan. "Use the Beta however you want, Tahir."

Tahir wraps his arm around my shoulder to move my body sideways, so my face will turn up directly into his. I shouldn't want this to happen. But I do. My eyes quickly dart to Ivan. He nods his permission, despite the scowl on his face.

Tahir's full coral lips part slightly, and so mine do the same. His face approaches mine, closer . . . closer . . . closer . . . and then . . . *magic*. His lips softly press into mine, and our mouths meet in soft exploration. My heart feels as if it could explode out of my skin. If this is 'raxia, I want more more more.

The gang claps in enthusiasm. "*There* is our Tahir!" says Farzad.

Tahir's mouth moves to my neck and up to nibble on my ear. Quietly so that none of the others could hear, he whispers into my ear, "You are the most beautiful girl I've ever seen. You are special. Different from all the other girls. You make me feel *alive*, Elysia."

19

I HAVE BEEN KISSED FOR THE VERY FIRST TIME.
And just as quickly forgotten.

"Nonsense. Clones serve parties, they don't attend them,"
said the Governor when Mother suggested she'd like to
bring me to Tahir's fancy birthday party at the Fortesquieu
compound.

Maybe I won't be a fancy guest at that party, but I have
something those other guests don't. I know that I alone
am Tahir's best gift, the only girl who makes him feel alive
again since his accident. At least, I was until the 'raxia wore
off and Tahir fell asleep. When he woke up, he was once
again totally "boring," as Dementia terms him, as if the light
switch to Tahir's lust had simply turned off. I will get it back
on. I know I can.

Ivan and Farzad speculated that it was the testosterone in

Ivan's 'raxia batch that brought Tahir's desires for naughtiness back to life again. I like Tahir's naughtiness. To experience disappointment at not being invited to Tahir's formal party would be naughtily inappropriate of me, and also a waste; what I want to further experience with Tahir, I would prefer to happen in private next time. If there is a next time. Please let there be a next time.

So, while the Bratton family is away at the Fortesquieu compound, their Beta will play. Left alone at the house, my prime mission is to jump into the pool as soon as they're gone. I do a running dive into the open infinity pool, swim across the length of it, and rise above the air at the edge, where Xanthe sits, cautiously dangling her feet and calves in the water. I splash water at her. "Come in!"

"I will drown," she says.

"You won't. Just step in right where you are. We will stay on the shallow end. I promise."

Xanthe looks around to see if any other clone servants may be around to report on her. We see no one. The staff are either resting or attending Tawny's Maximize Luxury for Your Human seminar in the Governor's conference space at the other end of the house. It's twilight now; the family won't be home till ten o'clock at the earliest, when Liesel's desire to attend a fancy party will inevitably meet with the child's need for sleep. There's so much swimming and diving and perhaps learning more about Tahir from Xanthe that can happen in the meantime, and I personally plan to maximize our use of this rare time when we are not on call to the humans. Maybe, even—chocolate will be pillaged. I work up such an appetite in the pool, and on this sweet evening after the afternoon when I have been kissed by a prince, and the air smells particularly succulent, the water feels extra silky, and the violet-orange sunset filled with promise, no mere strawberry shake shall satisfy it.

Xanthe takes the plunge, pressing down on her hands to lift her seated body from the ledge and into the water. The water comes up to her chest as she takes baby steps across the shallow end of the pool. She shivers, wrapping her arms around her chest.

"It's cold at first, but it will feel warmer as you move around," I tell her.

"It's"—she dips lower, until the water covers her shoulders and wets the ends of her bobbed black hair— "refreshing?"

I stand next to her and place my hand against the small of her back. "Try floating. I'll hold you steady if you're scared."

"I do not scare."

"Right."

We are programmed to not lie, except perhaps to ourselves, in the sense that we believe what we've been told about our programming even if experience tells us otherwise. Xanthe must experience some level of trepidation.

I say, "Tilt your head back and lift your legs up so you can float on your back. I promise you won't drown."

Despite her glazed fuchsia eyes, I sense trust in them. "I do want to try," she says.

I know she is scared of this simple task even if the fear is something she can't—or won't—acknowledge. Fear, perhaps, is not based on the chemical component of adrenaline alone. It acts also on inexperience, or venturing into the unknown, even if that unknown is as uncomplicated a thing as a swimming pool. At least, the pool feels uncomplicated to me, a natural extension of myself. To Xanthe, who has never been in one, it might seem like the great wild unknown.

Xanthe's head leans back as her legs float up. I place my arms beneath her back to make her feel supported and safe. I can't believe I took something so simple for granted. Having my First's abilities in the water was not my right but perhaps more a gift.

Xanthe floats!

Joy rises up too, I know it—but is that human feeling hers, or mine, upon witnessing her experience this new freedom?

"A-a-a-ah!" Xanthe says, staring directly up into the sky and, for the first time I've ever seen, with a smile on her face. "These humans must source this water with magic. Too good to be true."

"Shall I remove my arms?" I ask her.

"Yes, please. Slowly."

"Don't stiffen up. Let your body relax."

I slowly remove one arm, and she remains floating. I remove my other arm. She's on her own. Her body floats.

"I could stay here forever." She mimics a human's contented sigh.

"Are you okay on your own if I sprint to the other end and back?" I ask Xanthe. I want to check in with my underwater apparition man. I miss him. He has been ignoring me lately, now that the only boy I can think about is Tahir Fortesquieu.

"Mmmm," Xanthe sighs, closing her eyes as her body gives in to the floating sensation.

I dive beneath the water and swim to the other end, toward the entrance to the grotto tunnel, but I see nothing besides water and Xanthe's floating body. I swim through the tunnel, near which there are two floating chairs bobbing in the water. I retrieve the chairs, step out of the grotto to carry them back to the other side of the pool, and place the chairs in the water there.

"Let's do this like the humans do this," I tell Xanthe. She returns from her floating position to standing on the pool bottom, and I help her maneuver into one of the chairs.

I step into my own chair alongside her. It's a shame I didn't have the foresight to bring our strawberry shakes— or even better, some chocolate milk—to nestle into the cup holders. No matter. This evening is perfect enough already. That compulsory Demesne experience for humans, *leisure*, is for the clones tonight too.

"What was Astrid like?" I ask Xanthe.

Xanthe says, "She was hard to know. She just wanted to be in her room alone most of the time. Studying, I suppose. But she was very secretive, so it's hard to say. Why do you ask?"

"Just wondering. Am I anything like her?"

"In no way whatsoever."

"Should I be?"

"They seem pretty happy with you the way you are, so I'd say no."

"Your mate. What is he called?"

She smiles slightly at the thought of him. "He is called Miguel."

"Do you wish he was here now?"

She splashes water at me. "You'll do. For now. Besides, he is working at the Fortesquieu compound tonight. Making sure the oxygen for their party is particularly luxurious. The young man they are celebrating is very delicate since his accident."

"What was Tahir Fortesquieu like before his accident?"

"I didn't have much interaction with him except when he came to call on Astrid. He was very . . . datacheck the word *haughty*."

I do so and determine, "He does not seem that way to me now."

"Oh he doesn't, really?" Xanthe says, in a tone suggesting *He does, really*. "Do yourself a favor. Spare yourself the idea that a human will care for you like you're one of them."

"I would never expect a human to care for me." I don't know why Xanthe's words scorch me; all I asked her was what kind of fellow Tahir was before his accident. I didn't ask if I should hold out hope that I would be the clone to change the dynamics of interspecies love, that I would be the clone to be cared about rather than merely played with. But she should know there is a possibility of more for me. "Tahir Fortesquieu kissed me this afternoon," I confess to Xanthe.

Instead of setting her face to *surprise*, she allows it to go to *concerned*. She gently touches my arm and says, "Don't be like Tawny."

"A luxisstant?"

"A consort," Xanthe corrects.

"I could be more to him," I say.

"No," Xanthe says, definitively. "You can't."

I refuse to believe her. I don't respond.

"I know we are not supposed to want," Xanthe continues. "But please, promise me something. Want more for yourself than to just be a human's consort."

"What more could I possibly be?"

"You are smart, and strong, and brave. The humans will try to keep you from being anything more than their toy. It's up to you to rise above that."

"I can rise above that?"

"I believe you can."

"Do you know love with Miguel?" I ask Xanthe.

"I think that's what it is. With him, I experience . . ." Her voice drops to barely a whisper. "Contentment."

"How Demesne of you," I murmur. I think I'm as envious of her as I am pleased for her.

She's had enough of our cloned-heart-to-cloned-heart. "I can only float in this chair for so long. It's satisfactory for a few minutes, but I do not understand what the humans find so relaxing about resting under a waning sun while the cold skin shrivels up from idle lingering in the water. How can they sit still for so long?"

"Want to try a swim?" I ask her.

"Yes, please."

We get out of our chairs and place them at the water's ledge.

I place my arms beneath her back again. "Let's try a backstroke. Start by kicking your feet." She kicks her feet. "Now swing your arms behind you." She tries but gulps in water, loses her balance, and returns to standing upright on her feet.

"I don't understand," she says.

I demonstrate the backstroke, one length up and then back across the pool.

"I can't do it perfectly like that," Xanthe says.

"Perfection isn't important," I say, and we look at each other in recognition of the absurdity of my statement, the antithesis of the whole ethic of Demesne. It's like we want to . . . laugh? "Just try. I've got you."

She floats again on her back as I place my arms beneath her. She kicks her feet and then begins stroking her arms up and over, up and over. But the splash from her arms sends water up her nose and she returns again to standing upright. "A most unsatisfactory sensation," she says through unwelcome snorts.

"Let's try an easier way," I say.

I go to the water's ledge to retrieve a kickboard. I demonstrate how Xanthe can hold the kickboard against her chest and swim around the pool that way, or even venture to the deep end if she chooses. Xanthe takes the kickboard and begins kicking around the shallow end. I swim alongside her, a slow and steady breaststroke, as we find a peaceful rhythm.

Xanthe stops her kickboarding to stand again, and this time she changes direction. "I want to go that way," she says. "To the deep end. Like you."

"I'll be right there alongside you."

"I know."

We take off for the deep end of the pool.

The sun has set and Xanthe is exhausted from our swim. We lie on the humans' chaises, drying off in the cool nighttime air as we drink our strawberry shakes.

"You seem to experience love, not just mimic it. Are you sure you're not at least a little bit Defect?" I ask. I try to set my voice to *genuine* so Xanthe will know I am not trying to offend or accuse her. I want to . . . comfort her. Share this with her.

"Perhaps," Xanthe says, quietly. "Probably."

Xanthe says, "There's an army of Defects hiding out in the Rave Caves. They are making allies. It's true. They are planning an insurrection."

This news is shocking. Life on Demesne is too perfect to wish for their insurrection to be a success against impossible odds, and yet it's also liberating to know there are Defects out there who haven't been expired. They have created their own hope for themselves. They are planning a revolution.

"I overheard the Governor talking about it with the envoy. He said the protest people on the Mainland claim that Defects are not different from regular clones. The protest people say the difference is that Defects have developed a natural sense of outrage and injustice because they are being held in involuntary servitude."

I am frightened now. I want to rewind this conversation. "But we do not distinguish voluntary from involuntary servitude. We do not feel."

Quietly, Xanthe says, "You know that's not true." This time it is she who grabs my hand, and clenches. I feel so much at this moment that it's overwhelming. I feel connection with Xanthe such as I have never felt for the humans. I feel awe, learning that there are Defects planning an insurrection. I feel amazement that there really are protest people—humans!—who seek to free us.

I cannot deny. I *feel.*

"If this island is so peaceful, why are people on the Mainland protesting us?"

She looks around again, but sees no one. She leans in closer to me and speaks softly. "They are activists on the Mainland who believe that clones on Demesne are essentially slaves. They are fighting to emancipate us."

She has mentioned this concept before—*freedom*—but I am unclear what it would entail. "Emancipate us from what?" I gesture around us. To paradise. "Demesne is renowned as the most desirable and exclusive place on Earth. And we get to live here. We get to breathe the purest air. We are surrounded by scenery that has a perfect aesthetic. We want for nothing."

"Except choice about our servitude. The protesters want us to have choice."

"Why do we need choice if we have no souls? And where do the Firsts' souls go when they're extracted to make clones?" I ask Xanthe.

"I don't know. There are rumors. The Defects are determined to find out. They've discovered human feeling, and now they want it all. The feelings, *and* their Firsts' souls back."

Whoa.

Xanthe says, "Supposedly, there are people on the inside, military officers on the Base, who know where the souls are stored. Defects take the blame, but it's humans on the Mainland who are secretly really behind the Insurrection."

"There are *humans* behind the Insurrection?" I exclaim. "How is that even possible? They're the ones who created this paradise."

"Not enough to share," Xanthe says. "It's created problems."

"What kind of problems?"

Before she can answer, Tawny walks out onto the deck. She eyes Xanthe and me reclining on the Bratton's deck chairs. "My seminar is finished," says Tawny to Xanthe. "You should have attended. I will give you the talking points holosheet so you may review it."

"Great," says Xanthe. I know that Xanthe is doing the sarcasm, but Tawny does not appear to understand that.

"Yes, it is," says Tawny. "What are you doing out here?"

"Leisuring," says Xanthe.

Tawny does not recognize this sarcasm. "We serve. We do not leisure," says Tawny.

And then suddenly I understand what kind of problems the humans' leisure exclusivity has created. From way off in the distance, we hear a loud explosion. Xanthe and I jump to our feet and, together with Tawny, we look beyond the pool, past Io's waters, to the mountaintop on the other end of the island. We see the smoke rising, and then a ball of orange as the jungle lights up, on fire.

A bomb has gone off in paradise.

20

"NO WAY!" GREER LOOKS UP FROM HER RELAY. "The Governor has just told the residents that the bomb was an isolated incident, nothing for them to worry about. But he said they know who set the bomb off. The Beta!" The gang all gasp and turn their heads to look accusingly at me.

I gasp.

"I did not set off the bomb!" I proclaim. "Mother says I am perfect. I am *not* a criminal."

"Not you, Beta," says Greer, rolling her eyes. "The other Beta. The one called Becky."

We sit by ourselves on the deck of the floating pool at Haven as Demesne's residents are gathered inside the club for a town hall–style report from the Governor about the previous evening's incident. The teens have sequestered themselves from the adults' "boring convo" (per Dementia), which is turning out to be maybe not so boring.

No one was hurt by the explosion. It turned out to be a very crude—albeit loud—bomb, capable of more psychological than physical damage, besides some burned trees in the jungle. How could Becky possibly have obtained a bomb?

Maybe I'm just as guilty as the other teen Beta. I did not absorb *worry* into my human palette. I was too busy being the prized Beta and not the reject. Last time I saw her at the boutique, Becky looked different, and behaved strangely, and I knew something was wrong, but I did not concern myself. I walked out the boutique's door and back to my pampered life at Governor's House, and I did not give Becky another thought.

I failed Becky.

I failed.

Ivan looks at his Relay. "They're saying she was a Defect. That would explain it."

Dementia says, "The Defects are rising up to take over!" She raises her fist in solidarity. "They're *so awesome!* I want to cut one of my own!"

"This isn't funny," Greer scolds her.

"I didn't say it was," says Dementia. "But it is kinda cool, you have to admit. We need some Defects here. Something to make things more interesting."

A new Relay message comes through, causing Greer to say, "Holy crap. The beautiful Aquine who did the investigation just told the group that the Beta took 'raxia and that's what caused her to go Defect."

Farzad says, "Doesn't make sense. The 'raxia had no effect

on Elysia. The other Beta probably just went Defect because she didn't turn out to be a hot Beta like that one." He points at me. "Hell hath no fury like a runty clone, right?"

Greer says, "That Defect better be dissected fully. The chemistry of clones needs to be improved. You guys do know that Dr. Lusardi was brought here to supply clones before the science of cloning was actually ready to accommodate the service industry, right? It's true. My dad told me. They just didn't want to pay wages to the human workers who liked it so much here they didn't even pretend to work."

Ivan says, "Nah, guys, the bomb was mine! I did it!"

The group all laughs, except Tahir, who has yet to offer his opinion.

Greer sneers, "Everyone knows you're all bark and no bite, Ivan. By the way, do you realize you've eaten, like, ten pastries in a row? Leave some for us!"

Ivan's hand is midway toward reaching for another of the pastries set out on a platter for us by the servants on the deck. He stops for a moment as if to reconsider whether he wants another, then goes for it. He grabs a raspberry tart and gobbles it whole. "Raspberry! Almost as delicious as the air here!"

Farzad laughs. "Enjoy it now, 'cause the kind of decadent food you get here is not going to be available for you at the Base."

"Exactly," says Ivan. He promptly eats another tart, this time lemon. "Ah," he sighs, gulping in the succulent air. "Only some 'raxia could make this afternoon better."

Greer throws her hands up. "People! I'm trying to talk about something actually important here. A bomb went off on Demesne! Don't you think it's appalling that the Beta who did it was just sitting around waiting to be bought when she was a Defect all along? She should have been tested first." She turns to me. "Have you been tested as a Defect? It is weird how you can, like, dive and swim so perfectly. That's not normal."

Previously Greer encouraged me to risk death by diving for her entertainment; now she says these skills could brand me a Defect?

Ivan says, "Maybe the other Beta didn't really do it. Maybe she's just a convenient target to blame. She can be taken away quietly and no one will ever care, other than to be relieved that some nuisance with a taste for danger is gone. It's not like she's a real person who would get a trial and get to tell her side of the story." He looks at me. "Sweet, innocent Elysia. Do *you* think the other Beta did it?"

The gang laughs—imagine, soliciting an opinion from a clone!

I say, "If the Governor says Becky did it, then Becky did it."

"Right," says Ivan. "Just making sure *you're* not taking the bad 'raxia. Proving that if a Beta takes her owner's custom blend of new and improved 'raxia, she's obviously just fine." He pats the back of his own shoulder. "Job well done, Dr. Ivan."

So many *if*s.

If I hadn't been so busy showing off my aquatic skills and pleasing the humans, I could have tried to pass on my skills that the humans value to Becky, so she could have been bought and found an appropriate role for herself on Demesne.

If I had any control of my own life, I could have . . . what? What could I have done then, or now, or in the future, to help Becky? What could happen if I were the architect of my own destiny rather than a mere pawn in it?

Dementia says, "That Defect's gonna experience some gnarly torture. Jealous!"

My brain suddenly closes the knowledge gap. It hits me, what the infirmary at Dr. Lusardi's compound is really for. Becky will go there, and be dissected piece by piece to determine her faulty chemistry, but she will be living and breathing through the investigation. Suffering. There will be no anesthesia for the probing Becky will be subjected to. Poor, sallow Becky, who also loved chocolate. She will have her skin seared and her eyeballs extracted and every part of her body prodded with mental instruments to find out what went wrong with her.

"That's not true," says Greer. "The Aquine who did the investigation is also reporting to the Replicant Rights Commission, and he has just promised that the Defect will be humanely monitored under Dr. Lusardi's care. The Defect will be rehabilitated rather than destroyed."

From what I witnessed through the infirmary's windows, I know there's no way that's true. And I know Becky witnessed the torture in that room too.

Could it be that Dr. Lusardi wanted us to see through that window? As a warning?

Dementia, sitting next to me, turns her head to examine

my face up close. She announces, "You guys! Elysia actually looks concerned! Like, sad, even. I've never seen a clone look that deep. This bomb business must be serious!" She giggles.

"Dementia probably set off the bomb," says Tahir. Could I dare hope that Tahir hopes for such an absurd conclusion, because it would prove to him that Betas are not criminals? A Beta to him should be the girl he finds most beautiful, who makes him feel alive.

The gang laughs. He's joking like their old Tahir. The bomb hasn't *completely* rocked their world.

21

LATER THAT EVENING, SOON BEFORE LIGHTS-OUT
time in clone quarters, Xanthe slips into my bedroom.

"Where is Mother?" she asks me.

"Still with the Governor back at Haven," I say.

"Good," says Xanthe. She closes my bedroom door
behind her. "You heard?"

"I heard. Will Becky be expired?"

"Yes. But not immediately, because of the Aquine. His
report to the Replicant Rights Commission wouldn't look
so pretty if a Defect were placed before a firing squad. His
supposed advocacy of her 'rights' sealed the other Beta's fate.
Now she'll die slowly and cruelly."

"In the infirmary?"

"Probably."

"Where do you access your information, Xanthe? Is it a data modification I could also receive?"

"Hardly. The humans have their Relays. We . . . have our own network."

"Who is 'we'?"

"It is better for you not to know, for now."

There's something more pressing I need to know. "Have you taken the 'raxia? Is that why you are able to feel?"

"Miguel and I have taken the 'raxia," she admits. "Some clones at Haven got hold of some and shared. It seems to unblock something in our brains, and waken us."

"It did not wake me," I say.

"You took it?"

"Yes. It had no effect on me."

Xanthe's brows furrow. "I don't know why it didn't. Of the clones I know who have taken, it has taken only one hit of 'raxia to waken them. Perhaps because you are a Beta? Or your teen hormones are different?" Her facial expression suggests that her brain is computing further. "Which would, of course, invalidate the other Beta's conviction. If 'raxia did not affect you, it should not have affected her. Either she never took it and it never caused her to supposedly go Defect, or . . ."

I conclude, "Or Becky didn't set off the bomb, and the humans are lying."

Says Xanthe, "I blame the Aquine. Truly, I hate him."

"You hate?" I ask. Xanthe rages. Now there can be no denying: she is a Defect. Yet I am not scared of her.

"*Hate*," Xanthe affirms. "He is the ultimate hypocrite for what he has caused the other Beta. They are supposed to be spiritual people who maintain ethical relationships with nature. Aquine are not supposed to be military pawns. For the Aquine to pin blame on Becky is against their very nature."

"Maybe that's exactly why the Aquine turned in Becky. Because the Aquine do not believe that clones are 'natural.'"

Xanthe grabs her own wrist and suddenly slices her sharp fingernail across it, causing her flesh to bleed, and my heart to ache. *"I* am *real!"* Xanthe cries out. *"You* are *real!"*

In the zeal of our conversation, we did not notice a quiet figure enter my bedroom. Liesel stands at the doorway, holding a teddy bear and sucking her thumb. "Liesel!" I say. "You know Mother said thumb-sucking is for babies, not for big girls. What are you doing here, sweetheart?"

"I'm scared." She looks toward Xanthe's bloodied arm and whimpers.

I walk over to her and pick her up in my arms. She leans her head on my shoulder. Liesel asks, "Are you a Defect, Xanthe?"

"Of course not," Xanthe says. But her voice is not set to *reassuring.* "Shall I make you some warm milk to help you get to sleep?"

Liesel shakes her head against my shoulder. "No! Go away, Xanthe. You frighten me."

Xanthe looks at me, and I nod to her in tacit acknowledgement. I have this situation in control. Once Xanthe has removed herself from my bedroom, Liesel says, "You are not a bad Beta like the one who set off the bomb, are you, Elysia?"

I stroke her hair. "No, Liesel. I am a good Beta. A good

girl just like Xanthe. I will love you and take care of you as a sister should."

Her wet tears fall onto my shoulder. "I miss Astrid," she says. "But I'd miss you more, if you were gone. Please don't leave me, Elysia."

"I won't," I promise.

But there is no need for me to further try to soothe Liesel's nightmares. Once Mother got home and found Liesel still riled with anxiety about the bomb, Mother decided the only way to calm Liesel was to give her a small dosage of Mother's tranquilizing medication. Liesel does not need me at her bedside to help her sleep since she's passed out cold, which is a shame, as I wouldn't mind her nontranquilized warmth cuddling up against me on this night. I have only the room's darkness and emptiness to keep my company.

That is, until the Governor enters my room, without knocking, and turns on the light.

We have never been alone in a room together before. Seeing him without his usual collection of workers or family members around him makes him appear larger than usual, his imposing girth not dwarfed by the physical presence of others. He closes my bedroom door behind him.

"I need to question you about the incident," he says.

"Yes, Governor."

The Governor walks toward my bed. He does not smile genially at me as Mother does. He is all business.

"You knew this other Beta, Becky?"

"Yes. I was only at the boutique with her for a short period of time, before Mother bought me."

"Did she act strangely?"

"How do you mean, strangely?"

"The broker at the boutique said that Becky had recently been behaving differently. Wild and insolent, like a human teenager her age. Disrespecting authority, disregarding the rules."

"She seemed unremarkable when I knew her. She had only recently emerged, like me."

"Teen clones are only in the Beta stage right now because adolescent hormones are so unpredictable. The most advanced scientists still do not fully understand how to transition a teen clone from adolescent to adult. This unfortunate incident makes it imperative, obviously, that we understand if that particular wayward Beta's hormones contributed to her going bad." He sits down on my bed. Why does the Governor not acknowledge, as he's told the island's residents, that it was 'raxia that caused Becky to go Defect, and not teen hormones as he seems to be trying to tell me? "We don't want that to happen to you, right?"

"Correct, Governor."

"The Beta will be undergoing extensive chemical testing, obviously. We may have to run some tests on you, as well."

My body stiffens. *Fear*. It is real.

The Governor's index finger lightly touches my exposed knee, just below where my short nightgown falls. "I can't have a Defect living in my own household, can I?"

"No, sir."

His full hand finds its way onto my upper thigh.

"Unless you'd rather I do the tests myself," says the Governor. "Do you wish me to do the tests myself?"

I know I am being threatened. I know I am younger and would be considered prettier than Tawny, because of my innocent aesthetic, which Dementia has told me is appealing to certain types of "creeps." But I am also serving in the Governor's household as a daughter.

"I do not wish, Governor," I state.

"Good girl." His hand inches higher up, almost touching me *there*. "Tawny tells me that you and Xanthe have shared leisure time. Leisure is not meant for clones, you know. Unless the leisure is in service of a human." His breathing has gotten heavier and there's a slight trickle of sweat above his brows. "So beautiful," he murmurs as his hand presses between my legs. "So pure."

The sound of my bedroom door opening startles us, and we look to the doorway, where Ivan stands. He bounds into my room, calling out "Dad!" His utterance indicates he is looking for his father, but his face registers *concern*, suggesting that perhaps he was looking out for me.

In an instant the Governor's wandering hand is returned to his side. He hastily stands up.

"I was questioning Elysia about the rogue Beta," the Governor says.

Ivan stares down his father. "Mother is looking for you," says Ivan, his eyes seeming to dare his father, *Call me out on this lie. Just try.*

"Of course," says the Governor. "I'll go find her." He leaves my room.

Ivan walks over to my bed and places the blanket over my waist. He leans down to whisper in my ear, "Maybe you should sleep in Liesel's room from now on. But if you don't, be sure to always leave your door open. Okay?"

I nod. "Okay."

As he exits my room, he leaves the bedroom door partially ajar.

"Thank you, brother," I whisper to the empty room.

Worry is now safely embedded beneath my skin, and not because my database put it there.

22

XANTHE WILL EXPLAIN IT TO ME.

At dawn the next morning, I seek out Xanthe. I need her advice about what to do should the Governor make a surprise visit to my bedroom again. I need to know if she thinks they will really take me away for testing, because of what went wrong with Becky.

I sneak off to the servants' huts before the humans wake. Through the window opening in her hut at the row's far end, I see Xanthe getting dressed. I go to the window and call to her quietly. "Xanthe?"

She comes to the window and sees me. "What are you doing here? You're not supposed to—"

"I know," I interrupt. "Please. I need your help."

"Hold on, I need to finish dressing. I'll be right out."

While she puts on her work uniform, I inspect her

quarters. It's exactly as it sounds: a hut, furnished only with two twin beds and a basic set of dresser drawers. There is no art on the walls, no decoration to indicate anything about the workers who inhabit it. The floor is simply bamboo planks set over the grassy ground. But this time there is no nude male lover in her bed. Instead, on the bed next to hers lies Tawny, sleeping on her back, with her blond-blue hair so long it almost covers her rear. Tawny stirs while Xanthe dresses, but she does not awake.

Xanthe steps outside. "I didn't know Tawny was your roommate," I whisper.

She ushers me to a large tree where we can stand and talk partially concealed by leaves and branches. "Does it matter?" Xanthe asks me.

"She does not get in the way of your coupling time with Miguel?"

"Of course she gets in the way. Luckily, the Governor keeps her occupied most of the time. What's going on?"

"Last night, the Governor came into my room."

The threat of a smile that was on Xanthe's face disappears. She nods. "Are you okay?"

"He said they might send me for Defect testing, like the other teen Beta. He said only he could make sure that didn't happen."

Her face reddens. "Did he . . . you know?"

"Nothing happened. Ivan came in and told the Governor that Mother was looking for him. But what do you think I should do next time the Governor comes into my room and Ivan isn't around?"

It's the strangest thing, the hug Xanthe grabs me into. I

have never experienced one from my own kind before, only from Mother. The hug reminds me of a new word I recently discovered: *melancholy*. "There's nothing you can do," she whispers into my ear. "They own you."

She pulls away. Then, very quietly, she says, "Maybe the Governor won't be a problem to you any longer. To any of us."

"How do you mean?"

We hear Ivan calling for me in the distance, ready to begin our morning workout.

"Go," says Xanthe.

I don't care. I lean in to her for another hug, and squeeze her tight. "Thank you, Xanthe," I say. I don't feel better about the situation, but I do feel comforted.

Ivan and I end our morning run at the beach where the stairs lead up to Governor's House on top of the cliff.

Ivan is in fine form. In only a few weeks he will be shipped off to the Base. He should easily hold his own if not surpass his fellow recruits when it comes to physical strength and endurance. He has gone from bulky wrestler body to lean and agile young male.

He jabs at me before we take flight up the stairs—the play boxing ritual that ends our workouts. "So guess what?" he asks me.

I do not understand the human *Guess what?* game. Why not just say what you mean?

"That's what," I say, borrowing Liesel's favorite answer.

Ivan breaks some interesting news between jabs. "Bad news, champ. Mother told Tahir's mom about you and now his mom wants to test a Beta. The Fortesquieu family has asked to borrow you for a week, to see how it goes in case they make their own purchase. Mother said yes, 'cause since the whole bomb-scare thing, she thinks sending you there will be a great way to show the island how great a Beta really can be. One Defect shouldn't ruin it for everyone."

"Then why is that bad news?" I ask. Why does my heart feel like singing, *Hallelujah! A whole week with Tahir! And a week free of the Governor.*

Ivan's face suddenly darkens, the way it sometimes does when he takes his special-blend 'raxia laced with the testosterone. He hisses, "Because you're *my* Beta and I don't appreciate the Fortesquieus' thinking they can just take you away like that because they're so powerful and important."

"It's okay," I try to reassure him.

"It's *not* okay. But nothing I can do about it, either. Careful, champ," he warns, and I pull my hand away just in time for his hardest jab to hit the air and not me. He punched so hard I think he would have broken my hand.

Ivan and I knock fists against each other. Game over. Time for lunch, and rest. I am confused why Ivan wouldn't want his Beta on display at the best home in Demesne. If my week with the Fortesquieus goes well, it could only make the Brattons look better for having the foresight to purchase one.

As we begin our climb up the stairs, I see from the empty crevices that Ivan's bottles of cuvée seeds and steroidal components have been removed. "Where is your chemistry set?" I ask Ivan.

"I moved the materials to a secret spot I carved behind my bedroom wall."

"Don't you worry the Governor will discover it?"

"Sure I do. But he doesn't know I do 'raxia, so it's doubtful he'd come looking. He's too concerned that I be in great shape for the Base; he cares more about how many carbs I eat and how long I work out every day. Me doing 'raxia isn't even on his radar. Ha-ha, stoked for me! And I am liking having easier access to my stash now. It's gotten too risky to leave the materials out in the open here."

"Why so risky?"

"Too many investigators poking around the island, looking for 'raxia. But they'd never look inside Governor's House."

Everyone on this island wants something kept quiet.

I want to roar.

As Ivan and I finish the stair climb and head back toward the house, we hear a commotion coming from the grand manor. There is a shrill female scream, followed by what sounds like gunshots, and a flutter of motion—feet running, in our direction.

It's Xanthe. She's being chased by the Governor and Mother's bodyguards. "Defect!" the Governor yells at Xanthe. "How dare you rage in front of my little girl?"

No! Liesel must have told her father about seeing Xanthe cutting herself.

Xanthe whips past us, stopping at the edge of the cliff. I think she's going to jump. But—

"Don't look," Ivan says. His arm goes around my waist and he pulls my head to his shoulder.

I still can see.

The bodyguards surround Xanthe. She has nowhere to go.

"*In—sur—rec—tion!*" she howls, dragging the word out into an epic battle cry.

The Governor points a rifle at her. But he does not shoot.

Instead, one of the bodyguard shoves Xanthe off the cliff.

Her screams echo across the estate as she tumbles down the cliff, hitting its jagged surfaces on the way down.

The screams cease before she hits the water.

She must already be dead by then.

My body goes numb. All I can think is, Surely the sunbathers down on the beach could hear her. That can't be good for business.

Alone that night in my room, I cannot control the depth of this sadness. I feel epic rage and despair, and guilt. I knew Liesel was frightened by Xanthe's actions, and I should have realized she would go to her father with that fear. I should have told Liesel that Xanthe was only playing, lied to her and said that what she thought she saw was not what she saw. Why did my chip not self-modify for self-preservation, or to protect the preservation of my real sister, Xanthe? Maybe she was a Defect, but Xanthe was my friend, my protector, more kin to me than the Brattons ever could be.

I taste the bitterness in my mouth. My body hunches into fetal position, to shut out the world. What I am feeling now affirms what I've always known but refused to acknowledge. I am not just a Beta with quirks.

I am a member of the Brattons' family, like Astrid, so long as I behave like a fake girl instead of a real one who has feelings, and desires, and darkness. Unlike Astrid, I am easily expendable to them.

Like Xanthe: I am a Defect.

Grief [greef]: Keen mental suffering or distress over affliction or loss; sharp sorrow; painful regret.

Retaliate [ri-TAL-ee-ate]: To return like for like, especially evil for evil.

I dedicate these words to Xanthe.

23

I MUST REMAIN A TOY IN ORDER TO STAY ALIVE.

"Poor, dear Xanthe," I overhear Mother explain to the Aquine, who is interviewing her in the Governor's study. "She had a terrible sense of balance. I always begged her not to stand near the stairs because of it. Such a shame."

If I am drowned by these people because I am a Defect, will Mother tell the Replicant Rights Commission that I simply never learned how to swim?

The conversation I am trying to eavesdrop on is itself being drowned, by the noise from the gardener's power tools outside the study window. I can distinguish the words between Mother and the Aquine but not their tone.

"You're sure she wasn't suicidal?" the Aquine asks. Along with not being able to hear the tone of his voice too clearly,

I am disappointed not to see his face, which Dementia and
Greer and all the other ladies on the island find so striking.
From my peeking spot inside the closet, I can only see his
backside. I want to see the face responsible for sending
Becky back to Dr. Lusardi. I want to remember it.

"Clones don't get suicidal, young man," says Mother.
"They are not like real people. Do you know anything at all
about them?"

What's better, I wonder—to be a toy for the humans, or
to control your own destiny, even if the only way to do so is
suicide? What kind of message would taking one's own life
send them? Probably none at all. The humans on Demesne
thrive because of their culture of disposability; a clone is easy
enough to replace. They would not grieve over objects unless
the objects had some material or monetary value.

There's no way Xanthe would have chosen the path
of suicide. She had a dream of emancipation. She hinted
that she was involved with the Insurrection; she was part of
something big, something hopeful. I never got the chance to
find out more about what she was doing in secret. But I will.

"Actually, Mrs. Bratton," says the Aquine, "with all due
respect, there are quite a lot of data showing that clones are
not the unfeeling automatons we've tried to believe they are.
In fact, much of the latest research suggests—"

"Nonsense," interrupts Mother.

The Aquine says, "For the record, then, can you confirm
to me that the expired Lamb, Xanthe, fell to her death in an
unfortunate accident?"

"Yes! I told you that already! Now, leave me. I have a
headache."

"Thank you, Mrs. Bratton. I hope you feel better."

He stands up, shakes Mother's hand, and leaves. I never even got to see his face.

By the time Xanthe reached the ocean, her face was probably smashed and bloodied to bits.

My sister-friend was killed in cold blood, while I could only watch, helpless.

He should know that.

One day, I will look into the Aquine's face, and I will tell him.

Later, while Mother lies in bed with her headache, I pull down the silk shades in her room, darkening the floor-to-ceiling glass windows in her bedroom. As I close the last one, I look out the window at the bluff overlooking Io, to the exact spot where Xanthe was pushed off.

Her screams echo in my memory.

Screams equal suffering, is my understanding.

It's probable another girl suffered too. Whatever happened to my First that caused me to be made from her, she very likely experienced great pain. Could she have been killed like Xanthe? Ivan has told me that pirates roam the open seas in the perimeter many miles outside Demesne, where the ocean is particularly violent and unpredictable because the ice caps at the bottom and top of the planet melted away and caused the sea levels to rise and churn in anger. He said that thrill seekers risk their lives to venture onto those seas to attempt illegal entry to Demesne, or just to reach the Rave Caves, and many are captured by pirates and killed—then sold to Dr. Lusardi. Is that how I came to exist? Because my First was murdered, her body duplicated but its soul extracted, so that a family on Demesne could have a plaything?

The humans create life, and senselessly cause death. For nothing. I can't let Xanthe's and my First's deaths be in vain. How do I fight back? Can I, even?

The thought of their pain—Xanthe's and my First's— sears my brain, making me dizzy, buckling my knees. I did not ask to be emerged. I did not ask to understand human feelings of rage and unfairness. Their pain is my pain. It thunders through my skull and ripples across my body. It suffocates and overwhelms me. I fall to the ground as the room spins before my eyes. I lose consciousness.

When I awake, I am lying facedown on the floor. I can hear snoring coming from the bed next to me. Mother still sleeps.

I must have passed out. My brain must have needed escape from so many thoughts of suffering.

Escape.

Like Xanthe, maybe that's what my First was trying to do, when her ending came.

I clench my fists and wiggle my toes to reawaken. I make a promise to myself. When the time is right, when these feelings of rage and unfairness once again overcome me, I will not faint. I will fight.

24

IT'S A SHORT DISTANCE TO AVIATE FROM Governor's House to the Fortesquieu compound, and Mother has used every second of the journey to instruct me on how to behave with my temporary new owners. I am to do as they say, wear what they want, and be who they want me to be. But I am to be returned the same as I am delivered. If they want to change my hair or aestheticize me in any new way, I am to remind them to please contact Mother first.

Mother and I sit facing each other from opposite seats in the back of the Aviate, with an antique trousseau trunk opened on the floor between us. She still hadn't decided what I should pack by the time we had to leave Governor's House, so she brought along the trunk to pillage while we transport. The trunk is filled with dresses Astrid never wore but that Mother saved in case one day Astrid became not a grungy peacenik but instead a fashionista with a taste for vintage. Mother pulls out a champagne-pink frock from the trunk and holds it up against her body. "I'd have to stop eating for a month to get into this dress," Mother sighs. "But you will look exquisite in it. Yes, let's add it to your suitcase. You can wear it to dinner with the Fortesquieus."

"Yes, Mother."

"I wish clones had Relays so you could tell me everything that happens there, as it happens," Mother chirps.

Ivan says I am lucky not to be able to Relay. Clones don't need that much live information: everything we need to know is on our chips, which must be such a relief, according to Ivan. He says Astrid had her Relay disabled when she left for university because being at Mother's constant Relay was Astrid's worst nightmare. Mother adds, "Although it's possible Tahir's mother will want to dress you up herself instead of having you wear what I've sent over with you. She'll have access to all the best designers. But, knowing Bahiyya, she will abstain from the newest trends in favor of frump. People who grew up poor can be like that. No sense for the finer things."

"Tahir's mother was poor?" The Fortesquieu prince is descended from poverty? I never realized humans on Demesne could come from anything less than elite backgrounds.

Mother says, "Such a tragic and inspiring story. Both parents—Bahiyya and Tariq—were poor. Can you even imagine, such grand people came from total squalor? They grew up together in the slums in one of the old floody cities. They're both descended of a common French-Tunisian ancestry, I believe. They were childhood sweethearts who were torn apart as teenagers when the wars came."

"So how did Tahir's parents form a love story, then?" LoveStory is Liesel's favorite FantaSphere game. Apparently it is based on human truths and possibilities.

"They found one another again years later in Biome City. The story goes that Bahiyya had gone to BC to seek a new life after losing the husband she'd married as a young woman, and the children they'd had together. Her entire family was wiped out in the Water Wars. Horrible. But losing her first family opened her up to rediscovering her childhood love, who had become one of the richest men in the world. Bright side! Tariq Fortesquieu was a confirmed workaholic before Bahiyya, married to his science. But once they reconnected, she became his whole life."

I datacheck *Tariq Fortesquieu*. The biographical reference interface reveals that he was the mastermind behind the development of Biome City. He was a science prodigy as a child, who left home to study astrophysics on scholarship at the Biome Institute, the precursor to Biome University. At the Institute, he developed the mechanism that eventually brought some semblance of peace back into the world fractured by environmental warfare. He created artificial clouds that brought rain and water to previously uninhabitable lands. Because of him, the barren desert could be harnessed for urban development. This invention allowed millions of war refugees to build and populate the new desert cities such as BC, the brightest jewel in Tariq Fortesquieu's crown. With new cities came new economies, and new hope.

Mother continues, "Tahir's surfing accident was particularly cruel for his parents. They had lost so much already, and struggled so hard to create him."

"Struggle is very nonataraxic?" I ask.

"Absolutely, pet. That's why Demesne is such a respite for those who've earned it. Certainly, Bahiyya and Tariq struggled to produce Tahir. You see, they were both in their late forties by the time they found one another again in BC. They immediately married, and desperately tried for a child. But she was near menopausal, and her body was weakened from years of war and hardship. She was not able to carry a pregnancy to term, and not even her husband's money or his cherished science could help. Their time was running out. So they did what comes naturally. Tahir was born to them via a surrogate."

"Is Tahir their biological child?" I ask, suddenly curious as to whether their prince could be a different human entirely from what I'd been led to believe.

"Yes. But poor Bahiyya was too old to be farmed for another child, and after the children she'd already buried in her previous life, she did not want to be greedy. She said one child with her first true love was all she could hope for, and she got her wish. Tahir is his parents' shining light. I mean, I love my children, of course. But they love Tahir with a fierceness I won't even pretend to know. It's no wonder they retreated into privacy in BC after the accident."

"They needed to have quick access to the best medical experts and facilities available to make sure their beloved son recovered and had the best care possible."

"Right. You are so perceptive, precious. Demesne provides paradise, but not medical miracles like you can get in BC. Now that the Fortesquieus are returned here, it can only mean that Tahir is safely on the mend. What a relief. The Fortesquieus are Demesne's wealthiest residents; the Governor says their tax money alone could sustain the island. Our whole way of life here could be altered if they weren't property owners on Demesne. You must be the very best Beta you can be with them, Elysia. It is important that you represent to them how special this place really is."

The Aviate begins to make its landing on the grounds at the Fortesquieu compound as Mother's bodyguards in the front seat communicate our arrival to the Fortesquieu staff on the ground. "Will Bahiyya be coming out to greet me?" Mother calls to the front seat.

"We've been instructed to drop your companion in front, Mrs. Bratton. The butler will take possession of her," is the answer.

Mother's face falls; she's either disappointed or angered that the lady of the house will not be coming out to greet her. She looks wistfully at the party frock still draped over her body. "You will be such a comfort to Bahiyya. The Fortesquieus deserve to have a Beta on loan for a week after all they've been through. Be a good girl. You'll miss all the excitement at home as we prepare for the Governor's Ball, but you can report back to me everything that happens at the Fortesquieu compound once they return you. As you can see, they can be snobs, but . . . I suppose they've earned the right to be." Has Mother earned that right, I wonder? Is snobbery even a "right"? Mother leans over to me so her cheek is near my face. "Give Mother a kiss good-bye." I place a kiss on her cheek. "Tell me you will miss me, Elysia."

"I will miss you, Mother."

I feel. I want. I lie.

A clone butler ushers me into the main foyer after Mother passes me off to him and takes her leave in the Aviate. The foyer's floors and winding staircase are made from the finest marble, its walls gilded and lined with masterwork paintings depicting gods and goddesses from ancient myths. Tahir arrives in the room wearing wrinkled shorts and a tee, the braids lining the front top of his head loose and unkempt, his casual attire a direct contrast to the formal state of the room.

"Hey," he says. Perhaps the floor has radiant heat, because when I look at him, I think I will melt. But his glance at me suggests only remote interest, and for the first time I understand why girls sometimes fawn over boys who are unattainable or unknowable—because they can't help themselves; the reaction is involuntary. Luckily, the momentary warm sensation from the sight of him is my private satisfaction. I am physically incapable of fawning and therefore will not have to experience that unfortunate nuisance called unrequited love. I am here to serve.

"Hey," I mimic back. I pick up my suitcase to bring to my quarters, but Tahir shakes his head and gestures to the butler.

"It's not heavy, I'm fine," I say.

But Tahir says, "No, that's his job." I loosen my grip on the suitcase so the butler may do his job. I guess letting his butler carry my bag is as gentlemanly a greeting as Tahir is capable of. My job is to be a companion to Tahir and I am hoping we will start right away, until Tahir says, "I have physical therapy now. See you at dinner." He leaves as abruptly as he came in.

No *I'm so glad you're here, beautiful girl who makes me feel alive* or *Would you like to know the level of naughtiness I attained with Astrid, and how we might use your week here to surpass your predecessor?* Just "See you at dinner." Not even a *Whoa.*

I start to follow the butler down the hallway but stop when a husky voice at the top of the grand staircase calls out, "You're here, darling! Stay there so I can come greet you."

It is Tahir's mother, and I watch as she steps down the staircase to approach me. I'm almost shocked when I see Bahiyya Fortesquieu's face as she nears me. What's different about Tahir's mother in comparison to Mother's other lady friends is not just that she's richer than all of them combined; it's that she actually looks her age. She's beautiful in the way humans idealize, with a radiant, coffee-colored complexion punctuated by high cheekbones, thickly arched black eyebrows, full coral lips, and hazel eyes rimmed in thick eyelashes like Tahir's. What's startling about her face are the small crevices marking it—laugh lines around her mouth, crow's feet at the corners of her eyes, bold wrinkles indented into her cheeks. Even more astonishing is her hair—long and wavy, falling unrestrained to her hips, and completely, unabashedly gray. I've never seen such an aesthetic on a human. I didn't know it was possible for a later-aged human to actually desire to look their years.

She reaches the bottom of the staircase and I stand before her for inspection. Like Mother when she first saw me for sale at the boutique, Mrs. Fortesquieu eyes me from head to toe, then circumnavigates me, touching my hair, testing the firmness of my upper arms, looking carefully at the features that define my aesthetic—my long neck and full lips, high cheekbones, the delphinium vining at my left temple. Mrs. Fortesquieu peers into my fuchsia eyes before quickly looking away and pronouncing, "A most exquisite Beta, indeed."

"Thank you, Mrs. Fortesquieu," I say.

She holds her arms out to me and places her hands on my shoulders. "Please call us by our first names. I am Bahiyya. You will meet Tahir's father later this evening. You shall call him Tariq. We will welcome you more properly at dinner."

"Thank you, Bahiyya," I say. "Which level of formal is dinner? I have many dresses."

Bahiyya laughs softly. "We're very informal here. Wear rags to dinner for all I care."

Her hands pull me to her for a hug. She is as warm as her beautiful son is cold.

25

ON MY FIRST EVENING WITH THE FORTESQUIEUS, I learn that their family operates very differently from the Brattons'. The Governor and his wife communicate via argument, raised voices and threats, and they parent their children by negotiating with or berating them. The Fortesquieus seem to achieve an easier family ataraxia. Bahiyya and Tariq Fortesquieu compliment rather than taunt one another. She is vivacious and outgoing, with a dramatically beautiful aesthetic. He is a slight man, tall but gaunt, with thinning black hair, quiet brown eyes, and an introspective disposition, someone who would seem to prefer science to people, except when his wife and son are around, in which case his attention and affection are centered on them. Now retired from industry, he seems content to lavish his time and attention on his family. Tariq and Bahiyya

Fortesquieu regard each other with constant tenderness and kindness, holding hands whenever they are in proximity, always aware of where the other is and how they could best serve their partner in any moment, repeatedly punctuating their speech with endearments that sound sincere: "Yes, my love," "Whatever you wish, my darling." (As opposed to the Governor and Mother, whose endearments such as "my darling" sound more like they mean to hiss *my albatross* or *my most reviled enemy.*)

The Fortesquieu parents can't hug, kiss, and dote on Tahir often enough. They may have all the wealth in the world, but their son is clearly their most precious accomplishment. Tahir does not appear to return their physical affection, but Mrs. Fortesquieu informs me that's because he's a hormonal boy. The teen he is now, she says, can be prone to sullen moods and wants to keep to himself, but he's a good sort who has struggled since his accident. She's sure that once Tahir becomes a man he will more closely resemble the boy he once was: tender, affectionate, sweet.

On our first night together, I join them for a quiet meal on a terrace that juts out from the compound at such a distance that it feels like a deck floating several stories over Io. Farzad and his family do not join us this evening. Ivan has told me that Farzad's father is a drunk and his mother, Tariq Fortesquieu's sister, suffers from depression and rarely leaves their private apartment. That wing of the family lives on Demesne year-round because they have no income or desire to assimilate back in the real world.

I have worn the last dress Mother picked out for me, which indeed looks as if it were made of rags, with asymmetrical pieces of fabric quilted together to form a frock that offers a plunging reveal of my cleavage, but Tahir does not notice my finery. He sits at the dinner table focusing on what's on the table instead of the feminine flesh exposed by my dress. "Would you like another strawberry shake?" he asks after I finish the shake that's been set out for me. "Or do you consume human food?"

"I consume it," I say. His parents have been so warm and welcome to me; I can't help but offer sincerity in return, even if my sincerity is probably a Defect's trait. This home presents an opportunity for me to reinvent myself, as my real self. I am tired of pretending I'm someone I'm not. I admit, "I particularly love the chocolate. It is delicious."

"You *taste*?" Bahiyya asks me. She looks pleased rather than shocked.

"Yes," I say, emboldened.

The Brattons would think I was joking to charm them, but the Fortesquieus take me at my word. "Something new to Beta models? Excellent innovation by Dr. Lusardi," says Tariq.

"Marvelous!" Bahiyya agrees. "We will have chocolate every night for dinner, then!"

"Thank you!" I say enthusiastically.

Tahir has barely touched the food on his plate, preferring the green superfood shake that's been prepared for him. His mother chides him, "Tahir, darling. Try to eat something on your plate. It will make you feel good, I promise." She informs me, "Since his accident, Tahir has had a hard time getting food down, so cook prepares liquid calories for him so at least he gets nourishment. We're hoping his appetite and digestion will improve in the superior air here. Perhaps you can work out with him as you have with the Bratton boy, and help Tahir gain back some appetite."

That seems weird. A young man, once so athletically inclined, with so little appetite? Before his accident, his lust for life probably equaled a similar lust for taste. If he wants so much to improve his health now, wouldn't sampling some of this delicious food help?

"Yes," I say. To Tahir, I ask, "Shall we go running later?"

"That would be satisfactory," Tahir replies.

"You should really try some of the osso buco," I tell him. "It's amazing."

"I will," says Tahir. His fork spears a piece of the tender meat on his plate, and Tahir takes a bite. "Yes, that is pretty good."

His parents nod at each other knowingly, satisfied. "Good boy!" says Tariq.

"I am not a boy. I am eighteen. A man," says Tahir.

Bahiyya smiles affectionately at her son, perhaps trying to stifle a laugh. "Indeed you are, Tahir."

Tahir calls over to the butler standing in the corner and tells the clone, "Could you bring us some chocolate ice cream for Elysia?" Tahir turns to me. "Have you had ice cream before?"

Score! as Ivan would say. I shake my head. "I have not had ice cream before."

"Tonight you will," says Tahir.

Bahiyya says, "Tahir, wouldn't you like to ask Farzad to join us for dessert? I know he longs to spend more time with you now that you're back on Demesne."

"Maybe not tonight," Tahir mumbles.

His parents share a concerned look.

"Tomorrow, maybe," says Bahiyya. "Tomorrow we'll try to have Farzad over."

"Whatever," says Tahir. "I have decided what we will do after dinner."

"What?" his parents exclaim eagerly.

His mother asks, "Shall we go for a long walk together on the beach? Remember how we used to do that when you were younger?"

Like any ripe, exquisite teenage boy—make that *man*—he ignores his mother's nostalgic request. "I shall take Elysia up in the hovercopter after dinner."

His father starts to say, "I suppose we could all do that tonight—" but Tahir interrupts him.

"I meant just Elysia and me. We're fine on our own."

Mrs. Fortesquieu touches her fingertips to stroke Tahir's arm, but he pulls his arm away. "I don't think that's a good idea, my darling," she says.

"It is a matter of record that I'm a certified pilot," says Tahir.

Tariq says, "That was before the accident. You haven't been up since."

"I'm ready now," Tahir states.

Bahiyya and Tariq exchange another concerned glance, and then seem to telepathically acknowledge how they'll respond.

Bahiyya says, "You may go."

Tariq says, "But you must take the instructor to pilot the plane."

Bahiyya adds, "I'll Relay the club to have them send the instructor over."

"If you say so," says Tahir. "This dinner is a waste." He places his napkin onto the table, and stands up—the meal is clearly over for him. And we haven't even had our chocolate ice cream yet. He looks at me. "Let's go."

Perhaps this is the scoundrel Dementia and Greer promised. I couldn't imagine having any desire to resist his sullen request, even if it means sacrificing dessert. But I must wait for his parents—my temporary owners—to excuse me from the table. I look toward Tahir's mother, but her bright countenance is gone. She cries out, "Why must you be so hurtful to me? I'm your mother! You used to love me."

"So you tell me," Tahir says. He returns inside the house.

Tariq grabs his wife's hand and places a kiss on her palm. "He still loves you," he promises her. "He will find that again."

But there shall be no hovercopter ride tonight.

Tariq, displeased with Tahir's attitude, has decided our evening would be better spent giving Tahir a refresher course on what kind of boy he was before the accident. Dessert is brought into their entertainment arena, where we sit on plush lounge chairs formed in a circle. In the middle of our circle, a 4-D composite of footage from Tahir's surfing glory days beams for our entertainment.

Perhaps it would have been interesting to take an air ride tonight, but this experience is also rather excellent. I get to watch a wet, shirtless Tahir ride monster waves while I gulp down spoonfuls of chocolate ice cream slathered in hot butterscotch sauce. I might be in girl-clone ataraxia. We watch as pre-accident Tahir surfs through the barrel of a modest twenty-foot wave; he looks so near to us I expect to feel a splash. We watch as he rides down the slope of an eighty-foot wave, a feat so daring to observe at close range that I feel as if my body crests the danger along with him. We encounter Tahir, regal in a formal tuxedo suit at a gala event, shaking the hands of a head of state but distracted by a beautiful girl walking by, causing him to turn his sweet half smile and say, "Hey, beautiful" to her while the president grins. We see shirtless Tahir being draped in championship ribbons as he smiles brightly and holds on tightly to his beaming parents, standing on either side of him. In one shot, his mother leans over to place a kiss on his cheek, but he does not push her away; instead, he crooks his arm beneath her chin and affectionately reaches his fingers to rub her cheek as she kisses the side of his face in motherly pride. An interviewer asks him how he maintains his focus while riding the waves. Self-assuredly, he says, "I believe in my own talent. And I know my parents are always right here supporting me."

At this sound bite, Mrs. Fortesquieu gazes over at her son expectantly, as if to say, *You remember now, right?* She reaches over to touch Tahir's knee, but he recoils from her touch and stands up. It is hard to believe the quiet but beautiful boy watching his holographic former self, so alive with arrogance and exuberance, could possibly be the same person.

In fact, I don't believe it.

Tahir has stared in silence at the presentation, but it's as if he was looking straight through the beam to the wall in the distance behind the images, completely uninterested in his previous glory—bored by it, even.

"Are we done for the night?" Tahir asks his father.

His mother flees the room. Weeping.

Tahir's father sighs. "I suppose so. I will go comfort your mother. Tomorrow, Tahir, you will do better. Try harder with her."

"Yes, Father," says Tahir.

Like my room adjacent to Astrid's bedroom at Governor's House, my quarters are in a room adjacent to the study in Tahir's quarters. A bed has been made up for me on a long ottoman decked with silk pillows in bright purple, gold, and fuchsia. Tahir has been silent while leading me to where I will sleep. He's not the most engaging fellow, which is not at all distracting from his appeal, and might just heighten it.

I try to make conversation by asking him, "Was it outstanding to ride waves so big?" I know from my own diving experience since I emerged that there's a weird sense of connection I feel in the water, to something so totally more powerful and volatile than anything I can comprehend, and also something that must have felt simultaneously welcoming, and natural, and fulfilling to my First. Surely his human experience was similar?

Tahir answers in a nonanswer. "Yes."

Could *scoundrel* possibly also mean *bore*? For a gorgeous Prince Chocolate, he's most disengaging. How can this even be the same boy who held me on his lap and kissed me on his birthday, who told me that I make him feel alive?

This boy can often seem dead.

I try another question. "Do you have fond memories of Astrid? I am her replacement."

He answers in facts instead of feelings. "So you have stated already to me. Astrid and I shared time romantically when I was on Demesne, but it was not a serious relationship. As the daughter of an employee of Demesne, she was not an appropriate mate for me. Astrid scored in the ninety-ninth percentile on her university entrance exam. Gaining admission to her top-choice school was her primary concern, not a relationship."

If Greer and Dementia were here, they would share a moment of sadness for their friend Astrid, who has just been easily dismissed by the boy they claim broke her heart. I will waste no time mourning her loss. I determine to be remembered more fondly by this boy. My mission is clear: to break down whatever barrier has risen within him since his accident that causes him to be so aloof and removed where once he was charismatic and gregarious. I have a deep suspicion it's a barrier that only I know best how to handle.

We reach my quarters, and I sit down on the bed, from which I can see through the study to Tahir's bedroom. In this compound where there are dozens of luxurious bedrooms, and likely dozens of huts for clone sleeping quarters, I wonder why they want me so near to Tahir.

I ask him, "Am I here for your mother to try a Beta, or to be your toy? I have made an excellent workout companion to Ivan. He will be leaving soon for the Base in the best shape of his life."

"You are here so they can watch how a teen Beta behaves."

"Because they are worried I might be a terrorist?" I ask.

I worry I might be a terrorist.

"No," says Tahir.

"Shall I guess why?" I ask.

"Yes."

I have felt sure of nothing in my short life so far—except this gut feeling. The data are all there: His long absence from Demesne. His indifference. He eats liquid foods because he probably can't taste regular food and has no desire for it. He appears to go through the motions of his life, reciting facts from his past but seeming to make no connection to his present, or a desire for what his future might bring.

The data may be circumstantial, but my Defect's instincts aren't wrong, I suspect. If I *am* wrong, I will have posited something so scandalous there's no way I won't be labeled a Defect for identifying its truth. But if I'm right, perhaps I'll gain something for myself—my own companion.

I can't resist this leap. It could lead to my premature expiration, or to a new world of possibility, both frightening and exciting. I say, "I am here because you are also a teen Beta, and your parents want to see how you will interact with one of your own kind."

Tahir says, "Correct. My First, the real Tahir, died in that accident on the *gigantes*. I am his clone."

26

"MY PARENTS HOPED YOU WOULD FIGURE IT out," says Tahir. "That is why they brought you here."

"Did *you* hope?" I ask.

"Hope is still a vague human concept to me. I am different from Dr. Lusardi's other clones because I was created to continue my First's life, not to just be cloned for a fresh start. His parents wanted—"

"*Your* parents," I correct him. Already I am working in support of Bahiyya and Tariq.

"Yes, they keep telling me that. *My* parents wanted every factual detail of my First's life to be embedded into my chip. It is their hope that I will also know how First Tahir actually felt, but I experience no such desire. I feel no connection to his life. I am living out someone's else life. Perhaps with you here, I could experience my own."

So much energy has gusted inside me, I feel that I could explode. "Please can we run somewhere?" I ask Tahir.

We enter the FantaSphere room in Tahir's quarters. He sets the game to FloodQuest. To survive, we must run through the ruined remains of one of the old floody cities. We scavenge in alleys and climb stone walls and sprint past sentries until we reach the apex of the central castle, the high sanctuary that ends the quest. To get there, we must beat off hordes of panicked refugees, thieves, and plunderers, live rats and dead dog carcasses. And we must not get swallowed by the flood.

We can get there together.

Tahir tells me what happened to his First as we quest.

It had been a surfer's dream day. The wind and swells were cooperating just right. The First Tahir got towed out to the *gigantes* by hovercopter, determined to take advantage of the optimal conditions surfers dream about, wait for, long for. But the ocean is so feisty and unpredictable. Once he'd arrived, the swells had changed, moving faster and harder. The tow-in captains urged him not to make the jump, but he saw a liquid mountain rising that he just had to conquer. They dropped him down to catch the swell. It was a fifty-footer, by far not the biggest wave he'd ever ridden, but this one was different: mean and angry, heavy and thick, with unbelievable power and velocity. Nobody should have been on that wave. First Tahir took off onto the wave a few seconds too late, as if he'd contemplated in those last moments whether he should even take the plunge, but he went in anyway. He managed to make the drop onto the wave face by standing on his toes. It should have been a miraculous and wondrous surf down that moving mountain, but instead he appeared to struggle throughout the entire ride. He recovered at the bottom of the drop, and attempted to pull up under the wave's lip, but it crashed on him and sent him under. He fell from his board and was pulled under by the beast, which blasted his board out into the white-water. He drowned.

The surf team was able to retrieve the body and return it to the Fortesquieu compound. Bahiyya went crazy with grief. She'd already buried five children. Her anguished screams could be heard across the entire estate. Tariq secretly called in Dr. Lusardi. He asked her to create a clone from his son's deceased body. So he could always pass for human, clone Tahir was not vined, and his First's hazel eyes were trans-planted into the new body.

As clone Tahir emerged, while he was waking and aware but his eyes still closed, one of the first things Tahir heard was Dr. Lusardi telling her assistant she had not wanted this dangerous job, but she also couldn't deny such powerful people.

"Why did she not want the job?" I ask Tahir. I couldn't imagine Dr. Lusardi resisting a direct commission from one of the most influential families in the world.

Tahir says, "Dr. Lusardi told my parents that she was only in the Beta stage of creating teen clones. She said she could not create a teen clone that would live past the approximate time of its First's adolescence. My parents had very little time to make a choice. They decided to take the risk and hope for a cure."

"Risk? A cure? For what?" This makes no sense. There is

no "cure" needed for a clone, unless he means a cure for soul extraction. Could this Tahir clone have a soul?

"A cure for the Awfuls," says Tahir.

"What are the Awfuls? Do you mean how adults say teenagers become awful but it's just a stage that will pass?"

"*Stop!*" Tahir yells out, invoking the safe word that ends the game. The FloodQuest city and its vices instantly disappear.

We both fall to the floor, out of breath, exhausted.

I had been about to execute a marauding thief running at me to stab my heart with his sword, but apparently Tahir's news about the Awfuls is more important than my side maneuver of a karate kick to the head of the marauder. Tahir couldn't wait to call stop until I'd had the glory of the kill.

"You seriously don't know about the Awfuls?" Tahir asks me.

"I thought I knew, but I think you mean something else. Do you mean . . . could you possibly have a soul?"

"I have no soul. There wasn't enough time for Dr. Lusardi to prepare. She had to do the standard extraction in order to replicate the body. To try otherwise would have risked the cloning not working at all."

"What is so awful about that?" I ask, curious about how a standard cloning could be deemed so terrible.

"The Awfuls is the built-in stage Dr. Lusardi's teen Betas go through. They terminate before adulthood."

"*What?*" I yell. These humans—they are cruel monsters. Liars. Deceitful. For the first time, I want to hurt them the way they hurt me. This is so unfair. My body feels numb, my energy spent, my mind deceived and angry.

I'm barely emerged, and I'm already marked for death?

Tahir says, "Is this really the first you've heard of it?"

I nod. I know so little other than what's been told to me.

Tahir says, "You are upset. Legitimately upset."

"Aren't *you?*" I demand.

"Before, I was indifferent. Since I took the 'raxia, I am confused. I feel surprising anger. Do you want to know why we experience Awfuls?" I nod. Tahir continues. "Because they haven't figured out how to transition a teen clone to adulthood, and they didn't want to risk human owners experiencing attachment to teen clones that wouldn't make it to adulthood. So Dr. Lusardi designed the teen Betas to go through a stage she termed 'the Awfuls,' around the same time that human teens would be transitioning from the end of adolescence into adulthood. Basically, we become so rebellious and obnoxious that we alienate our humans, who then can't wait to get rid of us."

"Surely your parents with all their wealth and power could have asked for a clone with no such predetermined problem."

"They could ask. But Dr. Lusardi has not figured out how to accommodate this request. Cloning as a science was intended to replicate humanity, not to undo a tragic death."

"So what is a human supposed to do with their Awful?" I ask. "Are we expired?" I have sudden visions of being thrown from a cliff just for the crime of being a teenager.

"They don't have to expire us. It happens naturally. Once we turn Awful, we burn out quickly, and die. The point is that by then, no one would miss us. They'd *want* to get rid of us. The whole thing is a safeguard for the human buyers, but also for Dr. Lusardi."

I don't want to believe. "There have never been Awfuls here. We are the first teen Betas."

"We are not the first teen Betas. Who told you that?"

I realize no one actually told me that. I had just assumed. I shrug. I have no answers. All I've ever had is questions.

Tahir says, "Dr. Lusardi created a crop of teen Betas before us. They were used in experiments at the Base. They all died within months of turning Awful. Except for the ones who escaped. No one knows what happened to them."

There are others out there like me. Like us. How ignorant I was to have thought I was special. Different.

It never occurred to me I would live only a few years at best, just to descend into madness and die. Is there any comfort in knowing that this other teen Beta probably will too?

Xanthe knew hate.

Now, I know hate. I hate the humans who programmed me to die before I will barely have gotten a chance to live.

With his human eyes transplanted from his First, he easily passes as human. He has no aestheticizing tattoos. Teen clones have a very different hormonal balance from humans, which is why I do not suffer the usual PMS-y girl problems that Dementia and Greer complain about, and why Tahir has no chest or facial hair. Tariq and Bahiyya think they are subtle when they affectionately rub their hands over Tahir's chin and cheeks, but he knows they are hoping for signs of facial hair. Maybe if his face and body were no longer smooth and perfect, it would mean he might transition to adulthood rather than Awful. They want so much to hope. They have everything in the world, but without that hope, they seem to think they truly have nothing. Strange humans: they'd rather their clone look and behave exactly as their real son rather than set it free to determine his own course.

They have gone to extreme lengths to make sure no one discovers their son is a clone. When he was first emerging, when his parents thought he was asleep, Tahir heard what happened to the five members of the surf team who recovered First Tahir's body from the *gigantes*—the only people besides Dr. Lusardi and Tahir's parents who knew Tahir had actually drowned. They all received first-class passage and a lifetime of wealth to disappear to the farthest settled colony in the galaxy.

And yet, by inviting me into Tahir's life as they have this week, his parents have now entrusted me with his secret information. The humans must assume that as a soulless clone, I am an easy repository for their secrets. Knowledge equals power. How can I harness that power?

Tahir has spent the time since he emerged as a clone cloistered with his parents in Biome City, being tutored on the life that was his First's so that he can act out that life's continuance since the accident. The family is now back on Demesne for Dr. Lusardi to give Tahir secret "treatments" to prevent his teenage hormones from descending into Awful. Tahir is anesthetized during these treatments and does not know what happens during them.

"Do you feel changed after the treatments?" I ask Tahir.

"I feel nothing," he states. "Before, during, or after. I am empty."

Impulsively, I grab his hand. "You are not empty. You have me."

He clutches my hand in return, but his face is set to *disbelief*. The extension of his hand is a mimicked behavior, not based on a real desire to touch me. "Thank you," he says politely. "Shall we resume our FloodQuest game now?"

I need to make this Beta *more* like me. Before we both die, I need to make him *feel*.

"Let's run again," I say.

Even if there's nowhere real to go, I'd still rather get there with him.

27

SLEEP IS MEANINGLESS TO HIM, TAHIR SAYS, just another human exercise in empty time. He mimics it to keep his parents from harping on his need for it, but while I am on loan, they will not bother him about it. They are too hopeful that his wakeful time with a female Beta will somehow improve his dispassionate disposition.

When I awake the next morning, Tahir is lying on the floor on his stomach, with his arms bent and his head propped on his fists. He has been watching me sleep.

"Good morning," says Tahir. "Have you slept satisfactorily?"

"Yes, thank you." *I might sleep so much better nestled against you. So would you.* Datacheck: *spooning.*

"Who is Z?" he asks.

My eyes go from bleary and half open to instantly wide and alert.

"Why?" I ask.

"In your sleep," says Tahir. "Several times you mumbled, 'You know you own me, Z.'"

I turn over in bed, away from him. "I don't know who Z is," I say. Technically, I am not lying. I don't know her. I *am* her. But I never knew her.

I hear him move closer to me from the floor and feel his breath hot against the back of my neck. "There is no need to lie to me," says Tahir.

"How do you know I lie?" I ask. *Please say it's because you're also a Defect. Please.*

"A guess," Tahir says.

"An intuition?" I ask, understanding now how just the smallest sign from Tahir might give Bahiyya and Tariq hope that their son will "wake."

"Unlikely," says Tahir. "So who is Z?"

"Please will you keep it secret if I tell you?" I whisper.

"Of course," says Tahir.

I shouldn't, but I do.

I trust.

I turn over to face him and just say it. "Z was my First. I have memories of her. Not a lot, actually, just one specific memory. Of a boy she loved."

Tahir nods, with no expression of shock or disapproval. "Yes, that is not information that should be shared except between us."

I like that. There's an *us.*

"Do you think I'm a Defect?" I ask him.

"Whether or not you are a Defect has no relevance to me," says Tahir.

His indifferent reply is somehow comforting. Nonjudgmental. Maybe it shouldn't matter if *any* clone is a Defect. Maybe being a Defect or not has no relevance to our existence as living, breathing, sentient creatures.

"I am a Defect," I confess, surprised how easily the words come forth, and how relieved I feel to let them go.

"So what?" says Tahir. It felt like the biggest admission in the world to make, but he clearly couldn't care less. "Father says we are all Defects, in our way. Humans and clones. He says the word is really just a scare tactic to incite disobedient beings into subservience. He says that's all it really is—just a word."

Tariq Fortesquieu is freaking *cool*, for someone's dad.

Tahir adds, "Father would consider it encouraging that a Beta could make this connection with their First."

"Do you have real memories of your First?" I ask Tahir.

"If you mean, do I feel the memories, or relive them, the answer is no. The memories are basic ones, with no real details. Just data. It's like having a coloring book with all the pictures outlined in black and white, but no color to the images. And in case the chip does not do its job enough, his parents—*my* parents, I keep being reminded—continually ply me with flash-card exercises, to associate names and faces with people and events particular to his life. They fear that I am a wooden approximation of their real son. They want me to play the part of my First without anyone knowing I'm a clone. But it's not just for show. They actually want me to feel like I am the real Tahir. Of course, I cannot."

"You are better." He will think I mean he is better because he is *science*; I know he is better because he is kinder and gentler than the real Tahir.

"I am a continual disappointment to Tariq and Bahiyya. I am incapable of returning their affection and love, or sharing in their fond memories. I can mimic First Tahir, but the feelings are not there. They know that."

"Do you *wish* you could have his real feelings?"

Tahir's face adopts the expression our databases label *curious*. "For a moment, when I took Ivan's 'raxia, I did. But then the sensation passed. I cannot wish, Elysia. You know that."

That afternoon, we are called to join Tahir's parents for a picnic lunch on the beach. Bahiyya awaits us in the hydromassage pool built into Io's waters for her. It's a small, triangle-shaped tidal pool with jade walls, offering a soft contrast to the violet seawater lapping over the walls and feeding into the pool. She wears a purple velvet turban on her head, covering her gray hair and giving her slightly wrinkled but serene face a more youthful veneer.

"You look very relaxed," Tahir tells her as we stand on the shoreline. The servants are setting up the picnic lunch on the beach, placing a blanket on the sand, and setting up tables to hold our drinks. "The air here benefits you, I can see."

"I can't get enough of it." Bahiyya inhales a gulp and lets it out with great content. "I told you it was magic here on Demesne, didn't I?"

"You did," Tahir states.

"Do you love being here?" she asks him.

"I love being here," he repeats.

She recognizes his mimicry and tells him, "Your generation, you don't understand these pleasures. You don't understand war and suffering. May you never have to."

"Thank you," says Tahir.

Perhaps she also recognizes the futility of her hope for her cloned son to appreciate all the hardship her generation experienced, because she is eager to let go of the topic. She gazes at me wearing my one-piece swim costume. "Elysia, I've been told you are an excellent swimmer."

I exhibit. I step from the shore onto the jade rim of her pool and dive from the pointed edge where the pool meets the ocean. I swim a butterfly stroke a distance equivalent to the length of a competitive pool and return to the ocean side of the hydromassage pool. "My goodness," Bahiyya enthuses. "Your First could have been an Olympian. Such speed and grace. Come over to my side, darling."

I glide over the wall and into her pool. The warm water swirls over my skin and massages my muscles. The water offers pure silken warmth.

"You too, Tahir," Bahiyya says. "Come sit with me. I love having you children near." Tahir complies, stepping over the jade wall and into the pool. "It's wonderful here, right?"

Tahir nods and I can see him start to say "Yes, Mother" again, but her face is directed at him and not at me, so I smile and try to twinkle my eyes, so Tahir will know the expression to offer his mother. He sees my look, smiles, and opens his hazel eyes wider so they appear brighter and sweeter. I mouth the words *Marvelous, Mommy*, and Tahir answers, "Marvelous, Mommy."

She has noticed his gaze at me and is not unaware that his response was coached, but she is not displeased. Instead, she claps her hands together. "Excellent, Tahir," she exclaims. "You told Elysia?"

"Elysia knows I am a clone," Tahir says.

"Sssh," Bahiyya says softly. "There are servants on the beach. We don't want them to hear. We thought she might figure it out." She turns to me. "Did you?"

I nod.

She smiles at me. "You realize what this means?"

That I will be expired if I reveal this secret information?

Bahiyya says, "We might just have to keep you forever, Elysia."

They could easily coach him via Relay or hologram, but Tahir's parents choose to prepare him for the Governor's gala using old-time flash cards. I nibble freshly baked, warm chocolate chip cookies on our picnic blanket as I watch Tahir drink from his green shake and answer his parents' queries.

Tariq holds up a photo of an older gentleman wearing a crown. "The king of Zakat," Tahir identifies.

"What was special about him?" Bahiyya asks Tahir.

"He gave me an island for my thirteenth birthday," Tahir says.

Tariq asks, "And what else did he give you?"

Tahir says, "Access to his private harem."

"Correct," Bahiyya says. "Horrible old man."

Tariq holds up a photo of a soccer player in midkick at an international cup match. "Who is this?"

"Bhekizitha Danjuma, a.k.a. 'the Sphinx,' the world's most revered football champion, three-time Mainland Cup Most Valuable Player," says Tahir.

"What was special about him?" Bahiyya again asks Tahir.

Tahir says, "He wanted to visit Demesne so he came as your guest and he gave me private football lessons two years ago when I was sixteen."

Tariq flashes the other side of the card, which pictures a voluptuous young brunette. "And?"

Says Tahir, "And First Tahir seduced the Sphinx's girlfriend, causing the Sphinx to vow revenge on Tahir."

Bahiyya laughs. "Sore loser."

Tariq adds, "Sore loser who will be at the Governor's Ball as the guest of the envoy, I've been told."

Bahiyya says, "The Sphinx is married now. Surely he doesn't care."

Tahir sifts through his father's cards and holds up a card of the most famous young actress on the Mainland, a knockout beauty of mixed descent, with dark cinnamon skin, glossy black hair, and amber eyes. "The Sphinx is married to her now," Tahir says.

"Excellent work, Tahir," says Tariq.

"May I take Elysia to the ball as my companion?" Tahir asks.

I've been asked to the ball!

But Bahiyya says, "Of course not. She is a clone. That simply is not done."

* * *

"I have always been afraid of water," Bahiyya tells me. She's invited me to join her for the day's last soak in her hydro-massage tidal pool before dinner. "It's only on Demesne, where the water is so refined, that I can feel comfortable immersing myself in it. Tariq had this tidal pool built for me as a present after Tahir's birth. It's shallow enough that I can relax in it without fear of swimming."

"You don't know how to swim?" I ask.

She shakes her head. "Hard to believe, I know! Especially with such a dolphin of a son." She looks fondly in Tahir's direction. "At least, First Tahir loved the water. Especially here." She calls to Tariq and Tahir walking along the beach. "Men, please come join the ladies."

They step inside the jade walls of the triangular pool. Tariq says, "Shall we maximize the whirlpool setting?"

"Delicious!" says Bahiyya. Her husband adjusts the pool setting and the lapping waters warm and begin to whirl harder into a massaging stroke against the skin. Bahiyya asks Tahir, "I don't think you have been swimming in Io since the accident. You used to love doing swimming drills here before big meets. Perhaps you would like to try now? Before the sun goes down. Elysia can join you."

Elysia is quite enjoying the view of steam clinging to Tahir's bare pectorals. But I know how to do my job. "Shall we have a swim?" I ask Tahir.

"You swim beautifully. I like to watch you swim. You are very graceful and strong. Admirable."

Tariq says, "Good observations. I think you are making progress since Elysia has joined us, Tahir."

"I would like to make progress," Tahir says. There is a new confidence and sincerity in his voice. He turns to me. "I think we should tell them our secret."

Why not? I'm marked for death anyway. This air and water feel so, so good. I feel so, so good. The euphoria the humans experience on Demesne: I'm starting to understand it.

"I am a Defect," I say, trying to set my voice to *bold* and *fearless*. "I feel things."

The shocked gasp that comes from Bahiyya's and Tariq's mouths is not caused by my revelation. It's caused by Tahir, actually laughing at my admission.

Tahir shakes his head. "I didn't mean that. I meant tell them about the 'raxia."

"You laughed!" Bahiyya exclaims. It's as if I never spoke the blasphemous words: *I. Am. A. Defect.*

Tahir says, "Did I? I guess . . . I am comfortable when Elysia is around. I didn't try to make it happen. It just did."

"Excellent!" says Tariq. He turns to me. "Are you a Defect because you took 'raxia?"

"Actually, the 'raxia had no effect on me."

Tahir's parents turn to him, their faces shocked. "*You* took 'raxia?" Bahiyya asks Tahir.

"Yes," says Tahir. "For a brief moment, it made me feel alive."

Tariq shakes his head vigorously. "No. 'Raxia is not the answer. It's a highly addictive opiate. Any benefit it gives you by making you feel more human will be just as quickly undone by your increasing need for it. It will make you feel so human you will become a monster for it."

"Won't I become a monster anyway, Father?"

"Don't say it!" Bahiyya scolds Tahir. "We won't let that happen to you. Or to Elysia. We will find a cure before it sets in."

Tariq says, "We have the best scientists working to find a cure. You must not take 'raxia. First Tahir had addictive tendencies. You were not supposed to inherit them."

Tahir datachecks and then his face turns to *confused*. "I do not find evidence of First Tahir's addictive tendencies."

"That's because we wrote them out of your programming," Tariq says. "First Tahir was an excellent young man, but a playboy, who had vices, a susceptibility to alcohol and girls. Nothing that got him into too much trouble, but the potential was there. We knew there was the risk it would get worse as he aged into adulthood. We feared his tendencies could turn to more dangerous, desperate addictions, if left unchecked." His voice dead serious, he tells Tahir, "Do not take 'raxia again."

"But—" Bahiyya says.

"I mean it!" snaps Tariq. "Where did you get the 'raxia?"

I quickly compute the only person we can pin the blame on who will not get in trouble for it. "Demetra," I say.

"You are forbidden from spending more time with her if 'raxia is involved," Tariq says. "I understand that teenagers like to experiment with narcotics, but it is more dangerous for you. You are still too delicate, Tahir."

"Okay," says Tahir, who couldn't care less.

That matter settled, Bahiyya's face settles fondly on

mine. "I prayed you would be a Beta who could feel. If you can, maybe it's possible for Tahir too."

"You will not have me expired?" I ask.

"Of course not, child!" says Bahiyya. "Your secret is safe with us."

"We will cherish you as our own," says Tariq. "*You* can teach Tahir how to feel. Not the 'raxia."

28

LAST NIGHT, I FOUND OUT I DON'T HAVE LONG to live.

Tonight, I discover what's worth living for.

Tahir acts more human at dinner that night—eating the food on his plate, saying "Delicious" about the dessert, letting his mother stroke his hand without flinching, and reciting anecdotes about Governor's Ball attendees for his father. Having another Beta in the household is proving beneficial to Tahir's "recovery." Therefore, we are excused early to play FantaSphere. We do not have to sit through another night of holograms of First Tahir with his parents.

As we walk back toward his quarters, Tahir asks me, "How is the ataraxia at the Bratton household?"

"They mimic it like clones," I say.

"Really?" says Tahir.

"Not really," I have to admit. "Not only do I have memories, but I seem to be capable of making a joke."

"Oh," says Tahir, in a tone sounding close to pity.

I answer his question. "The Brattons strive for ataraxia, but it does not come as easily as it seems to here. The parents bicker constantly. Their daughter on the Mainland seems to want nothing to do with them—she never calls them, so far as I've seen or heard."

We've reached a long hallway where there are holographic displays of his First, a walking family album shining across the length of the walls. It's like watching his First grow up before our very eyes. There's real Tahir crawling on the floor as a baby. Tahir taking his first steps. Toddler Tahir blowing out the candles on his second birthday, surrounded by a beaming Tariq and Bahiyya. Prep school jacket–attired Tahir being escorted by his parents and their bodyguards for his first day of school. Tahir and his cousin Farzad as young boys on Demesne, riding their first small waves. Nearing pubescence, Tahir at age thirteen, winning his first surf competition. A close-up shot of Tahir, aged seventeen, dressed in tuxedo finery at last year's Governor's Ball; in the vague distance behind him stands blond Astrid, regarding him furtively while he flashes a megawatt grin, not noticing her glance.

And then it feels like my heart stops cold.

There is First Tahir, who is no longer a boy but a buff and strapping young man, surrounded by fellow competitors on the beach at a big-wave surf competition. There is Tahir, yes, looking insolent and confident and ready to be towed out for an epic ride, but there is someone else, a blond man standing in profile behind him. The bronzed man is taller and beefier than Tahir, and appears to be a few years older, and even though I cannot see his turquoise eyes from the angle of the shot, I know who the man is.

Her surfer god. The man who belonged to my First. I expected to see him next somewhere under water, not on the walls of the Fortesquieu compound.

I stop Tahir and point him out. "Who is that?"

Tahir's eyes close as he struggles to pull out a memory. "I know his name came up in the memory lessons. I'm not sure. Maybe Alexander? He was a rival to my First at surf meets. Why do you ask?"

"He looks like the man I have visions of. From my First."

"How unnecessary for you," says Tahir.

Maybe Tahir is right. Suddenly that godlike man from my visions about whom I've been so curious intrigues me not at all. He is a ghost who must be exorcised from my subconscious.

The surfer god belonged to my First's life.

I want my own.

Especially if it's going to end so soon.

Tahir and I enter the FantaSphere room.

"Shall we act out LoveStory tonight?" Tahir asks me.

"Yes, please." *Hurry.*

He sets the game to LoveStory. "What backdrop?" he asks.

I have played this game with Liesel before, using our Prince Chocolate creation. Out of habit, I start to ask for the honeymoon suite backdrop, a tropical bungalow that sits on stilts over a sapphire lagoon. Inside, the suite has the usual romantic furnishings, along with a taffy candy machine that Liesel thinks any honeymooning couple would want. Outside, the bungalow's steps lead directly down to lagoon water teeming with vibrant marine life, rainbow-colored fish who like to nibble and tickle toes, and beyond the blue water, an endless vista of cloudless skies, white sand, and coconut trees, all bathed in sunshine and ocean breezes.

I've had it with paradise. And I don't have to share Prince Chocolate with Liesel this time. This one's all mine, and his flesh is real even if is a replication, and the game does not have to stay at a kid-friendly rating level.

"Biome City," I request.

Instantly, we are in the penthouse of the Green Cactus Hotel, BC's most famous luxury hotel, built to resemble a towering cactus, with balconies crafted to look like cactus needles. Tahir latches his index finger through mine and leads me to the palace suite's windows so we may admire the view. Bright stars burst across the black night sky while the city's tree-themed office towers complement the stars with their own flashing jade lights atop each building. Beyond the central business district, the avenues stretch out to the individual communities, where the housing structures are biomimetically modeled on termite mounds, anthills, and bee honeycombs, creating living and livable art from creepy-crawly-pesky inspiration. Past the suburban communities, pyramid-shaped dunes give the appearance of a desert-sand fortress rimming the city.

Tahir loosens his hand from mine to open the window. Crisp, dry air smelling of desert wildflowers wafts in through the window screen. He reaches his arm around my back as his hand parks itself in the curve of my waist. I nestle my head against the side of his neck.

We have both been programmed to know what to do.

"What about your parents?" I ask.

"They won't bother us. They want us to be alone together. No one will interrupt us. I promise. We have all night, every night you're here."

His warm, strong arms offer such comfort. With Tahir, now: this is my choice. I can physically experiment like other teenagers, but without their worries. If our lives are destined to be so short, why not try some nights of LoveStory before the Awfuls set in?

"Why me?" I ask Tahir. He could have any girl. He could have a real girl, like Dementia or Greer.

"I know I can't feel. But if I *could* . . . you are the girl I would fall into lovestory with. You are strong, and brave, and beautiful. You are kindhearted. You have all the best qualities a human should seek in a mate."

You do too, I think. You just don't know it yet.

"I programmed a game for you," says Tahir. "Close your eyes."

I close my eyes.

Tahir tells the FantaSphere, "Elysia's PromNight."

My eyes still closed, I datacheck the words *prom night*. The interface informs me that prom night is a teenage rite of passage from the pre–Water Wars period, a gala event commemorating a teen's high school graduation.

"Open your eyes now," he says. "If you can't be my date at the Governor's Ball, you can be mine at our own dance."

I open my eyes. We are in the ballroom of the Green Cactus Hotel, and it's decorated for PromNight, with strings of soft white lights dangling from the ceiling centered around a chandelier crafted in the shape of a desert rose and emanating a soft pink light. The room's perimeter is lined with shrubbery, rows of silk trees with bright-pink blooms at their tops, their branches strewn with pink lights. The gala's music is in surround sound, in the form of a robust power ballad from ancient times, something about how someone's heart will go on and on.

We are not alone here. Surrounding us are many teen couples slow-dancing. The dancers are all clones with fuchsia eyes, vined in fleur-de-lis and delphinium, and the word BETA aestheticized at the back of their necks.

"A gala night for us, and our people," Tahir announces. He is dressed in a formal suit made of caramel-colored raw silk, with a brown fedora hat, so handsome in his finery I actually gasp. I look down at my own finery. He did not dress me in the princess ball gown in which Liesel likes to outfit me, but chose a classic LBD—Little Black Dress—a strapless but not immodest configuration that covers my chest but leaves something to the imagination, and falls to my midthigh.

"Look there," says Tahir, pointing to the center of the room beneath the rose-shaped chandelier, which is beaming down holographic images of the dancing couples along with text labels, so each girl and boy gets a chance to be PROM QUEEN, PROM KING, or MOST LIKELY TO . . . The chandelier selects Tahir as PROM KING and me as PROM QUEEN and I see my whole getup for the first time. My hair has been styled in a braided upsweep and strung with diamonds and pearls. My face has been cosmetically altered, with dark red lips and metallic gold shadow streaking my eyelids. My long legs are bare and glitter with gold, and my feet wear couture black high-heeled shoes with red ribbons wound up my calves.

"Is your aesthetic satisfactory?" Tahir asks.

I gulp, and nod. I don't look at all like me—but the aesthetic is more than satisfactory. I imagine I look the way Z did, when she owned the ghostly surfer god's heart. Sexy. Mysterious.

Tahir pulls me to him, and we slow-dance. Our bodies draw heat from each other as we press close. "You lean your head on my shoulder now," Tahir informs me. I place my head on his shoulder. I look around at the other couples who seem to be taking their dances to the next level with shared kisses to go along with their embraces. Tahir notices too, and asks, "Shall we mimic them?"

I lift my head from his shoulder and stare into his hazel eyes as his mouth moves close to mine. I want time to stop right now, so I can capture this exquisite second of antici-pation before our lips touch. *Snap*. The second makes its everlasting impression in my heart. I vow to hold on to it so I can extract the moment whenever I want in the future, when my world returns to being about service to humans and not about a lovestory with this beautiful Beta boy.

First Tahir was a noted lover of women, but clone Tahir is raw in these arts, as am I. So close, his lips to mine. We have done this before at Hidden Beach, but then we were surrounded by the gang, who were daring him to go further. It didn't really count.

I want so badly for it to count this time.

My mouth parts and his lips descend on mine. *Sizzle.* The sensation is scientific after all, pure electricity, these lips touching. His hands encircle my waist as mine reach up his back, beneath his jacket, to pull him closer, tighter. The kissing begins innocently, just two mouths meeting, but quickly becomes deeper, to lips guiding and exploring, answering each other's longing with more longing, more kissing.

The strings of lights overhead could be fireworks in my heart.

This is what matters. It's what brings connection, and purpose, and human love.

But the song ends and Tahir pulls away. He says, "It does not matter if I do not actually feel it. Tariq and Bahiyya say it is important for me to experience it."

I feel it.

I will make him too.

29

"I DON'T LIKE YOU, BETA. GO KEEP DEMENTIA entertained."

Hidden Beach today is perfection as usual, except that Farzad has decided he hates me. In his opinion, his aunt Bahiyya trying a Beta for a week has completely ruined the time he was hoping to spend alone with his cousin Tahir. They were boyhood best friends. Surely Farzad should occupy the majority of Tahir's time now that he's back on Demesne, and not this Beta companion toy?

Dementia and Tahir are a few paces behind as we step from the sailboat that brought us here onto the cove's sandy beach. "I am sorry you don't like me, Farzad," I say. I am not sorry, but my language abilities are programmed to respond appropriately and comfortingly to human verbal cues. "How shall I keep Dementia entertained?"

"I want to take Tahir out on some baby waves here. You stay with Dementia so she doesn't bother us. I promised my aunt and uncle someone would keep an eye on Dementia if she was allowed to hang out with us today."

"Tahir is not allowed to surf," I remind Farzad. Actually, Tahir is supposed to say he is not allowed to surf or play Z-Grav, but only because that's a logical course for someone with his First's injuries. Clone Tahir can participate just fine.

"Tahir is not allowed to surf the *gigantes*," Farzad asserts. "These waves here are nothing."

"What if he does not want to surf?" I ask. The boys are carrying boards to the beach, but the intention (at least as promised to Tariq and Bahiyya) had been for Dementia and Farzad to go wave riding this afternoon, not Tahir and Farzad. Greer and Ivan did not join us this afternoon as their families are busy preparing for the upcoming Governor's Ball.

"Of course he will want to. Tahir lives for the dare."

"*Lived* for the dare," I correct Farzad. "That was before. Maybe now he's different. Maybe now he'd rather not."

From behind us, Dementia and Tahir have stopped walking to remove some seaweed that's attached to her feet, and so, out of their earshot, Farzad shoots me a look of pure hatred and says, "You don't know him, Beta. How dare you be so bold? You're *nothing*. Created to be some island whore. Don't tell me what my cousin should and should not be doing."

What I could tell Farzad: his Beta cousin and I have spent the last four days and nights wrapped up in each other through endless games of LoveStory. We've walked hand

in hand with the earliest humanoids across the land bridge
that once connected Asia to North America. We've climbed
Mount Vesuvius in ancient Italy in the time before its mighty
volcanic destruction. We've danced with kings and queens
and chatted with the great philosophers in Renaissance-
era parties. We've strolled along the Seine in Paris wearing
berets and eating croissants, stopping to model for Jazz Age
painters. We've thrashed in the mosh pit of CBGB's in
New York City while the Ramones played onstage. We've
made out through the night while snuggled together in a
sleeping bag inside an igloo perched on an ice floe that's
broken off from land and floated out into the ocean during
the time of the Water Wars. We've gone night dune riding
on the outskirts of Biome City as the stars in the sky above
spelled out TAHIR + ELYSIA. We've merged the complicated
LoveStory with the simplicity of Z-Grav as we've risen
through space together for hours on end, the goal of the
game changed not to reach the ground but for our hands and
lips to attach to one another as much as possible, whether
we are on the ceiling or floating through the middle of the
room or while literally bouncing off the walls.

We are Betas, freaks of nature, but that's okay, great
even—because we share it. We reckon that since we are
biological mates of a sort, we should therefore behave as
physical ones too. And we accomplished all this without
the bothersome courtship rituals that humans have to go
through: *Does he/she like me, or like–like me? Should I risk my
heart letting him/her know how I feel? What if I'm no good at
this? You're pretty.*

But something is still missing. I *feel* our connection; Tahir *experiences* it. Farzad will probably be in possession of the drug that could bridge that gap. I've counted on that today; it's why I encouraged Tahir to accept Farzad's invitation.

Why should I always be a good girl? That routine is old; boring. I was so stupid when I first emerged, so naïve and eager. Maybe it's a sign I'm starting to turn Awful, but I plan to get Tahir to disobey his father's order for him not to take 'raxia. It is time we took charge of our own destinies, like grown-ups. Tomorrow I will be returned to the Bratton household. Today, we must *live*.

More and more, I understand Tariq and Bahiyya's desperate adult need for Tahir to feel the way they do. I want him to feel the way I do, not just mimic.

If we're going to die, I want us to die sharing something real first.

I tell Farzad none of this. Instead, I look down at the sand and murmur, "Okay."

Farzad quickly finds out what I could have told him to begin with: I was right.

Tahir does not want to ride the baby waves. He wants to kick a soccer ball around on the beach with the girls. He meant it when he told Farzad his surfing days were over, and not just because of doctor's orders. "I've emerged a new guy since the accident," Tahir says to Farzad, but looking at me. "I want a new sport. Football is the sport of the people. Surfing is for privileged, elitist boys." He is repeating information from his database, but only I know this; the others think Tahir is expressing his opinion.

Dementia's eyes seem to almost bug out of their eye

sockets as she raises a fist in solidarity. "Yeah! I *like* the new Tahir!"

I like watching shirtless Tahir's taut stomach muscles flex and ripple as he runs across the beach and kicks through the sand. If he were out in the water, my view of him would be nearly as good. I've gotten so used to having him so near. How will I survive once I return to Governor's House?

Farzad glances at me as if Tahir's new attitude must be my fault. "Whoa, Tahir. How much pain medication are you on, anyway?"

"None," says Tahir.

"'Raxia to the rescue!" Dementia calls out, as she goes to pull out a few pills from her tote bag.

Finally, opportunity.

Farzad sulks. "He thinks he's too cool for that too, now. And my aunt and uncle were very specific that Tahir was only allowed out with us today so long as no one—*Dementia*—indulges in the 'raxia those irresponsible teens love."

"So what," says Dementia. "Let's have some fun. This is pure high-grade 'raxia, not that weirdo steroid mix Ivan makes. This is the good stuff."

Tahir looks my way and we have one of those knowing moments that we've seen Tariq and Bahiyya share. I lean over to whisper in his ear. "If 'raxia can make us feel, maybe it can also guide us toward circumventing the Awfuls?"

Tahir nods at Farzad. "Yes," Tahir says. "We shall try the pure high-grade 'raxia."

Farzad throws his hands up. "Who do I appease here? My bro-man, who needs the 'raxia, clearly, or my aunt and uncle."

Dementia says, "Your bro-man!"
Farzad says, "Let's do this."

I do not understand the human teens' love for this drug. All it does is sedate them. Dementia and Farzad come from the most privileged families in the world. They lie on their sides on surfboards to stare at one another as they fall into 'raxia bliss; their tanned, beach-attired bodies reveal them to be healthy, fit, and beautiful. The world practically belongs to them. These teens could do *anything* they wanted instead of just what others tell them to do. Instead, they choose to lie still on the sand, their eyes half closed, their lips slightly upturned into contented smiles.

"Your aesthetic is awesome," Farzad murmurs to topless Dementia.

"No, *your* aesthetic is awesome," Dementia murmurs to Farzad, who has forsaken his usual board shorts for a tight pair of black swim briefs that reveal his endowment to be of an aesthetic Dementia apparently finds pleasing.

They latch index fingers from across the sand and soon fall into a lazy-hazy sleep.

Tahir and I sit on the sand nearby them, tossing the soccer ball back and forth. This pure high-grade 'raxia has had no effect on us. We each took a pill, but perhaps we are too Beta to respond to the real thing. So far.

Tahir reaches over to tickle my feet. "'Your aesthetic is awesome,'" he mimics.

I lean over to press the funny bone on his knee, causing his foot to momentarily fly up. "'No, *your* aesthetic is awesome,'" I say.

Some charge of something passes between us in this moment, something indefinable and untouchable but very real. I feel it, weirdly, in my heart. A pang of wanting. I can tell by the look in his eyes that he feels it too.

"Maybe the 'raxia really is working?" Tahir says. "Something feels different. I am not sleepy like them. I feel—*something*. Not mimic excited but truly excited. How strange. My heart, it is surging."

"Mine too!" I am starting to feel so . . . alive. Tingly, awake, exuberant. This 'raxia that doesn't have Ivan's chemicals mixed in indeed feels like it's awakening me to something bigger and brighter than anything I've experienced before. I feel more than so, so good. I feel *great*. I look at Tahir. I feel *hungry*. For boy.

Tahir's hazel eyes light up again, as they were the last time he did 'raxia. I see in them: lust. This is no FantaSphere fake. His eyes reflect urgent *want*.

Tahir crawls closer to me and places his hands on my shoulders. He strokes. I put my hands around his head to pull his face closer to mine. I feel my pulse rate rapidly rise and my heart clench—*fluttering* is the word I believe the humans use. Suddenly, I need Tahir next to me, on me, now. The urgency is unexpected and visceral. Tahir must feel it too, because his lips press into mine, but this time his kiss is hard and needy instead of soft and exploratory. It's as if we are back inside another game of LoveStory all over again, except now we're out in the world, and time and space are real, and this time there are stakes involved way beyond mere experimentation.

Tahir's tongue finds its way into my mouth, lightly tracing

my teeth before sweetly coiling itself around my tongue. Wow wow *wow!* For a quick second, he pries his lips from mine and murmurs aloud what I am thinking—"Wow!"— and then his lips reattach to mine. I want this moment to never end, but I also need it to accelerate. I need more than a kiss. Tahir presses his torso into mine as I surrender into the sand, loving the feel of his weight on mine. I trace my hands through the parts between the braids that run along his scalp before my hands venture down, softly scraping his bare back with my fingernails. Something else is different from our FantaSphere LoveStory sessions this time. For all our kissing and caressing during the previous week, the bodily sensations have never progressed to this point.

And then came pure high-grade 'raxia.

His hands reach behind my back to untie the string of my bikini top. Once untied, I fling the top off and onto the sand and then immediately return my hands to his body. My fingers go beneath his board shorts, wandering below his chest for the first time, toward his pelvis. His bare chest presses against my breasts and I now understand how and why the humans try for that aesthetic of two hearts beating as one. We've found it. *Thump-thump.* Such sweetness, it's almost unbearable!

But Tahir stops. He removes himself from my body and falls onto his back next to me. His beautiful face looks flustered. He reaches to touch my hand.

"It's weird with Farzad and Dementia right there," he whispers.

I pull his palm to my lips to kiss it. Then I stand up, pulling him up to his feet along with me. "Come on!"

I run down the beach to the water and dive in. Tahir follows.

We swim and swim, not stopping until we're nearly out of sight range of sleeping Farzad and Dementia. For the first time, I understand the humans' obsession with Io's water. It is pure *magic* gliding over my skin, luxurious and exquisite. I could understand the compulsion to kill, to protect access to this heaven-sourced water.

Our feet sink into the shallow seabed while the violet water laps over our bodies and our lips lead us back to each other. Tahir's hands press against my bottom as he lifts my body. I wrap my legs around him as our bodies press together. I hold on to him tight and cannot seem to stop kissing him—his neck, his cheek, his forehead, his eyelids that close over First Tahir's eyes. I want to drink in every inch of his flesh. My thirst feels unquenchable.

Yes, the 'raxia definitely has a different effect on Betas than on the comatose humans lying on the distant sand. My body feels different, and somehow my brain does too. It's as if a locked door inside the neural pathways inside my head has not just opened, but has flung wide to let flow into it a whole new level of experience and understanding. Deeper, purer, real.

Then Tahir's hand is there, between my legs, and my back arches in pleasure as Tahir's lips find my neck.

Tahir pulls my back upright so that our chests press hard against one another. He stops the kissing madness long enough to ask me, "Do you want this?"

I experience a feeling of gratitude, sharing this moment

with a being who would seek assurance of my consent—
unnecessary as it may be from a manufactured servant. "Yes!
Please!"

I need to know what this is before it all goes away.

He presses his precious lips against my ear. "I love you,
Elysia," he says.

"I love you too," I say back.

This time: He means it. I mean it.

There's no turning back. We are both fully awakened
now.

30

THE FIRE HAS BEEN LIT. NOW IT CAN ONLY GROW.
An interesting thing happens after some 'raxia indulgence causes a Beta prince boy to proclaim his love for a
store-bought Beta girl.

He's nicer to his parents.

It could just be that Bahiyya asked the chef to prepare
a chocolate dinner for my final night at the Fortesquieu
compound, where Tahir and I have joined Tariq and Bahiyya
for a last supper. Any kindness extended to me seems to
brighten Tahir. The first course was white chocolate with
caviar, followed by a spinach salad spritzed with a dark
chocolate vinaigrette. The main course is venison stew
prepared with shavings of bittersweet chocolate.

The bittersweet part for me is that the chef could have

tossed all the nonessential ingredients such as caviar, spinach, and venison and simply served course after course of chocolate. Before the 'raxia, I found the taste of chocolate delightful. Now, post-'raxia, it tastes incredible at an epic level. But the bittersweet part of the meal is the recognition of the inevitable. Soon I will leave the sweet freedom of the Fortesquieu home and return to the dysfunctional Bratton one.

I don't know how I will survive at Governor's House after this week away. Having Tahir to myself. Becoming one with him.

"Won't you eat some stew?" Bahiyya asks Tahir. "It used to be your favorite. Taste it. Perhaps you'll remember?"

Tahir truly does not care for human food, but he knows she's had the meal prepared to somehow honor me, and he gulps down a spoonful.

"Delicious, *Maman*," he says, using First Tahir's term of endearment for Bahiyya. Her face glows, hearing the word.

"My darling Tahir, you are coming back to us. I know it. I see it!" Bahiyya turns to smile beneficently at me. "Elysia, my divine angel. How can we ever live without you now?"

Tariq says, "It's true. Tahir is happier with Elysia here."

Softly, Tahir reminds his father, "I cannot experience happiness, Papa." But Tahir's eyes meet mine when he says this; Tahir knows now that happiness is not to be an entirely elusive emotion for us.

Tariq's face falls slightly, saddened by his son's words. "Of course you can, Tahir. Elysia is proof that it's possible. Give it time."

Tahir takes another gulp of stew. "But . . ." Tahir pauses,

as if to make sure he should say what he's about to say. Then he proclaims: "I *want* to experience happiness."

Tariq's face lights back up as Bahiyya lets out a small cry. She says, "That's all I could ask for you, my darling. That's all." The emotion of the moment gets the better of us as her hands move to cover her face; she needs a full-on cry. Once it passes, she wipes the tears from her eyes and looks to her husband. They seem to share another of their telepathic decision glances. Tariq nods at Bahiyya, and then she turns to me. Bahiyya says, "It's settled, then. I will be calling the Brattons after dinner and making an offer."

"An offer on what?" I ask.

"On *who*?" Tahir asks.

Bahiyya nods as her face brightens again. "On you, Elysia. I shall purchase you from the Brattons and then you may bring happiness to my son all the time. You will have to return to their household tomorrow until we can settle on the terms, but once the Governor's Ball has passed, I'm sure we can reach a quick agreement with the Brattons."

Bahiyya reaches over to place her hand over Tahir's. He does not pull back but instead takes her hand and places it to caress his cheek. As she touches his face, he dips into her hand like a cat, rubbing his face sweetly across her hand.

She beams.

And then suddenly, her face falls as her hand finds something of concern. She gasps, then rubs her hand more aggressively over Tahir's chin.

"Stubble," Bahiyya says to Tariq, as if Tahir weren't even there.

Their faces, a moment ago so excited and pleased, have

paled. No one is in the mood for more dinner, judging by the looks on their faces.

Except me.

I'm *starving*.

This boy said he loved me. We are mates. Now we can be together for however long our Beta hormones will allow us to survive. We may be robbed of long lives, but we won't be robbed of precious time together.

His stubble will either make him a man or make him Awful.

Either way, he'll get there with me.

"Tahir is due to see Dr. Lusardi tomorrow," says Tariq. "She can test a sample of the stubble."

"Yes," agrees Bahiyya.

But.

"No," Tahir says.

"What?" his parents both exclaim.

"No," Tahir repeats. "I am finished seeing Dr. Lusardi."

"That's not for you to decide," Bahiyya says.

Tahir gives her the same loving look he's seen on First Tahir's face in the family's holographic family album, and for the first time I've ever seen—that his parents have probably ever seen—he flashes his First's megawatt grin, gleaming white teeth and pure charisma. "*Maman*. Please. I get terrible headaches after Dr. Lusardi's treatments. There is nothing more she can do for me." He leans over to nuzzle his cheek against his mother's.

The reaction from his parents for his insolent refusal is ecstatic. Their faces glow with surprise and pride. Their clone finally looks and reacts like their son.

"Then it is settled," says Tariq. "For now. If you are capable of expressing choice and affection, you are clearly on your way to becoming more human. Perhaps you don't need further treatments. I'm not convinced her treatments improve you any more than what the doctors were doing for you in BC, anyway."

"Finally," says Bahiyya, "we have hope."

31

HIS PARENTS PROVIDED CHOCOLATE TO COMMEMORATE
my last night on loan to their home.

Tahir provides me with an Olympic pool, FantaSphere
version.

"How would you prefer to spend your last night here?"
he asked me after dinner.

I said, "I would like to dive. My First was a diver, I
think. I would like to experience her competitive world.
TeamDefect version."

"TeamDefect version will probably be an improvement,"
said Tahir. "More strength and agility, without all the
humans' bothersome aspirations and distractions."

And so, I'm at the Paris Olympics at the height of the
Water Wars. While countries and nationalities are being
decimated and realigned, the need for a common hope,

as exemplified by the Olympic tradition, has never been stronger. The games must go on.

It's my turn to dive.

I pace behind the platform diving boards, playing a game of hot/cold, trying to determine which board fits me best. I stop at the five-meter tower but feel frigid to its potential. Too safe. I step to the seven-meter stairs. There is possibility here, but it's lukewarm. Finally I step over to the ten-meter platform and my body goes hot with want. This is where Z would have chosen to dive. She would have sought the ultimate DD—degree of difficulty.

I climb the stairs, my bare feet pressing down as I bear up, and there is something about these hard, wet steps against my feet that feels familiar, and comforting, and challenging. Although I am not yet immersed in water, I feel her spirit rise to me from the pool, the first time I have channeled Z so strongly in the open air. *Do it for me*, she requests. *Because I can't.*

I reach the top plank and step onto it. From ten meters high, I can look past the pool and the spectator stands to a panoramic view of the city. The Eiffel Tower looms large over the fabled city as an orange-pink sun casts the sky in a soft twilight. I narrow my focus down into the stands and see the spectators from all over the world. They are different sizes and colors but all are fuchsia-eyed. My people. My eyes zone in on the best spectator in the crowd, seated in the front row above the pool's center point. His eyes are hazel, his hair is half-braided, and he's gazing at me with eager antici-pation, perhaps even pride. He flashes his First's megawatt smile but then changes it, closing his mouth so that his bright teeth are not flashing, and he raises an eyebrow to me, a distinctly sexy gesture that announces, *I own this face now*. He gives me the thumbs-up gesture and my heart sings because this person in the crowd believes in me. I give him the thumbs-up as I walk to the end of the diving board.

Now, I must forget about Tahir in the stands and focus my energy. Up here, towering over the city but also over the center point of where I know her soul belonged—the pool—I let the surge of nothingness sweep through me, obscuring my view of the stands and city stretched out before me. This is her concentration taking over, blocking out everything but the dive to come. Yet, through that nothingness, a familiar face zaps into the frequency—the turquoise-eyed, barrel-chested surfer man. It's then I realize what happened to Z's diving career. She lost her focus because of him.

Go away, I will him. He complies. My mind returns to nothingness, by *choice*. I will *not* be distracted by him. I will own this dive. I can do this for Z, and do it better than Z. I can divine my Defect power for this dive.

At the precipice of the ten-meter-high board, I place my hands onto the floor and call forth my legs to spring up over my body. I do not think about the risk to my body being suspended upside down ten meters above the ground, held upright by nothing more than my core strength; rather, I focus my mind on the physics of what I am about to do. My body holds the handstand for the required five seconds as I visualize the dive I am about to perform, an arm stand forward with two somersaults. *Five . . . four . . . three . . . two . . . one*: I push off with my hands and propel my body into one flip, a second flip, and then I curl my head into my chest, point my toes, and rip into the water with barely a splash.

Flawless.

Beneath the water, I feel exhilaration and pride. I did this for her, but for me too. I am not alone at the bottom of the pool. This time, when the face of Z's lover appears, he is different. His blond hair is braided in cornrows and his eyes are hazel. The face is melding into the one I want it to be. His gravelly voice does not say, *You know you own me, Z.* Instead, the voice I hear is Tahir's, asking me, "Why should *anyone* be allowed to own you?"

It's Tahir's turn to choose our final FantaSphere game. We go from Paris to Biome City.

"Hovercopter BC," he says. "Since we can't experience the real thing without human oversight, we can fly through space alone in here."

Tahir pilots the copter at a low altitude over the Honey Quarter in BC. The copter's ceiling, floor, and sides are made of clear plastic, allowing us infinite night-sky views heralding thousands of stars twinkling above the plain, and below us, direct peeks into the honeycomb homes of the neighborhood's residents, who we watch through their windows as they go about their nighttime rituals: preparing dinner, putting the children to sleep, making love.

I nuzzle my head into Tahir's neck. He takes my hand, puts it on his knee, and covers it with his hand. He leans over to place a kiss on my cheek. The distraction of our kiss causes the plane to crash into a honeycomb apartment complex. Another advantage to flying in a virtual plane piloted by an inexperienced clone: no harm, no foul. The copter merely bounces off the complex as if the building were made of rubber. The residents inside are not disturbed, and the pilot can choose to set the plane to autonavigate so he and his passenger may resume making out.

Our kisses are slow and searching and inevitably must include hands and graduate to full body contact. When our seated positions can no longer accommodate these ministrations, Tahir calls out, "Land. Sand dunes."

The plane lands itself on top of a pyramid-shaped sand dune outside the city. Tahir and I step outside the plane and fall onto the sand. He crawls on top of me, cupping my face into his hands as his hazel eyes gaze intently into mine. I open my mouth for another kiss, but he's got discussion on his mind.

"I am filled with sadness," he says. "So much ache. It's horrible. How do the humans survive it?"

"Why?" My hand lightly caresses his newly stubbled cheek. I wanted him to feel, but not sadness. That he could hurt causes my heart to clench in pain.

"I don't want us to be separated. That lady you call Mother has already told Bahiyya she's glad to entertain offers for you, but nothing can be finalized until after the ball. I'm sure she's just leveraging time to try to get a bigger price from my parents."

"I don't want to go back," I say. I don't tell Tahir what looms for me back at Governor's House. The lord of the manor who intends to make me his whore. The crazy Mother who won't care less if I get shoved off a cliff.

"It makes me sad for you to be leaving. It makes me

furious—yes, furious!—that you are even considered property. But," Tahir pauses and takes a deep breath, as if gathering his resolve, "I need you to go back, temporarily. I need to buy us some time."

"Why?"

"If you are around me all the time, I cannot resist you. Now that I am fully awake to you, to this life and its possibilities, I want you with me all the time, so we can forge our own new path. In order to accomplish that, I need to not be distracted, so I can formulate a plan."

I understand his need for focus. It's how I could nail a perfect-ten Olympic platform dive in the previous FantaSphere game. By blocking out everything and everyone else.

"A plan for what?" I look into his hazel eyes, which before seemed soft and dreamy. Now, they are lit in determination and anger.

"I get it now. We are lesser beings. But our feelings should matter just as much. Who knows how soon till we turn Awful? We need to experience everything they will never allow us before we expire."

"Maybe we can survive the Awfuls. Maybe we can figure out a cure on our own."

"I agree. But our only hope for survival is if we flee. I am working on a plan for our escape."

"Escape? But what about your parents? They love you so much."

"I know. I get that now too. It does not please me that my running away will grieve them. But escaping is something I need to do for myself. Otherwise I will never be able to have my own identity. I want you to share that new life. You are part of me now. I can't let you go. Do you agree?"

So many times I have said this word to appease the humans. This is the first time I proclaim it for myself, and for Tahir, and for all our kind: "*Yes!*"

There is elation, and then there is reality. "But . . . how?" I ask.

"We are going to *fly* away together. I am going to spend our time apart practicing how to pilot a real hovercopter. Then I am going to steal my parents' plane and take us away from here."

"To where?"

"I don't know. Does it matter?"

It doesn't. So long as we get there together.

"I read about it in one of First Tahir's books. The French called it *la petite mort*," Tahir tells me, stroking my blond hair. We have awoken in each other's arms as dawn rises over our sand-dune bed. The hovercopter is parked in the distance, waiting to return us to real time and space. "That moment of release with the one you love, they say it's like a little death."

"A mighty mighty one," I murmur. Greer's terminology makes more sense to me now. That moment of utmost release and surrender as waves of pleasure crests through the body—I get it. It's mighty mighty exquisite. Thank you, 'raxia.

Tahir says, "I would rather die than for us not to experience our own freedom."

"Me too."

Now we can add a death wish to our escape pact.

And, the promise of a deed.

So far, in Io and in the FantaSphere, we have professed our love to each other. We have experienced *la petite mort* together. But, technically, we have yet to do the actual deed, that act of coupling for which the humans have so many different words, all meaning the same thing: Sex. Coitus. Doing it. The mighty mighty. Making love.

Tahir and I have decided to save ourselves.

We will share the real thing when we are free.

32

BACK HOME AT GOVERNOR'S HOUSE, I AM JUST like the Astrid girl whom I replaced—I did not miss the Brattons at all while away. It would appear the household barely noticed my absence, anyway. With the Governor's Ball coming up tomorrow, the household is in a whirl of activity. The fuchsia-eyed workers have never appeared so hurried or so busy as they do upon my return.

I flee immediately to the sanctuary of my room, which isn't even mine. I am to wait there until Mother calls for me. It's only a short time that I have to remain here, I reassure myself. I can pretend the room is my own private FantaSphere with Tahir.

But privacy is not to be mine. Ivan bursts into my quarters, looking sweaty and sallow. He closes the door behind him. He presses his body against the back of the door, almost as if he wants to throw himself against the hard surface to induce pain—or to show he can handle the pain. "Guess what?"

I shrug. These humans and their guessing games are starting to annoy me.

"The Aquine did a sweep of the island, looking for Defect 'raxia, and they found a major stash hidden away in the construction site at Haven."

"Whoa," I say.

I feel so not whoa. The Brattons' companion toy, now lacking her own Beta companion, just wants to throw herself on the bed and wail in a tantrum like a toddler.

"Dad has the 'raxia stored in a safe here at Governor's House. I have the combination! There's so much, I can take just a little bit and no one notices. I've been doing all kind of experiments while you were away." He flexes his bulging biceps—it looks two times bigger than the last time I worked out with him.

Double whoa, for real! I must get that combination, and supply myself and my love. "You are looking very strong, brother," I compliment him. He looks *too* strong—manic, even. I suspect a little bit of 'raxia will never be enough for him anymore. How will he survive at the Base?

"Right?" says Ivan. "I ought to personally thank the clone they're saying was stockpiling the 'raxia. They say he was leading the Insurrection thingie. You missed a lot while you were gone!"

There is a leader? How can I connect with this clone?

Another wish, unattainable. Ivan adds, "Luckily they took that guy away. They're saying he was a rageful Defect who was plotting to build more bombs."

I assess: I am a clone with no Relay to communicate with others of my kind. I am chipped with information—some of which turns out to be false, the rest of which are only basic facts—and I am chipped with a locator device that can identify my whereabouts to the humans at any point. I can only expand my knowledge base by experience and not by inherent design. I have no privacy and no power. Realistically, how can I truly hatch an escape pact with Tahir? We're going to need help. Our own resources will not be enough. We need to find this alleged Insurrection leader.

"So the Defect was returned to Dr. Lusardi, then?" Tahir and I could storm Dr. Lusardi's compound and free the Defects! Wouldn't that be a beautiful dream.

"No way. The Defect was expired immediately."

Or not.

"What was this clone called?" I ask Ivan, although I'm sure I already know.

"Not sure. Mike or something? He was an oxygen leveler. They're saying he was scheming to sabotage the atmosphere here."

The oxygen leveler must have been Miguel, Xanthe's love. At least now their hearts might be joined in the hereafter, if such a thing even exists. If the humans haven't ruined that for them too.

If Ivan had any idea of the Defect I am, he might perceive that he should back away from me right now, as I have a sudden urge to hold him accountable for his brethren's transgressions.

Ivan has not a speck of concern. He pulls a bag of pills

from his pocket and says, "I have this small stash of 'raxia I swiped from the safe, but it's too hot for me to keep in my room now. I doubt they would come looking in there, but I can't take the risk, especially so close to my official departure for the Base. Just a few more days, dude!"

Seriously, sweat is almost pouring down his face and his breathing seems heavier, and forced. I suspect he is an addict now.

"Are you okay, brother?" I ask him. Are you okay with the rage percolating inside me that suddenly would like to be expressed openly, somehow? Because I am starting to feel okay with that prospect, even if it could reveal me as a Defect.

"Just a little jumpy, maybe." He places the bag of 'raxia in my dresser drawer. "Keep this safe for me, okay, champ?"

I'll take the risk. Tahir and I will be able to put Ivan's stash to good use for ourselves soon enough. This bad news at least comes with an upside for me.

"Yes, brother," I acquiesce.

"So how was it at the Fortesquieus'?" Ivan asks me.

"Harmonious and beautiful, of course," I say. *Sink back down, rage. I'm not ready to deal with you yet. I have no idea what I'm supposed to do with you.*

"So do you like totally think you're better than us now that you've been a guest at the Fortesquieus'?" He's kidding. I think.

"I was not a guest there. I was a worker companion."

"Maybe you did your job too good. I heard they want to buy you now."

"We can still be workout companions when you return home from the Base," I reassure Ivan.

Ivan's eyes narrow at me, displeased, as if I have done something wrong in being too good a Beta. "We owned you first," Ivan reminds me, and he leaves my room.

Alone in my room after Ivan leaves, I look around at its sterile walls, at its window view out toward the path that leads to the cliff where my friend Xanthe was killed. I cannot pretend this room is my FantaSphere with Tahir. It is a prison.

I go into Astrid's room and sit down at her vanity table. I observe myself in the mirror, looking at my fuchsia eyes, high cheekbones, peachy perfect skin—all of it created for me, but is it any of it truly mine? I'm just a replication of a prior being. How do I claim my own identity without blatantly announcing to the humans, *I am a Defect. Please torture and then expire me?*

We are lesser beings. But our feelings should matter just as much.

I remember Tahir's words as I tug on a strand at the blond hair hanging below my shoulders. I twirl the hair around my index finger, this hair that Mother so loves to braid.

This hair that I hate having braided. *Hate.*

Mother thinks she owns this hair. Ivan thinks he owns *me.*

They don't just think they own me. They do own me. This is a fact.

This fact will change. *I* will change.

I open the vanity drawer and find a pair of scissors. I place a strand at the front of my hair between my fingers, and I cut. I will have bangs: *my* choice. Snip. Snip. Snip. I look in the mirror at the uneven fringe hanging above my eyebrows. It's not enough. I want more hair gone. I reach for the back of my hair and don't just cut it. I let the scissors go into reckless assault mode. Snip. Cut. Slash. *Gone.* With each long wad of blond hair that falls to the floor, I feel more and more free.

I will become my own person whether they like it or not.

I have been called to Mother's study.

I enter the room as she is looking down at her desk, reviewing her guest list. She does not look up immediately at me but says, "So, pet. I guess you were a big hit at the Fortesquieus'."

"Yes, Mother," I say.

"It's a shame, really. Now I'll have no choice but to sell you to them. You have made me look good to the Fortesquieus, but at such cost—I was not prepared to let you go permanently. The Governor would not hear of me denying a request from that family."

"Yes, Mother."

Yes!

Mother looks up from her desk. Her eyes go wide and her jaw drops. She points a finger at me. "I *told* you to ask Bahiyya to speak with me first if she wanted to alter you in any way." She stands up and walks to me, and swipes her fingers through my newly shorn hair. While I am not yet free of this house, I am free of the hair that Mother so treasured. My new short cut is wild and unkempt, pixieish—*so* not the boring, refined Demesne clone aesthetic. Mother says, "My goodness, Bahiyya has horrendous taste. Is this supposed to be the new hair fashion in BC?"

"I don't have that data," I say. I do know Mother will not protest about the haircut to a figure as socially powerful as Bahiyya; I may very well be living at the Fortesquieus' before Mother even realizes I cut the hair myself.

Mother sighs. "This new hair is not going to suit your ball costume, but nothing to do about that now."

"My ball costume?" I ask. "Am I to be a server there?"

"I may have no choice but to sell you to Bahiyya. But if you are so special as to be purchased by no less than the Fortesquieus, well, then, I have convinced the Governor in turn that you are suitable to be my companion at the ball. You won't be a guest, obviously. But you also won't be a server. Rather, you will be on display. So everyone will know *I* was the early adopter. You were mine first."

33

I AM THE FIRST BETA INVITED TO THE BALL.

I am neither guest nor servant here. I am a piece of performance art, seated on a white swing hung from the high ceiling, where I overlook the ceremonies from twenty feet above the floor to provide overhead aesthetic entertainment for the crowd.

All of the families of Demesne have come to the island for its annual gala, held in the ballroom at Haven. The party is stocked not only with the most powerful people in the world, but with their human playthings, posing tonight as their guests—entertainment stars, politicians, world-renowned athletes—who have scored rare invites to experience this one-night-only chance to mingle on Demesne. In the crowd, I spy Mother's mahjong friends, Ivan's friends, the Fortesquieus, and many of the people from Tahir's tutorial flash cards, including the king of Zakat and the world-renowned soccer player known as the Sphinx.

For the richest and most powerful people in the world to gather for a party is no small occasion, and neither is their venue. The grand ballroom at Haven is designed in the style of the Hall of Mirrors at the Palace of Versailles in ancient France, modernized with accents reflecting Demesne's own distinctive culture. The ballroom is floor-to-ceiling spectacle. Like its predecessor, Haven's Hall of Mirrors has seventeen grand arched windows separated by marble pilasters decorated in gilded sculptures. The windows face outside, allowing the 357 pieces of mirror inlayed into the arched windows to reflect the lavish outdoor display of coral-red cuvée torchflowers back into the room—a mesmerizing effect. Seventeen large crystal chandeliers and twenty-six smaller ones made of solid silver hang from the ceiling; from these chandeliers, a thousand candles light the room. The ballroom's floor is patterned in Demesne's distinctive Parquet du Nouveau Versailles, found in many of Demesne's homes—large squares of bamboo parquetry, laid on the bias, with interlaced diagonal motifs representing Demesne's fleur-de-lis symbol. While the artwork in Versailles' Hall of Mirrors depicted the victories of Louis XIV and the symbolism of France, the frescoes lining the walls and ceiling at Haven's ballroom depict Demesne in all its glory: the lapping violet ocean, oceanside cliffs, towering volcanic mountaintop, and interior jungle; homes like the Fortesquieu compound's limestone-cliff pueblo and Governor's House; an aerial view of the whole island with Io's violet ring separating its perimeter from the rest of the world; sunrise over Haven; portraits of perfect faces tattooed with violet fleurs-de-lis at their temples.

In one corner of the room, a platform has been set up for the night's musical entertainment—Demesne's RSO, or Replicant Symphony Orchestra. The all-male symphony is comprised of every caste of island clones—from bamboo- to holly-vined, grunt worker to tennis pro—who wear black-and-white tuxedos. With their extremely fit bodies and aesthetically pleasing faces, they are possibly the best-looking orchestra in the world.

But everyone's a critic. Says Mother about the RSO's sound: "Perfect pitch. No passion." Mother fans a peacock feather across her unimpressed face as the RSO completes its Mozart piece.

She stands below my swing in the corner of the room opposite the RSO, at the head of a procession where newly arriving guests greet the Governor and his family. This year's gala has a Greek-gods theme, with Mother costumed as Hera, the goddess of home and marriage, the jealous and vengeful wife of Zeus, whose chariot was pulled by peacocks. The Governor is mighty Zeus, of course, while Liesel wears a rainbow-hued frock to symbolize the goddess Iris, the personification of the rainbow and messenger of the gods. Because he is about to enter the military, Ivan is dressed in formal military uniform, but with a cloned black vulture resting on his shoulder, to symbolize Ares, the Greek god of war. Vultures, which prey upon dead carcasses in the battle-field, were sacred to Ares.

Not all families are attired in the Greek-gods theme. A gala event heralds peace and prosperity, but what was lost during the time of the recent Water Wars is not forgotten. Those families who still mourn wear traditional black to formal events. Among them are the Fortesquieus, who have chosen to bring Tahir after all. During my week at their house, they had debated whether Tahir was indeed ready to be reintroduced to society, so the flash cards—and perhaps his Beta companion—must have done their job satisfactorily to prepare him. Tahir's shaggy bush of half-braided, half-wild hair is gone, replaced with neat cornrows lining his scalp in eight perfect rows. He and Tariq both wear custom-made black silk suits, simple and elegant, while Bahiyya, who perhaps lost more family than anyone else in the room, wears an outfit custom-designed for her queenly stature. Instead of a dress, she wears graceful, tailored black silk slacks similar to her menfolk's, but with a feminine black jacket over a corset accented at the front with crepe trim, ornate embroidery, and lace decoration, made from pieces of one of Queen Victoria's mourning dresses, which Tariq bought for Bahiyya at auction from a now defunct royal museum. Bahiyya's long white hair, sweeping down to her waist, is interlaced with strings sparkling with small precious jewels—sapphires, diamonds, rubies, and emeralds—and offers stunning contrast to the black of her modest but stylish costume, which reveals a minimum of flesh.

Such restraint of flesh was not provided for my costume. Mother decided my angelic appearance best befitted Artemis, the Hellenic goddess of young girls—i.e., virgins. For my outfit, she chose a short white frock designed as a maiden huntress's costume. The dress leaves little to the imagination. Although it falls just above my knees, and is belted at the waist by a braid of gold, the bodice of the dress is cut with a plunging V-neckline that covers my breasts—barely—and is open down to just above my belly button. My newly shorn hair is not long enough for the upsweep Mother had planned for it, so she settled on a garland of white pearlflowers on my head, with blond tendrils framing my face. My lower eyelids have been lined with copper pencil, while my upper lids are accented with violet eye shadow. My eyebrows have been defined and shaped with light-brown pencil, and black extensions added to my eyelashes. My lips are tinted a pink-violet color.

Mother's Beta, soon to be bought by no less than the Fortesquieu family, was too prized a possession to not show off this year. The whole island should be able to check out what the Fortesquieu family covets. Now that they can see me so vibrantly on display on the swing, everyone will want a teen Beta, and all because Mother started the trend. Or so Mother hopes. My early reviews from the night's first set of guests have pleased her. The guests admire me up on the swing, and offer their commentary on my appearance: "Exquisite." "The best Beta yet!" Chuckle chuckle titter titter.

I merely swing overhead, neither a participant nor a worker at the festivities.

I watch Tahir in the middle of the room as he is engaged in conversation by the king of Zakat. Over the music, I cannot hear their conversation, but I can see Tahir's body language reacting with familiarity to the King, and Tahir throws his head back in laughter at something the King says, which causes Tariq and Bahiyya to have one of their shared glances, an approving one.

All I ever get to do on this island is watch. But I have a pact with Tahir now. Soon, we are going to make things *happen* for ourselves. Soon, we are going to seek freedom. I can survive until then, I tell myself. Hold on just a little longer, Elysia.

I can barely contain my desire to jump off this swing, take hold of Tahir, and run away with him this very instant. I wish for Tahir to look up at me, to acknowledge me up here on this swing on my own, to acknowledge our pact so that I may be reassured during my vacant performance art swing ride, but his eyes do not find mine.

Perhaps he is too embarrassed to look up. Or too angry.

There's no music playing, but Dementia has a dance in her heart. She can't not perform it. And so, alone on the middle of the floor, she slithers her arms around in sylphlike movements while gyrating her bare belly and pelvis up and down, back and forth. Dementia's dance is notable not only because of its lack of musical accompaniment and her solo stature on the floor, but also because of the way her costume moves (or rather, doesn't) with her gyrations. Tonight Dementia is dressed as Aphrodite, the goddess of love who rose from the sea. For her costume, Dementia crafted an outfit involving no fabric whatsoever. Instead, she "wears" (if it can be called that) a stiff chemical concoction made to resemble sea foam, sprayed to cover her private parts and not much else. Dementia's Aphrodite is all flesh and foam, and exactly no dress. The pink-hued white of the sea foam plays off beautifully against Dementia's olive skin.

Greer, standing below my swing with Ivan and Farzad at her side, mutters, "In five . . . four . . . three . . . two . . . one . . . and, yes, there they are, right on schedule." Dementia's shipping-baron parents, the Cortez-Oliviers, who made their fortune developing tankers strong enough to withstand the ocean's new might, make their late arrival into the ballroom just in time to witness their daughter's brazen show for the whole room. Greer says, "By the look on their faces, Mom and Dad didn't check Dementia's costume for themselves before they left for the ball."

"Demetra!" Mrs. Cortez-Olivier cries out. "Come here this instant! This is completely inappropriate!"

Dementia's father takes matters into his own hands rather than yell at his daughter. He motions to a nearby security clone, who races over to Dementia, takes off his jacket to place over her near-naked body, then sweeps a kicking and screaming Dementia into his arms and whisks her away from the ballroom.

Apparently Demesne social code requires *some* semblance of modesty.

"Dementia strikes again," says Ivan.

"I think you will miss Dementia most when you desert us for the Base," Greer teases Ivan. Tonight Greer is dressed as Selene, the goddess of the moon, who was often depicted riding a pair of serpentine dragons. Greer wears a white robe with a half-moon on her head of flowing red hair, and carries a talon carved in the shape of a serpentine dragon. "At least she makes things more interesting here on Boring Island."

"Elysia is the one who I will miss the most," says Ivan as I swing above him.

"She's not even yours anymore, practically."

Farzad glares up in my direction, looking at me in unrestrained disgust.

"Bloody damn!" Greer says, suddenly distracted. "Dementia's going to be so sad she missed this."

"What?" asks Farzad.

"My beautiful Aquine!" Greer sighs as a new arrival enters the ballroom.

"Who?" Farzad asks.

I see a few officers, guests from the Base on the Mainland wearing formal military uniform, stopping to speak with the Governor and Greer's father.

Greer says, "That guy in the middle? The really tall one. That's the Aquine. This must be his final hurrah. His assignment on Demesne is ending. I am so going to weep when he leaves this island."

I strive to locate this Aquine, the man who Xanthe informed me is supposedly on Demesne to protect clones' rights, but who is in fact a direct threat to our kind. Because of him, Becky was sent back to Dr. Lusardi for "experiments." Because of him, rumors of the Insurrection have grown more rampant . . . and Xanthe was shoved to her death from a cliff. Because of him, Xanthe's lover was expired. But before my eyes spot the Aquine, they settle on Tahir, and linger. I only want to take in Tahir, now in conversation in the distance with the Sphinx, who is playfully (or not) shoving Tahir, trying to get some reaction from him. Whatever is said between them causes the Sphinx to cry out, "You're a fake, Tahir Fortesquieu!" before the king of Zakat interjects to calm down the athlete. Tariq and Bahiyya look less than calm; they quickly escort Tahir out of the ballroom, out of my view.

I should be with him, to help him.

Farzad follows the Fortesquieus out of the room, leaving Greer standing idly below me.

"Come to me, Aquine," she murmurs sexily, as if practicing her most seductive pickup line. She looks up at me. "Sounded ridiculous, didn't it? Help me think up something better to say."

"Point him out to me and I will try to datacheck something clever to say to him," I say.

Greer says, "The tall blond guy in the center of the room, surrounded by the gaggle of panting middle-aged women."

Without Tahir to distract me, my eyes quickly hone in on the Aquine. It's hard to get a good look at his face, but I can see that he has buzz-cut blond hair and a studly build. When he finally gazes up from his admirers, his eyes catch mine for a split second. His eyes, so turquoise. His look at me: it registers recognition. A lightning strike hits directly into the core of my being, that same electric current I've felt when I'm submersed in water.

It's him. The Aquine is the man who belonged to my First, the lover whose heart she owned.

34

THE GOVERNOR STANDS BELOW MY SWING. "Elysia, come down at once. Take Mother to her suite to rest. She's had too much to drink."

"Yes, Governor," I say, as I climb down the ladder the server clones have attached to the swing.

I try to look over my shoulder for another glance of the Aquine while I have the benefit of height, but he has disappeared. Did I dream him?

The Governor leads me to Mother, who is arguing loudly with Ivan, and sloppily slurring her words. "Yew are just a mean, mean boy. Yew can't tell me what I can dew wif my own property-y-y-y, Eye-van-n-n."

The Governor intones, "Time for a rest now, dear. I reserved a suite for you at Haven for tonight so you can sleep it off."

Mother hiccups. "Don't wanna miss the sunrise cocktails. Tradition!"

"We will wake you in time for morning cocktails," the Governor reassures his drunk wife.

"And a liter of coffee," Ivan adds.

Mother places her hands on my cheeks. "My precious Beta-a-a. Are you to put me to rest?"

"Yes, Mother," I say.

She slurs as she tells me, "Such a sweet girl. I shall mees you sooo when those snobs take yew away." She is too tired to protest her leaving; she yawns, eager—or relieved—for me to guide her away from the biggest night of the year on Demesne.

Mother passed out cold within moments of me bringing her to her suite. No one will come looking for me for hours. They will be expecting me to tend to Mother.

Opportunity.

I must find him. If I am right about him, and if he wants to seek me out in private, there is one place I know he will go—to the pool. I head toward Nectar Bay.

I sneak outside Haven and take cover behind a thick hedge rimming the gardens. Am I being disloyal to Tahir, seeking out the Aquine? No, I'm not. I need some answers, is all. The Aquine can tell me about my First. Tahir already has the luxury of knowing everything about his. I want the same. I have a pact with Tahir. Nothing—and no one—can interfere with that. Tahir and I will die together rather than fail to achieve it.

I sprint past the gardens and down to the beach inlet at

Nectar Bay. I walk the long dock that leads to the floating pool in the middle of the bay. The plank is festively lit with hundreds of tangerine-colored votive candles lining its edges, giving the violet-blue water below a serene glow. No guests have found their way this far from the club yet. Haven is far enough away that I can only hear the faint murmur of the party going on in the distance, but not so close that the festivities extend this far. I remove my costume's huntress sandals, sit down at the dock's edge, and dangle my feet and calves into the pool.

At last, my body starts to relax, as it always does when it meets the water.

I wait. He will turn up. I know it.

I listen to the water lap. I'm trying to think about Tahir and our imminent escape, but my mind keeps wandering back to the Aquine. My imagination decides to go buck wild—buck-naked wild. I envision the Aquine swimming in the pool, a robust butterfly stroke. He swims nude, a vision of glistening male perfection, bronzed and muscled, gliding across the water, swimming the stroke named for an insect, but this chiseled, blond-haired man has the speed and strength of a dolphin. This vision is not my imagination, I feel sure; at some point, my First saw him swim like this.

Oh, my. Oh! *My!* That now familiar, never not exquisite shiver passes through my body, a remembrance of what I've experienced with Tahir. An extra petite *petite mort.*

I have to wonder: Was my First a slut?

Away with you, beautiful Aquine. I love Tahir. It's not possible another male could make me feel so warm and alive. Not. Possible.

"Z!"

I whip my head around to see who's there.

It's the Aquine, real and not imagined. I knew he would find me here. He's almost as beautiful in his formal military uniform as he was naked in my imagination. Almost. When I've had visions of him underwater, his dirty-blond hair was longer, his face warm and inviting. Live and in the real flesh, his hair is in a trim military cut, and he looks dashing but stiff, as if he would much rather be wearing surf shorts and communing with water than being adorned in fancy military finery.

His voice is as gravelly and masculine as when I heard his apparition speak to me underwater. "Z! Is that you? I thought I saw you inside earlier but you hopped off that ridiculous swing before I could get a good look at you."

I remember: this Aquine comes from a sect who hates our kind. I remember there were things I wanted to tell this Aquine to his face.

The quarter moon's light is so dark save for the candles lining the pier. He crouches down to see my face closer. "Zhara?" he asks. There's a gentleness to his deep voice. It's unexpected.

He reaches for the tangerine votive and places the candlelight closer to my face. I let him look, glaring with my glassy eyes directly into his deep blue ones. Now he can't not see the vining and the fleur-de-lis on my temples.

"Who's Zhara?" I ask him.

He drops the votive into the pool, shocked. For a moment, it's like he can't breathe. His chest seems to choke as his face drains of color. It appears as if he is about to faint.

But the moment passes, and as he regains his composure, his blue eyes stare into my vacant clone eyes. Finally, the Aquine speaks. He says, "Zhara was your First."

I don't know why I am so compelled, but I suddenly shove him, so hard his rear end falls onto the deck from his crouching position. This rash stunt from me will surely reveal to him that his First's clone is an irrefutably crazy Defect. Great first impression. But I don't care.

Actually, I do know the reason for my irrational act. The reason is unmistakably human. Hate.

I hate him for being part of a human sect that considers clones to be unnatural. I hate him for being the cause of Becky's return to Dr. Lusardi, and Xanthe's lover's expiration.

I hate Zhara, for passing the lust she felt for him into me.

"Hey," the Aquine says, shocked. "What did I do?"

I crouch down opposite him, so he can get a good look at my cloned face. His hand reaches out to try to touch my vining, but I take his hand and slap it away from my face.

"Back down, tiger!" he growls at me. "I was trying to see if your vining was real. When I saw you up on the swing earlier, I thought you must be Zhara, playing some kind of joke. That's the kind of inappropriate thing she did." He pauses. "She also liked to slap."

"I am not Zhara," I proclaim. "I am Elysia. I am a clone, and"—I might truly be malfunctioning at an epic level, because I tell him the truth—"and I hate you. I don't care what that hate makes me."

"Don't hate me," he says. "You don't even know me yet. . . ." He pauses, searching for the right word. *Defect?* "Elysia," he finally concludes, as if reluctant to speak aloud the new name of my First's clone. As if enunciating the name aloud could make me real.

"I know enough," I say.

He starts to stand up but looks cautiously at me first. "Don't strike, tiger! I'm just standing up. Let me regain my equilibrium."

He stands up. I stand up too, but my knees feel weak, my heart smashed to bits, my breathing hurried and bothered. He is so tall and so—freaking—gorgeous. I totally get why she was obsessed with him. I datacheck this horrible sensation and discover what it is. *Swooning* is what I am experiencing for this man I just a moment ago so impulsively slapped.

Appalling.

Unnecessary.

I refuse.

There's so much I want and need to know about Zhara. I cannot waste this time with the Aquine on swooning or slapping. I must return to being docile, measured Elysia. Fact finder. I ask him, "How did she die?"

"I don't know. Until now, I didn't know she *had* died. We only knew she was missing. Where did you come from?"

"I came from Dr. Lusardi. Like all of us here."

"All of you here don't come from Dr. Lusardi. Where did you get that misinformation? Dr. Lusardi only makes the ones whose Firsts die within the Demesne archipelago."

Who do I believe—this stranger, or Dr. Lusardi, my maker?

I don't know how I can get in all my questions before someone comes looking for me, or him. Maybe he feels the same. "When did Zhara disappear?" I ask. Based on the amount of time since I emerged, I know how long it's been since she died, but I don't know what happened to cost Zhara her life.

Zhara. I exist because she once existed. She is me.

The Aquine says, "Zhara went missing after a class camping trip a few months ago. She and some kids slipped off in the middle of the night, into the jungle, to do some 'raxia. When they woke up, she was gone. She hasn't been seen since. Presumed dead."

"Was she a diver?"

The corners of his mouth curl up slightly, as if in fond memory. "Yes. How did you know? That's how I knew her. We were on the same team. Zhara was an incredible athlete. She bronze medaled at the Junior Olympics."

This is such a silly question, but I can't help myself. "Was she nice?"

He lets out a bona fide laugh. "*Nice* isn't the first word that comes to mind. *Hellbeast* is what her father called her. *Spirited* is the word I'd choose, if *I* were feeling nice. I can see some of her passed into you."

Defect, I will him to say. *Just say it.*

"I am my own person," I let him know.

"Clearly," he says.

"Do you have a name, Aquine?"

"My name is Alexander Blackburn."

The name feels already etched in my heart.

Then, Alexander Blackburn does the weirdest thing. He extends his hand to mine, as a welcome, as a greeting. His hand touches mine and it's like—*zap!*—a direct connection to my First surges through every fiber of her artificial reincarnation. "Nice to meet you, Elysia."

"You mated with her," I pronounce.

Alexander looks at me quizzically. "How could you possibly know that?"

He sits back down on the plank, and extends his long legs lengthwise. He momentarily buries his face in his hands. I think he might be . . . crying? This very tall, barrel-chested, superstud Aquine?

"Are you okay?" I ask him. Maybe he's the Defect freak, not me.

He looks up. It wasn't a big cry, but there are tears welling in his blue eyes. "I didn't know she had even died. There's no chance to even grieve . . . her clone is right here. It's sick. It's not right."

"You have no right to judge me," I say.

I cannot believe so much insolence continues to escape my lips. I am writing my own death sentence talking to this Aquine. There's just something about him that prevents me from stopping myself. I hate him for that too.

"I'm *not* judging you," says Alexander. "Don't make assumptions you have no idea about. Your datacheck is wrong. I'm grieving for Zhara. Can you allow me that?"

He asks my permission? There can be no doubt. The Aquine race are definitely Defects.

He whimpers slightly, such a feminine sound that somehow sounds masculine from him. "Zhara was a beautiful girl, but so reckless. Look what's become of her. Her lost soul, now resurrected soulless. It's a lot to take in all at once. Please forgive me."

What game does he play with me, this master-race human asking a manufactured clone for absolution?

I want to know everything about Zhara. Her family. Her friends. Her diving. Her life as a free human.

But I have no opportunity to further question the Aquine. We hear shouts coming from the beach, and the Aquine immediately stands up to and heads toward the scuffle. Or perhaps he needs a reason to cease his crying jag. I follow him.

On the beach, the Sphinx and Tahir are engaged in a brawl.

"Spoiled brat," the Sphinx snarls at Tahir, and shoves him.

Tahir's response is a right hook directly to the Sphinx's jaw. Clones are usually too passive for that kind of instinctual human response to threat. Something is very, very wrong with Tahir.

"Your wife asked me to dance. I did not seek her out," Tahir says to the Sphinx.

The Sphinx answers with a jab that Tahir ducks. Tahir grabs the Sphinx into a chokehold, pinning him down to the ground.

"Break it up!" the Aquine shouts and tries to tear Tahir's arms from around the Sphinx's neck. Tahir is in such a rage that his eyes appear engorged and glassy, sweat pours down his face, and his breathing is fast and furious. He doesn't even acknowledge me. Tahir lets go of the Sphinx long enough to shove the Aquine to the ground. The Sphinx uses this opportunity to jump on top of Tahir, but Tahir flips the Sphinx over his back, sending the Sphinx directly onto a boulder in the sand.

"My knee!" the Sphinx screams.

Tariq and Bahiyya come running down the beach in search of Tahir.

The Sphinx is too injured to stand up. He hisses at Tahir, "Your eyes—like a clone! You are too strong—like a clone! Not even a clone. A Defect!"

I go to Tahir and place my arm on him, trying to calm him, comfort him, but he shrugs me away. "Get off me. I don't want you right now," he snarls at me.

There can only be one explanation for Tahir's rage. Tahir has gone Awful.

35

THE SPHINX MAY NEVER PLAY FOOTBALL AGAIN.
Everyone on Demesne is talking about it. No one knows
the full story of what happened; they only know he was
injured in a brawl on Nectar Bay, and departed immediately
thereafter under cover of night. He was airlifted back to the
Mainland for emergency surgery.

Traditionally, many Demesne families stay overnight
at Haven after the Governor's Ball and commune together
over sunrise cocktails and on into late morning brunch,
depending on when the revelers straggle onto the patio
lounge tables following the night's festivities. This morning
time is sacred to them. It's when they discuss the annual
gala's highlights and hookups. The scandals.

Mother has me sitting next to her so I may rub her neck
to help her overcome her hangover pain. The Governor has

not yet awoken, but we are joined for brunch by Ivan, Mrs. Red Whine, and Mrs. Former Beauty Queen. Over poached eggs and caviar, the group discusses the high and low points of the evening.

Mrs. Former Beauty Queen tells Mother, "Everyone just adored your Beta. What a brilliant idea to put her on display on the swing."

Mrs. Red Whine says, "But such a shame about your headache this morning, darling."

Ivan says, "So what already! The real questions is, who here knows how the Sphinx got injured?"

Mother says, "No one is talking. Not even the clones. Which must mean the reason is scandalous. Once the Governor investigates and finds out, he will tell me, and I will tell you. Promise."

I know the reason, but I remain silent. *Please let Tahir be okay.* If he is Awful, I need now more than ever to be with him. But I am too busy rubbing Mother's neck and trying to be invisible.

The plan for my escape pact with Tahir needs to be accelerated. His parents hustled him away so quickly last night, without even acknowledging my presence on the beach. All they could focus on was removing Tahir swiftly from the scene. The Aquine escorted me back to Haven and then said, simply, "I'd suggest you keep what happened here tonight to yourself."

But panic simmers beneath my skin. Tahir and I do not have time to waste for him to relearn how to hover-copter. Because of what happened with the Sphinx, his parents might return Tahir to Dr. Lusardi to be "fixed," and

Tahir will be ruined. Tahir is perfect the way he is, maybe even more so now. I like his Awful. It means he feels. The arrogant Sphinx probably had it coming.

The Governor arrives and sits down at the table. Mrs. Former Beauty Queen tells him, "Your Beta was such a success last night. I think you should ask for a higher price from the Fortesquieus."

The Governor sips from a Bloody Mary. "The deal is off. The Fortesquieus left the island early this morning. Tahir was having problems with headaches, so Tariq and Bahiyya decided to return to BC, where his doctors are, just to be safe."

Just like that? Tahir is gone? And my hope to achieve freedom with him?

It is so hard to rub Mother's neck at this moment. I want to strangle it in epic frustration.

Tahir did not leave Demesne because of a headache. He is gone because of what happened last night with the Sphinx. Tariq and Bahiyya must have decided to sidestep Dr. Lusardi completely and cloister Tahir with their private specialists in Biome City. They will try harder to train Tahir to be more like his First. I am certain: Tahir will never return to Demesne again unless he has successfully passed through the Awfuls stage, and until he has unequivocally absorbed his First's life and memories that his parents have tried to implant. Until they can make him be the son they want, Tahir will be a prisoner in his own home.

So I must find a way to get to him.

If he has turned Awful, so too shall I, in all probability. And if madness is all I have to look forward to, what do I have to lose by trying to escape on my own, so I can join my Tahir? It would be madness for me *not* to pursue my own freedom. If Tahir can't make our pact come true, *I* will.

Mother grabs at my hand on her neck and gives it a soft pat. "My sweetest Beta," Mother sighs. "I'm glad the deal is off. I didn't want to let Elysia go."

Mrs. Red Whine asks Ivan, "When do you leave for the Base, dear? Thank goodness your mother will have her Beta to console her while you're away."

"Two days," says Ivan. "Can't wait."

Ivan! Of course. Ivan is leaving the island. He will sneak me on board his private flight to the Mainland. He will help me. I am his champ.

Escape. It's the only word my head can process through their chatter. Escape escape escape.

Before, I was going through the motions of being the pet Beta at Governor's House because it never occurred to me I had other options. I emerged, and I did as I was told, because I had no reason not to, no understanding of what other possibilities existed for me. Now, I go through the motions of being their pet Beta—I have no choice—but I am calculating. How can I get out of here?

I *will* be reunited with Tahir. We will go Awful and die together. But we will do it as free Betas. Not as puppets of the humans.

The thought occurs to me that I should seek out the Aquine, Alexander Blackburn, to help. He knows that I am a Defect, but there has been no sign yet that he has revealed me as one to the Governor. While he was no stranger to Zhara, he essentially is one to me, and I've already revealed too much of myself to him. To seek him out and declare my desire for emancipation has too high a probability of leading to my expiration. No, not the Aquine.

Ivan. He is the key.

Late that night, back at Governor's House, Ivan comes into my room before I settle into bed. Ivan wants his 'raxia, as I knew he would.

"Do you want it all or would you like just one pill at a time, so you won't be tempted to use it up too quickly?" I ask him.

"Give me three," he says. "Lately, it's like, the more I do, the more I need for it to have any effect."

I hand him four pills. "Don't be stressed, brother. Are you excited to begin your new adventure at the Base?"

"You have no idea. Everything here is the same, all the time. Perfect. Boring. I can't wait to be somewhere else. To have some purpose. Action. I'll miss you, though, champ." He pats my arm affectionately. I hand him a glass of water and he gulps down the first two pills. "G'night, Beta," he says, and starts to leave my room, but I call him back.

"Would you like to play Z-Grav?" I need to buy some time for the 'raxia to take effect.

"Great idea! Awesome way to coast till the 'raxia kicks in."

We leave my room and head to the FantaSphere.

I don't need to let Ivan win this particular Z-Grav game. The double dose of 'raxia has quickly kicked in, and Ivan has no desire to race me from the ceiling to the floor. The game suctions us to the ceiling, and Ivan is content to stay there. He floats through the air and bounces against the ceiling but makes no attempt to work his way down to the floor. Nor do I. I've got him where I want him.

A big grin spreads across Ivan's face as he informs me, "Brilliant idea to play Z-Grav while on 'raxia. Why did I never do this before? I feel like I'm some psychedelic astronaut from forever ago. Everything is so upside down and gnarly and floaty." He waves his arms around and somersaults against the wall.

If there was ever a time to reveal to him that I am a Defect, this is it.

"Brother, would you like to know a secret?"

"You bet I would! I didn't know clones had secrets. Cool."

"During my time at the Fortesquieu compound, Tahir and I determined that we are mates."

"So? You and me are mates too. How's that a secret?"

"No, brother. The other kind of mates."

He bounces playfully against the wall, but his jaw drops in shock. "You think you experience . . . *love?*" He reaches his arms over his head to suction him back to the ceiling. "I must be trippin' *hard.*"

It's now or never. I proclaim, "I cannot bear the separation from Tahir now. I must go to him in Biome City. You could sneak me on your plane to the Mainland. Tahir will reward you for helping me. I promise you."

Ivan's eyes flutter closed. "No way, dude. Even feeling this mellow, I still know that's *insane.* You know I'm gonna have to tell Dad, right, champ? I just want to punch you and Tahir so hard right now, for screwing everything up like this." He tries to lunge toward me, but the Z-Grav just suctions him back to the ceiling. Frustrated, he kicks his legs in my direction, but he is too far away to harm me, and he is too tired to exert any real force.

And then he's asleep.

I end the game. We fall to the floor, and I leave him in the FantaSphere.

I have no choice now. I just wrote my own death sentence.

I must leave, on my own. *Immediately.*

36

I RACE BACK TO MY ROOM, TO CHANGE OUT OF MY pajamas into regular clothes.

I have no plan. I will jump from the window, and run like I've never run before. I'll figure it out along the way.

I must not worry, I tell myself. Worrying is for humans. Worrying distracts me from the mission.

Wherever he is right now, Tahir is safe. We will find a way to be together. Have faith.

I must not worry. I must not doubt the impossible.

If I repeat it enough times to myself, I will believe it.

The lights are out in my room as I change clothes, but I hear someone come into my room while I am standing over my bed wearing only undergarments. At first I think it's Liesel, seeking comfort. But it's not Liesel. The burly figure, visible through the faint moonlight coming through my window in the dark night, walks over to my bed. I gasp, startled. Who has come for me—the father, or the son?

"What else are you hiding, Defect?" he asks.

"Ivan?" I sputter. I hastily try to place the shirt over my head, but he grabs it from me. He shoves me down onto my bed and places his hand on my sternum, to hold me still.

"What did you do with Tahir while you were away? Did he make you his whore?"

I no longer believe that clones do not produce adrenaline. My mind knows my body is being threatened, and my heart pounds in response. Beads of sweat trickle on my forehead. "We did not do that," I reassure Ivan.

"You better not have. You belong to me. Are you the reason Tahir disappeared so suddenly? Because his parents can't have their precious son mating with a whore?"

"It's not like that, brother."

"Don't 'brother' me. Of course it's like that. You'd actually dare to escape from here to be with him? You think I would *help* you, Defect?"

"I . . . I . . . I don't know."

"Don't lie to me!"

"I'm not able to lie!" I lie. No wonder lying comes so readily to humans. It must be an instinctive response to fear.

Ivan's hands grip my neck as he lowers his body on top of mine, straddling me on the bed. His mouth is now so close I can taste his breath, making me drunk with fear.

"What are you doing?" I whisper. "Don't you want more 'raxia?"

"No. There isn't enough 'raxia in the world for what I need tonight."

"What are you doing?" I whisper.

I think I know.

I refuse to believe.

He insists on making me a true believer.

His lips descend on mine, covering my mouth in a sloppy joining of mouths that's an assault, not a kiss. I try to bite him, but that only excites him more.

"Don't," I gasp between attacks from his mouth. "Please. Don't."

I may have no soul, but I know enough to know: this is not right.

"Mother got you for me, you know."

Be a nice girl, darling Elysia, she said to me when I first arrived at Governor's House. *Let Ivan have his way.*

Was this what Mother meant?

His big hands hold me down, trapping me. I am powerless to what is happening. I try to push him away. I kick at him, I claw at him, I shove at him. I try. I am strong, but he is so much stronger. It's like the extra dosage of 'raxia now mixed with the awareness that his Beta is a traitorous Defect who loves another boy has turned him monster strong. And he likes the fight.

I close my eyes to shut out the face of this darkness. My mind removes itself from the present, going to memories of Tahir holding me through the night, Tahir touching my skin with tenderness, Tahir loving me so much he would escape all the wealth and privilege in the world to be with me, to liberate me.

Please let this not be happening.

Please let this be a dangerous FantaSphere game that will end any moment.

It happens.

"*Stop!*" I cry out.

But invocation of the safe word does not work here.

> **Violate** [VIE-uh-late]: To break through or pass by force or without right: to violate a frontier.

Ivan has stolen what I saved for Tahir.

I remind myself that what my body has just experienced was merely physical pain. My heart does not understand what to feel; it refuses to feel. Perhaps that's my true Defect power—not the ability to feel, but the ability to deny feeling.

This is why Mother really bought me. So that Ivan could have his way.

There is no such thing as safety.

Especially for a clone.

Who's now been made some human's consort.

37

ZHARA IS LUCKY TO BE DEAD.

I understand now why Astrid strived so hard to escape this hell home in paradise.

I know now why Mother does not want Ivan to soothe Liesel at night.

In—sur—rec—tion!

It's starting to make sense.

It is better not to have a soul.

Then it can't be slowly killed out of you.

38

IVAN KNOWS I AM A DEFECT, BUT HE HAS decided not to tell. Yet. He announces that by grabbing me in a chokehold when he awakes in the morning, and breathes his nasty breath into my ear. "Tell anyone about this and you are as good as dead, Defect," he hisses. "You keep quiet, and I'll keep quiet."

Last night in the FantaSphere, he threatened to tell his father on me. But this morning, everything is different. He won't tell. He wants to keep my silence.

He gets up and leaves my room, as if nothing has changed. Tomorrow, he leaves for the Base. I can only wait for him to leave. Once he's gone, my mind will be clear. I can devise a new escape plan. I must find my way back to Tahir.

Once Ivan is gone, I will train harder, until an escape

route becomes viable. Run harder, swim faster, dive stronger. I could learn to use weaponry, knives and guns—the real kind, not FantaSphere fakes. The Governor loves to hunt. He will eventually come for me anyway. Why not use him to gain skill and experience? Use him like they use me.

I could seek out the other Defects who are part of the rising rebellion. I could seek out the Aquine. Alexander Blackburn had a relationship with my First. Even if his kind doesn't like clones, his assignment on Demesne was supposedly about representing my rights.

I want to know my rights.

Ivan knows I am a Defect.

I know I am a Defect.

Does either of us know yet what a Defect really can do?

I could not save myself. But could I save others like me?

I want to be the girl Zhara once was.

Hellbeast.

Maybe I am, already.

I go to Astrid's secret drawer. I take: her knife.

In the siding of the drawer, I notice her scrawl carved into the wood. She wrote:

> *To open the blind eyes, to bring out the*
> *prisoners from the prison, and them that sit in*
> *darkness out of the prison house.* —Isaiah 42:7

Amen, sister.

Someone should pay for their sins.

* * *

The family is at Haven having lunch with friends for Ivan's
last day. Mother tried to bring me along, but Ivan sneered,
"Family only for last day. No stupid clones."

I use my alone time to take a walk to the cliff's edge at
Governor's House, to the spot where Xanthe was thrown off.

I press my fingers into the bump beneath the skin on my
wrist. I need this gone. I need to own at least one part of myself.

I use Astrid's knife to slit my skin. Blood gushes from
the slit as I maneuver to find that thing beneath. The flow of
blood actually helps me find it sooner. My locator chip slips
out from beneath the skin on my wrist. I press a rag onto
my bloody wrist to contain the wound. Then I toss the chip
down into their precious Io.

I feel no pain. I feel total 'raxia.

Isaiah was right. The prisoners need to be brought out
of the prison.

Bad things happen to clones on Demesne because no
clones speak up. They can't—unless they're Defects. They're
too comatose, being the humans' slaves.

I am a Defect and I am alive and I want someone to pay
for their sins before it's too late.

If I tell the truth, it will set me free. I can't even wait one
more day until after Ivan leaves. The outcome will be the same.

If Mother knows, she will send me away. The shame will
be too great.

I find Mother in the massage room after the family's lunch.
She lies on her stomach, face down. She speaks through the
opening in the massage table's headrest. "Elysia, darling, I
missed you at lunch, but Ivan is just so bossy sometimes.

Maybe you could take Ivan for a run to help him burn off all that brute energy he's accumulated for the Base. The cook is preparing a grand meal for his last night with us. Make that boy work up an appetite! You've been such a wonderful companion to him. He's in the best shape of his life. The Governor is very pleased."

"I did as you said, Mother. I let him have his way. Last night in my room."

I am as good as dead anyway. I just don't care anymore. Whatever they're going to do to me, let it begin. Release me from the agony of this home.

For a moment she looks up from the headrest, confused. Then her expression clears as she understands. "Good girl," she says.

Tears well in my eyes. They surprise me. I have never cried before. "There is more," I say. "Ivan takes 'raxia. He makes it himself and keeps it hidden. He is an addict. He will probably not survive at the Base without 'raxia." Tears gush freely from my eyes and I make no attempt to stop their wet shame from appearing on my face.

Let Ivan suffer some consequences too.

But Mother is not concerned that her son is addicted to the very drug that is leading Demesne clones astray. "You *cry?*" Mother gasps.

Her eyes meet mine, her look quickly turning from shock to rage. The clone masseuse drops his bottle of oil to the floor.

"Leave us!" Mother screams at him. The rippling-muscled, bare-chested man leaves the room.

Mother sits up on the table, covered by a sheet. "Defect!" she accuses me. "You cut your hair yourself, didn't you?

Bahiyya had nothing to do with it. You are a Defect!"

I've just told her that her son has violated me, and she is concerned that I cut my own hair?

"Defect!" I admit. "It's true! And I want to be sent away, or I will make sure everyone on this island knows that the Governor's son is supplying 'raxia to clones."

I just made that lie up on the spot. Good one, Elysia. Maybe you can survive out in the wild.

"I own you," Mother retorts. "How dare you." She lets out a howl of frustration, then redirects her yelling to me: *"Go to your room! And don't come out until I say you may!"*

Evening comes, with no communication from anyone, until a note is slipped under my door, written in a young girl's scrawl.

> Dear Elysia,
> I don't understand why everyone is so mad
> at you but I want you to know I love you
> and I will sneak you chocolate if you want it.
> Love, Liesel
> PS-Not JK!

I slip a note back under the door for her.

> Dear Liesel,
> Go away so you don't get in trouble. And
> please keep your bedroom door locked at night.
> I love you too.
> Elysia

There was never a lock on my bedroom door or Astrid's door, but there is one on Liesel's now. I put it there this afternoon while the family was at Haven. I told the butler it was Mother's orders.

My room is too distant from Mother and the Governor's quarters to hear them, but I can sense it. The household is in turmoil.

All I can do is wait. Guards are stationed below my window in case I try to jump.

Just after night falls, Ivan comes to my room. He quietly opens my door. From his stealth, I know he has been forbidden to visit me.

"You bitch," he whispers. "I ought to kill you."

He pushes me onto the bed and straddles me in that familiar way. He clenches his hands around my neck. He means it.

I gasp for breath, as his fingers burrow into my neck, pushing the life out of me. He's going to kill me. I start to lose consciousness, and only desperation and fear keep my heart pounding, hard.

Darkness descends, as Awful arises.

Ivan has no idea what's coming. Neither do I.

Last time I did not fight hard enough. This time, I will.

I reach for Astrid's knife hidden underneath my pillow and plunge it into Ivan's heart. He tries to fight me, but the shock of the sudden, direct hit is too much—he cannot match me. His is bigger, but I am more agile. I want to win more.

Again and again, I plunge the dagger into his heart the way he forced himself into me. I dedicate each cut: For

Xanthe. *Stab*. For Becky. *Stab*. For Tahir. *Stab*. For every manufactured slave on this island hell. *Stab stab stab*.

Someone should pay for their sins.

I'll show you Awful, humans.

I can't even see what I'm doing. All I know is rage, and panic, and darkness.

Finally, Ivan collapses on top of me. His dark red blood gushes all over the white sheets, spilling onto the mattress, soaking my back and bottom underneath where I lie.

I hear a deafening scream.

It's not my own.

It's Liesel, standing in the doorway, holding a steaming plate of macaroni and cheese she has brought for me.

Mother and the Governor hurry into my room after Liesel's scream.

I've pushed Ivan off me and I stand on my bed, trapped.

They see their dead son lying at my bloodied feet. They see their murderous Beta, splattered in their son's blood, quaking in shock and fear.

"Where's my rifle?" the Governor shouts. "I'm going to kill her right now. Liesel, get out of here." He turns to Mother. "See what you've caused us!"

Mother falls to the floor. "My baby!" she whimper moans. "My precious boy!"

What would a hellbeast do?

I look out the open window above my bed.

I should jump out of it.

I do.

* * *

There's no time to think. All I can do is run.

The guards stationed below my window didn't expect me to jump out of it. They heard the shouting and were returning inside the house to help the Governor just as I jumped. My feet land on the ground and I am able to get a running start ahead of them before they realize what's happened. I run toward the stairs that go down the cliff side. If I can get to Io's magical waters, the sea will save me. It has to.

They follow me, the Governor and his henchmen. They're faster than I would have expected. The henchmen catch me at the point where they had Xanthe trapped.

There's nothing to do but wait.

I face them dead on at the edge of the cliff. I'd rather die by the Governor's rifle than be thrown off the cliff. It will be quicker.

The Governor points the rifle at me as his henchmen stand on either side of me. They don't bother to hold me down. I have nowhere to go.

The Governor presses his finger to the trigger.

They'll merely toss my body into the sea once it's over.

Unless I toss it there first.

Either I'll make it or I won't. It's about one hundred feet down to the churning sea, with just a craggy cliff in the way.

I've changed my mind.

I'd rather die my way than by the Governor's hands.

I turn around, bend my knees and in an instant—

He shoots.

I dive.

39

MY EYES OPEN TO A CLOUDLESS BLUE SKY
that appears to stretch into forever.

Banana trees surround me overhead. A toucan is perched
on the branch of a eucalyptus tree near my side. The smell
of gardenias and jasmine flowers and a distant sea breeze
permeates the air.

I cough. Wherever I am, the dull, thin air here is so not
premium. And I am swaying.

A female voice that sounds familiar chirps nearby,
singing an improvised version of "Children of Hope."

> *"In these troubled times of darkness and fright,*
> *From them we receive the gift most sublime.*
> *They are our dreams, our loves,*

Our children of hope—
Nope, I meant dope—
Dopey children, ha-ha-ha. . . ."

Back and forth, I sway. I can't lift my head too far—it
aches—but my hands grasp pieces of rope beneath my body,
supporting it. I see the rope attached to banana trees at
either end of my bed. No, it's not a bed. I'm swinging on a
hammock. I think I'm in the jungle.
I'm alive.
That's all I know.

"You're awake," the female voice says. I try to turn my head
to identify the face attached to the voice, but pain grips my
neck and I must keep my head idle. I close my eyes again, to
block the hurt pounding my head. My body feels as though
it's been smashed to bits. I can't move.
Sway. Nice, gentle, breezy sway. Helps headache go away.
A hand, rough-skinned but warm, touches my arm.
The female voice says, "Welcome back, Elysia. Some of us
weren't sure you would survive. I never doubted."
"Who are you?" I mumble. My eyelids open slightly
and I see her face staring down at mine. She has slanted
black eyes with high cheekbones against skin burned a crisp
toasty color, and she is bald. The right side of her face, at her
temple, is scarred with purplish burn marks.
She must notice where my eyes are focusing, because
she touches the burn scars, a deformity rendered grotesquely
beautiful on her bold face. It announces: I survived. "This

is where my fleur-de-lis used to be," she says. "I am M-X. The Defects call me the Healer. Their leader found you and brought you to me. You were practically dead."

"You have healed me?"

"Time will tell. I have tried. You speak. That is a good sign."

"Where am I?"

"You're on the island at the farthest end of the Demesne archipelago. The humans considered this island so uninhabitable they gave it to no name. I call it Mine, because I am the only person who lives here. Well, you and your rescuer also. Just until you are strong enough for me to send you both away."

"Is this the Rave Caves?" I ask.

"The Rave Caves are a dream resort compared to Mine. Only the most bonkers clone alive would want to live here. That would be me, dearie."

"Are you a Defect?"

"Aren't we all?"

"Why do you seem familiar, yet not?"

"I use to be called Mei-Xing."

"The orientation video!"

"Yes, I used to be Dr. Lusardi's top prop. Until she discovered my gifts for healing. Then, I was labeled a Defect, and tortured."

"You escaped?"

M-X looks around her, at the wild jungle where only we and nature dwell. "Clearly."

"Are you sure I'm not dreaming?"

Her hard hand gives a sharp pinch to my elbow. I flinch.

"I'm sure you're not dreaming. You should be dead, Elysia."

Soon enough I will learn why I should be dead, and how I lived. For now, I must return to sleep.

"Tired," I say.

I can't stay awake one more second. Please, I think, if I am truly still alive, then let my sleep bring dreams of Tahir.

My dreams are not of Tahir.

My dreams are of blood and screams and terror. Murder.

I took a life.

Please, let me not wake back up.

40

THE NEXT TIME I AWAKE, IT IS NIGHT.

I have been moved. I am on a bed of juniper boughs placed on the ground, in a small enclosed space, a simple thatched dwelling with an open entryway through which I can see a campfire burning outside.

My headache is gone. I reach my arms above my head and stretch my toes as far down as they'll go. I feel born anew, ready to face the world. Or at least ready to face the (mostly) deserted island of Mine.

I stand up on my own, for the first time in I don't how long. My head momentarily processes a sensation of dizziness, but it quickly passes, and I walk outside. A blue-and-white batik-dyed sarong covers my body, and my feet are bare.

M-X is sitting by the fire, hand-feeding a banana to a small monkey nestled in the crook of her arm. She sees me and says, "You wake, and now you walk. I like this progress. How are you feeling?"

"Much better."

"Excellent. I guess you'd like to know how you got here?" I nod and sit down on a log opposite M-X. "What do you remember?"

"They were trying to kill me. I dove from the cliff. I don't know what happened after that."

"You have quite an abundance of strength and stamina— perhaps more even than your First. That plunge followed by that swim would have killed most anyone else. It's probably because your swim was within Io's ring that you survived. The nurturing waters sustained you."

"I swam all the way here? That doesn't seem possible."

"It's not. Mine is at least twenty nautical miles from Demesne. After you jumped, you managed to swim to a buoy farther out to sea. You tapped out there, dehydrated and incapacitated. You lost consciousness floating on the buoy, where you were discovered the next morning by a diver with a boat, who delivered you to me to be healed. You were close to dead."

"How long have I been here?"

"Just over a week. You have been in and out of consciousness."

"Are the humans looking for me?"

"Yes. But you were smart enough to remove your locator chip. They've tracked your chip to the bottom of the sea.

You are presumed dead, but no body has been found yet, either. They're still searching for a body, but they've got bigger problems on Demesne now."

"Like what?"

"Like, murder. There's never been such a crime on Demesne. And committed by a clone, no less. The island is basically under lockdown now, until the residents can be assured no more such mutinies can take place among their workers."

"How do you know all this? Do you have a Relay?"

"We have devised ways of communicating outside the humans' periphery. Those who are part of the cause have developed an underground network to Relay information to one another."

"The Insurrection? Is that your cause?"

"Yes. The Insurrection's first major strike was about to go down right before the murder."

"By who? How?" Xanthe and Miguel! They must have been part of the group planning this, I realize.

"All around you, there were clones and sympathizers who were setting everything in place to make the first attack. You probably didn't notice. Lusardi may have too precisely customized your chip to teen settings, so that you only saw the micro world of your own social interactions."

I believe I have been mildly insulted. "I noticed bigger things going on. I just had no understanding of what to do with the information. Sorry if I ruined the plan."

"Don't be sorry. You are a symbol of freedom to the clones now."

"I took a life. I am more sorry for that." My eyes go moist as tears roll down my face. The tears make me feel sad, but they also bring relief.

M-X says, "They have enslaved us. Tortured us. Expired us. They do not feel remorse. Neither should you."

"I can't help the remorse I feel." The tears on my face provoke a revolt in my body, which convulses into a sudden, bitter sob. "I did a terrible thing. I'm sorry. So very sorry." Ivan may have wronged me, but should he have paid for that with his life? "I killed my own brother."

"He was *not* your brother," M-X snaps. "And he would not cry for you."

I am the worst kind of Defect. I feel. I sob. I murder. "Am I Awful?" I ask M-X.

"It's possible your Awfuls are beginning. It's just as possible you acted in self-defense, which had nothing to do with raging hormones and everything to do with a basic instinct of self-preservation. Too soon to tell."

More than the possible onset of Awful, I should be worrying about the humans who are looking for me. "Is it safe here? How come the humans do not take back this island or the Rave Caves? Surely they have the capability to control these places for themselves."

M-X says, "By law, these islands in the archipelago are Mainland territory. Only the Demesne vacation haven exists independently. To the Mainland government, these other islands are unproductive dots on a map. One island was made a virtual eco-bubble because of wealth and privilege. But that's the island with the most lush and amenable vegetation. These other places are not worth the humans' bother. The terrain is too difficult. To tamper with those who do use the other islands could risk a full-scale war. They know that."

"But surely they are mightier. With their aircraft and weaponry and bombs."

"Mightier with technology. But those of us who live on these desolate islands know how to utilize the earth better. We can navigate the jungles and caves. The military has bigger problems on the Mainland than dealing with these specks of land in the middle of the ocean. It is not worth their while to use their expensive arsenal on us. So long as the Defects do not attack Demesne, basically no one cares."

"So we Defects are essentially worthless to the humans?"

"Yes."

"Awesome."

"Indeed," M-X demurs.

"Dr. Lusardi must care, though. She must want to control the Defects."

"Hardly," says M-X. "She needs to control the Defects that are on Demesne. The others, once they are gone, she does not concern herself about."

"How can that be? The humans brought her there to manufacture their clones. Surely her profit margin and reputation are affected if Defects run amok in the Rave Caves."

"That's the humans' problem, not hers."

"I don't get it."

M-X traces the burn scar on her temple with her finger. "When you were at Governor's House, did you never notice that Dr. Lusardi never made visits to check up on the clones that she manufactured? That she never attended social functions or involved herself in island life there at all, outside her compound?"

"I didn't notice. But now that you mention it . . ."

"Lusardi doesn't care because Lusardi herself is a machine. Like us, her only mission there is to serve."

"Ha! Like a clone."

"Not *Ha!* Lusardi *is* a clone. Duplicated from the original Dr. Larissa Lusardi, who was a brilliant scientist but with an unfortunate streak of righteousness. When she objected too vehemently against using her clones for servitude, they murdered her. They transferred her memory and skill into her clone, but extracted her First's soul, to get rid of those irritating ethics that prevented her First from dutifully fulfilling Demesne humans' purchase orders."

The fire crackles more quietly as the fire begins to die down. We will need to replenish the wood soon, or retire to sleep. I realize I have neglected to ask M-X the most important question: "Which Defect rescued and delivered me here?"

"Look behind you. He's human, not Defect. Although he has been chosen to lead the Army of Defects hiding out in the Rave Caves."

I turn my head and see a tall figure carrying freshly chopped logs for the fire. Over the logs, I see his blond hair, and as he walks closer and approaches the fire, the deep blue of his turquoise eyes.

It is the Aquine, Alexander Blackburn. He saved me.

41

"I DID NOT SAVE YOU," ALEXANDER INFORMS me. "You saved yourself."

It's the next morning. M-X has grown tired of her companions, and has retreated to the other side of the island to collect herbs, insects, and shells for her remedies. I have no job here yet, besides to rock in a hammock as I continue to regain my strength, which M-X says is my only job right now. It's kind of an awesome gig, actually, all this doing nothing in the middle of this tropical nowhere. It's also kind of boring. Eventually, sooner rather than later, I hope, I will have to get up out of this hammock, and get on with my life.

I have no idea how to do that. The hammock seems pretty cozy, for now.

"How did you find me?" I ask Alexander Blackburn, who has chosen to while away his morning rocking on the hammock opposite me.

"I was part of the search party sent to retrieve your body after you leapt from the cliff at Governor's House. I'm a commando diver. Or, was."

"What does that mean, was?"

"It means, I'm officially AWOL since bringing you here. The military thinks either I lost my life on the mission, or I've abandoned my job, which would cause me to be court-martialed if captured."

"M-X says you lead the Army of Defects? They're not just a myth."

"They're not a myth. They're why I joined the military."

"So you're a human traitor?"

"That's a matter of perspective. My people are eco-warriors. Joining the military was the best way to try destroy Demesne from the inside." My stomach rumbles so loudly that he glances over at me. "Are you hungry?"

"So hungry," I say. Since there's no longer any reason for me to deny the pleasure I take from food, it seems I grow hungrier and hungrier. He laughs. "Why funny?" I ask.

"Just like Zhara. The girl loved to eat."

His comment angers me. "My appetite is my own. I like to eat because food is tasty, especially chocolate. Not because of her."

"It's definitely your own thing, then," Alexander Blackburn says. "Zhara did not like chocolate."

"Barbaric!" I exclaim, then cringe, appalled by how much I sound like Mother.

The Aquine sits up on his hammock. "Then let's go get lunch. No chocolate in these parts, but we can forage up something good, I bet."

"Where do we get lunch, Alexander Blackburn?"

"We hunt it or fish it, is where. And please stop calling me by my full name."

"Then what should I call you? Aquine?"

He chuckles again. "Zhara called me Xander.'"

"I shall call you Alex.'" I stand up from my hammock. "Let's go fish some lunch, Alex. I would like to go to where the water is."

We traipse through the jungle brush toward the beach. Along the way, Alex tells me how he as an Aquine joined the military to train to become a covert operative, when he was in fact already a covert operative.

So, it's true what Xanthe once told me. There really are humans in power who want to help the Defects regain their souls, who want to abolish the legality of cloned servitude on Demesne.

Zhara's father became actively involved in the cause after the death of Zhara's mother, in a clash during an anti-clone servitude protest. He's a conservative, rigid man, says Alex—the last person one would ever think to be on board with the pro-Defect alliance. When Zhara was still a child, his wife abandoned the family because they disagreed about her joining the protest movement. But his wife's death, the loss of his daughter's mother, changed his opinions, and he became secretly involved in the movement. Zhara's father is a key "inside man" in the military. He recruited Alexander into the cause and introduced him to the small but growing network of military officers who want to abolish the practice of clone servitude on Demesne.

"How would Zhara's father feel about her clone?" I ask Alex.

We've reached the beach. I don't wait for the answer to his question. Instinctively, I run to the water. I don't realize until I see the white sand and the white-tipped waves rolling over the sapphire blue water how much I've missed the ocean. I step into it. This non-bioengineered water is more chilly than Io's and does not magically soothe and caress my skin, but it wakes me and pleases me to be in it.

"Help me," Alex calls to me from the beach. I turn back around. He stands at a canoe situated on the sand, his chiseled torso framed by the sunlight behind his back.

Together, we guide the canoe into the water. I step inside and he does too, launching the boat as he jumps into it. We sit on opposite ends of the canoe and paddle our way a bit farther into the ocean, still in shallow water, but away from the beach.

"I don't know how I will be able to tell Zhara's father," says Alex, acknowledging what I've suspected: Zhara's dad, who is my biological father too, I suppose, would not welcome his daughter's clone.

"I don't understand why you are part of this movement. Don't Aquine want to eradicate cloning because it's not natural? Isn't yours a cult of genetically engineered people?"

"First, we are not a cult. Second, the Aquine engineered themselves by choice, not because of profit motives. Our race was formed with the intention to pool the best elements in humankind, so that our people could live harmoniously and productively on Earth, outside the confines of greed. We feel that cloning is a form of slavery."

"So you are not an abolitionist?"

"I know cloning can't be stopped. My mission—my hope—is that one day clones will be given the same fundamental rights as humans, and never again used as slaves."

The fish are easily visible through the clear tropical water surrounding our canoe. But I have already killed a human. I can't kill a fish too. It's too soon. I refuse the spear gun Alex tries to hand me.

"I thought you said you were hungry," he says.

My head shakes vehemently. I can't even *look*. "Well, hold the bucket so I can drop the fish in."

I hold the bucket firm at his feet as he spears fish for our dinner. Hearing the dying fish flail in the bucket makes me want to throw up. I must distract myself from this murder, even if it does mean lunch.

"How did you end up on Demesne?" I ask him.

"I trained at the Base to become a commando. Demesne is the most sought after and difficult assignment to get, but we suspected I had a good shot at it, because I am Aquine. Because who supposedly cares less about clone rights than an Aquine? Who better for the job of rubber stamping the annual report to the Replicant Rights Commission?"

"I heard how you protected our rights on Demesne. You protected them so well you sent the other teen Beta back to

Dr. Lusardi's to be tortured. There's no way she set off that bomb."

"She didn't. But someone had to take the fall. She was an easy target. A 'raxia addict, close to death—or Awful—already." He says it so casually. "Collateral damage, they call it in the military."

"I call it an atrocity," I inform him. Then, I ask, "So, who did set off the bomb?"

"I did," Alex says. "On the orders of the Governor. The goal was to dismantle a small 'raxia ring hiding out in the jungle near Dr. Lusardi's compound. The teen Beta was blamed so the Governor could have cover for the real reason behind the bomb, which was in fact a very public warning to those supporting the Insurrection." He pauses and looks me in the eyes. "I am sorry," he says. "This battle requires hard choices. They will only get harder and harder."

Like the choice he made to go AWOL, for me, risking his own life—and his imminent death should the military recapture him.

I've lost too much to mourn more now for what's already gone. My life ahead should be an open canvas, filled with possibility. If only Tahir could be included in it.

"*Sorry* won't bring Becky back," I tell Alex. There's nothing left to say on the subject; I'm done discussing it. I stand up in the boat, preparing to dive. "I'd like to go for a quick swim."

But Alex looks at the clouds forming in the sky and says, "Rain's coming. But there's a great swimming hole on that atoll over there." He points to a small island about a quarter mile from our boat. "I'll take you there tomorrow if it clears up."

"Can I dive there too?"

"There are some elevated diving spots, yes. But maybe that's not a good idea in your delicate condition, daredevil." He says that last word with too much familiarity.

"Daredevil? Was that what Zhara was?"

"Yes."

"Then don't call me that. And I am feeling more than well enough to dive again."

42

ALEX MEDITATES AT SUNSET EVERY NIGHT.
It's some Aquine thing. Reflecting on gratitude. Whatever.
It's no FantaSphere adventure.

His absence allows me and M-X to share the evening
by the campfire, talking. Here on Mine, M-X does not treat
me as a companion, but as just a regular girl. Here on Mine,
it does not matter if I go Awful. I am wild and free already
here.

"I would like to stay here," I tell M-X.

"Now that you are better?" she asks.

I nod.

"Impossible," says M-X. "I heal, and I send away. It's no
fun for me having long-term guests."

"I don't believe you. Everyone desires companionship."

"Not true. And if you'd witnessed the things I did in Dr.

Lusardi's infirmary, you'd prefer a lifetime of solitude after that too. Besides, you will have to leave with the Aquine soon. He has imprinted on you."

"Excuse me?"

But I think I already know. *You know you own me, Z.* It's starting to make sense.

Aquine mate for life. Whatever happened to tear them apart, he is still bonded to Zhara. And by extension, then, to me. Whether I want that or not. Whether I desire Alex in return or not.

"You are his mate," M-X says. "He rescued you. He nursed you back to health."

"You said that you healed me."

"I gave you herbal remedies. He stayed by your side night and day, wiped your brow, held your hand, fed you broth, kept you clean. I think he even prayed for you."

If he thinks he owns me now, he's got another think coming.

I don't want to be owned by anybody, ever again.

M-X's pet monkey climbs onto her shoulder, jumps to the banana tree above her, and pulls down a new bunch of bananas. He pulls a banana from the bunch and hands it to M-X for her to peel for him, but she returns the banana to the monkey's hand. "Go over there and offer some food to our guest. She must be very hungry now that she's feeling better."

The monkey steps over to me and offers me a banana. I take it, but do not peel it. The monkey regards me quizzically. So I peel the banana and offer it back to him. "Here, you have it."

M-X says, "You need to eat. While you convalesced, you were fed broth enhanced with healing herbs, but you must be yearning for richer food now."

"I am, but for some reason the smell of bananas makes me nauseous. I guess you don't have a secret stash of chocolate somewhere here? Perhaps a strawberry shake?"

"Your days of strawberry shakes are over. Not only are they not available here in the wild, but your body should not process Dr. Lusardi's chemicals anymore either."

"Why not?"

"Because you are pregnant."

I turn my head around, checking. Am I in a FantaSphere game? Or is this some type of sick joke on M-X's part?

"Not possible," I finally say. "Replicants cannot replicate."

"That's what we thought. Until now."

"How do you know?"

"I am a Healer. I know. And your blood sample confirmed my suspicion."

"I refuse." My hands press into my belly. I feel nothing. "There is a thing inside me? I want it gone." The very thought of my body producing a new being is repulsive to me. I've barely started my own life. If indeed there is a new life growing in my body, it was conceived in violence, and it was not meant to be. This shouldn't even be possible. So many lies these humans have fed me.

This is so unfair! I want to scream.

M-X says, "That 'thing' is life, and it is just as much a fighter as you, apparently. You must respect it. If this is possible for you, perhaps it is possible for the rest of our kind. You are hope."

"I took a life. I am not worthy of being a symbol of freedom and hope. I am a coward."

"If that were true, I would not have bothered trying to heal you."

I protest! "I can't have a baby. I don't know even know how to be a person yet. Will you help it?" I ask her. "If it is emerged."

"Born," she corrects me. "It will be born. Not emerged."

"If it is born," I say. The level of desperation and fear I suddenly feel is as shocking as the news that my body, which was not supposed to be able to reproduce, can indeed reproduce. This news is more awful than losing Tahir, than learning of our imminent Awfuls. "Will you take care of it?" I beseech M-X. "I cannot. I do not want it."

"You do not know what you want. You've spent your short life being brainwashed to believe you're not supposed to even have wants. You can't make this decision now about what grows inside you. It's too early on."

"I can!" I assert.

I can't.

"Help me get rid of it," I plead with M-X.

"I have promised the Aquine I won't, in exchange for his taking you away now that you are healed. Aquine believe in the sanctity of life. He will take you as his mate now. He will love and raise your child as his."

"That's absurd! I do not ask that of him!"

"You don't have to. It's his biological imperative. He can't *not* do that, with his mate. Your First was his mate, regardless of whether he and she were old enough or ready to make that bond. It happened. And Aquine mate for life.

Which means you are his mate now, because she once was."

I may as well be living back at Governor's House. I am given no choice about where I would like to go, or how. I am just told. More and more, I understand why human teenagers become rebellious. It must be so they can take control of their own lives.

What control could I possibly take for myself?

I am a pregnant, teenaged Beta clone who has murdered the son of the chief executive lording over an island owned by the world's richest people. I have no education, no wealth, no resources. A choice in my own destiny is not really an option right now. I am obliged to go along with anyone who can help me survive this next stage of my life.

43

THE OCEAN STORMS OUTSIDE IO'S RING ARE particularly harsh; they're what caused First Tahir to lose his life. All of that energy used within the ring has made the ocean beyond Io's violet waters more and more unstable. There's a reason only random Defects and pirates try to traverse it.

I dream about this violent, nonviolet ocean that night, as a loud thunderstorm passes over our jungle fortress, dripping rain onto my body through the holes in the thatched hut's roof, filling my heart with terror with each bolt of lightning and crack of thunder.

In my dream, I have gone fishing with Alex.

As we set sail, I think, Humans amaze me. They have created the technology to replicate themselves, and the technology to craft eco-bubble paradise islands in the middle of nowhere serviced by their manufactured clones. They have built cities, destroyed cities, and built cities anew. They have gone to space and constructed colonies light-years away from their beloved Earth. And yet, for all their technical prowess, there are those among them who still travel via . . . inflatable boat?

Seriously? I shout to Alex over the roar of the ocean's waves. *An inflatable boat?*

This boat was all that was available from the Rave Caves, he replies. *They are not exactly teeming with supplies there. It was either this boat, or swim.*

The sky turns a dark gray as fog wraps around the boat. Quickly, visibility declines to nil. When we left the island of Mine, the sky was clear and the sea calm. He won't admit it aloud, but I know. We are lost. The churning sea has tossed us off course. The ocean must be punishing me for what I did to Ivan. The sky cracks open in thunderous fury, sending a bolt of lightning directly to the boat's hull. As the boat starts to deflate, the Aquine says, *Looks like it's a swim after all.*

The water is cold and bitter, furious. It wants to swallow us whole. Waves pound us, the current batters us, yet we manage to swim.

Stay close! Alex shouts at me. *We just have to make it to the atoll.*

He need not instruct me. My body knows just what to do. It has done this before.

This is how Zhara died.

I don't know if it's because of the lightning strike, the proximity to her mighty love man, or because I am just the most utterly defective Defect Beta, but here in my own dream, Z's visions return. I'm grateful for the vision, actually—seeing what she experienced allows me to separate myself from my nightmare's impossible swim through the stormy sea.

The previous visions I borrowed from her provided glimpses only of him. Beneath the water, he beckoned and enticed, a siren call. *You know you own me, Z,* Alex would say. It's Zhara's voice I hear now, for the first time. It's the same voice as mine, but harder, angrier. She was very bossy.

Woo-hoo! Death party! she shouts. I see the waves battering the dinghy she is on. I see two other people on the boat with her, a male and a female, perhaps around the same age as she, but their faces are blurry. I can't see them. I can only sense their fear and panic in direct conflict with the serene relaxation coursing through their veins. Zhara and her friends had gone on an unauthorized excursion away from their school camping trip. They wanted to sit on the ocean and do some 'raxia and swim as close to Io's ring as they could get. They never even got close before the storm set in. Quickly their 'raxia dreamscape turned into their 'raxia nightmare. To survive, they had to abandon ship. But the drug they'd taken worked directly against them, sapping them of the focus and strength they needed in the moment of crisis.

At least we'll die happy, Zhara thought.

Even she didn't believe it.

She doubted she was strong enough for this swim. Persistent, nagging doubts were what crippled her strength throughout her life. *I'm not good enough, not strong enough. I'm not worthy.* But she was.

It was the 'raxia that killed her, not the stormy swim. She took the 'raxia to feel ease, to feel something other than the pain that had welled so big in her heart that she wanted to die rather than experience one more day of such heartache, a hurt so big it had killed her competitive focus and cost her a place on the Olympic diving team. She'd discovered that doing 'raxia made the pain go away. But this time, the 'raxia made her too easeful to swim. Sober, she could have survived the storm. But in this moment of crisis, not only would she not make it, she'd be taking her friends down with her. They hadn't been keen on leaving their school group. But she'd begged. Teased. Gotten her way as always by promising an epic good time and an adventure to brag about to the group later, once they returned to the camping site.

Her nightmare is my nightmare. I struggle to swim through the churning waters, fighting for survival, just as she did. I see clearly what happened to Zhara. She drowned. She went down not for lack of strength, but because her heart simply stopped. OD'd. She wanted so badly to stop her heart from hurting. The 'raxia allowed her heart to comply.

44

AFTER MY NIGHT'S BATTERED SLEEP, THE
morning sun beams bright and peaceful, as if the sky had
never unleashed hell the night before.

"You promised me a swim," I tell Alex the next morning,
when I find him clearing the brush of downed branches
from the night's storm. "I want a nice, refreshing swim. In
calm water."

He drops the downed tree he'd been carrying away. "Let's
go," says Alex. "I'm always available for a swim."

We take the canoe to the nearby atoll he pointed out
yesterday. It's a coral-reefed island comprising a few miles
total of dry land with beach and trees, encircling a central
water source. On a bright, warm and sunny day like today,
without a cloud in the sky, while dolphins swim around the

atoll, green turtles waddle across the sand, and seabirds fly above us, humans might consider this stretch of beach some kind of paradise.

Zhara would have loved to be stranded on a deserted island with Alexander Blackburn. She might have called the experience a honeymoon. I think of it as yet another curiosity I must experience until I can ultimately be reunited with Tahir.

A pregnant Beta can dream, right?

Alexander and I are not the first to discover this island. Others have been here before us and scattered their relics throughout the island. They've carved their names into cactus flowers. *Amber* ♥ *Pierre. Jake + Nicholas. Alone with God and turtles, Ezekiel.* They've left pieces of clothing—T-shirts and swimsuits—hanging from tree branches.

Alex leads me to a spot in the middle of the atoll where emerald-green trees encircle a perfect blue-water lagoon lined in pink sand. Paradise, for real. Somehow, Alex thinks I need help with this paradise. *Ha!* Paradise might be the *only* terrain I am educated to navigate. He tries to take my hand, to steady my steps into the warm water, as if I am fragile. I pull my hand away from him.

"I am sixteen," I tell Alexander. "I know how to take care of myself."

"You are the equivalent of seventeen," Alexander says. "Zhara's birthday was last month."

I do not really know what to say to him. There is so much to ask him, but it's hard to focus when every time he looks at me, I know he is seeing her. He sees my vining and my fuchsia eyes, and I am sure he mourns. When I look at him, wearing only black swim trunks on his extremely muscled body, I see his turquoise eyes and the wisps of sun-kissed blond hair trailing around his face, and all I can think is, You did *it* with her. You did *it* with Other Me.

I cannot deny: it is a thing of utter beauty to watch Alex swim.

He doesn't just swim in the water; it's like he dances in it. His strokes, so powerful, are so graceful at the same time; he's like a human fish who belongs in this beneficent tropical water.

Perhaps he could teach the thing growing inside me to swim too. There's not much regarding the human feeling termed happiness I will be able to offer this thing conceived in violence. But an Aquine could love and protect it as I never will be able to.

I swim, following Alex to the middle of the lagoon where the water is deep, but our feet can still touch the bottom. I sink my feet into the warm sand of the seabed. The sun seems to shine directly around Alex, as if enshrouding him in a halo. "Tell me more about Zhara?" I request.

We both begin to tread water, to keep moving while keeping conversation afloat. Alex says, "I first met her when I was sixteen and she was thirteen. I helped coach her diving team. Zhara was an amazing diver, training for the Olympics, but she had a lot of family trouble. She lost her mother very young, and was always fighting with her father. She could have been a true athletic champion but her basic nature—rebellious, tempestuous—was always at war with her physical gifts. Soon after she turned sixteen, I was nineteen, and had decided to join the military. In the water, we were mates, because there, Zhara was her best self. But on land, she was too much to handle. She was willful and selfish. She was constantly trying to provoke me into a relationship with her. I was very attracted to her, but I thought her not mature enough to mate with yet. But then, one night, soon before I left for the Base, I gave in to temptation. She dared me. And I could not resist her any longer. But the next morning, I broke it off. Told her it had been a mistake, that she was too young, too impetuous. I left for the Base, and from what I heard, she slowly spiraled out of control until that camping trip, when she disappeared."

"I thought Aquines imprinted for life. How could you have broken it off with her after?" I ask him. I have no reason to defend her, but I can hear that my tone sounds accusatory.

Alex says, "Aquine engineering can have flaws, just as yours does. It's not one-hundred-percent perfect. That is my shame, my failure. My rejection of Zhara after what we shared should not have been able to happen, but it did." He stops treading long enough to stand again and observe me. "I acted callously, and in direct contradiction to the very nature of my people. I am not proud. And now, here you are."

Hey, sun, I want to say to the light's halo effect framing his muscled body. *Guess the Aquine's not such an angel, after all.*

He is honest. I have to respect that about him.

I swim around his standing figure, inspecting him the

way the humans have so frequently inspected me. Appraising. His sculpted biceps and pectorals. The bronze of his tanned skin. His sun-kissed blond hair. His turquoise eyes, staring so intently into mine now. Wanting.

Alex releases his feet from the water's bottom and returns to swimming—this time, chasing me through the water. I laugh as he darts beneath and around me, and I do the same, resurrecting this aqua dance I know he did so many times with her.

But *I* own this experience now. She is gone. He is mine for the taking, should I choose.

Do I even have a choice?

I let him catch me. We are breathless as his big arms encircle my body, and pull me close to him. I look up into the pools of his eyes, and I know. He is not Tahir. But he will do.

With Alex, I can join the Army of Defects in the Rave Caves. Alex can train me so that I may be part of the Insurrection. Be the symbol of freedom they want me to be. They want to rise up; *I* want to rise up. I want purpose and direction, not a life cut short like Zhara's. I want to finish what Xanthe and Miguel started.

Alex will take care of the being growing inside me. He is not my love. But he is an excellent solution. My choice is decided. I will join his call to arms. *His* arms, so beefy and strong—are so very enticing. Not such a sacrifice to want to be wrapped inside them.

Suddenly, everything Zhara felt for him—lust, love, passion, obsession, tenderness, desire—seems to flow fully alive within me. Here with him in the water, I lift my legs and wrap around them around his back. He holds me tight, his chest pressing into mine, and yes, I can't deny. My heart races. A swoon.

"Yes?" he asks in his gravelly voice.

"Yes," I murmur.

Alex's lips lean down to mine, and my mouth parts to meet his. The sun, the water, this moment: we have imprinted together.

Diving. Swimming. Kissing. Holding. Knowing.

The afternoon's setting sun lets us know twilight approaches. We need to leave the atoll's blue lagoon to make it back to Mine before sunset for Alex's meditation time, and for me to say my proper good-bye to M-X.

Tomorrow, we have determined, we will set sail for the Rave Caves, to our new beginning.

As we return to our canoe stored on the beach, we see a small sailboat in the water, coming in to land at the beach.

"I recognize that boat," says Alex, holding my hand as we walk toward the shore. "It belongs to the Army of Defects in the Rave Caves."

The boat lands and is drawn up on the sand by two burly men vined in holly. Alex says, "New recruits from Haven, I see."

The two men help a girl to climb out over the boat's side. A human girl, not vined, looking feral and punk, her long blond hair streaked with black and blue dye, turned wild by the ocean wind. She sees us and calls out, "Xander!"

Alex's hand drops mine. The Defects and the girl stand right in front of us.

The girl's face regards me. It registers *shock* and then *anguish*.

Her face is mine.

The girl is Zhara.

I do have a soul. I always suspected it to be true, and now I know for sure. Because my First never died.